Advance Praise for PULL

"Rich, engaging characters and a thrilling plot that's easy to
follow, even as the narrative maintains a brisk pace."
—*Kirkus Reviews*

"Memory, mystery, and mental mayhem are the trifecta driving
this inventive narrative, while authentic human touch-points
ensure readers remain fully invested in the characters."
—*Independent Book Review*

"Who is telling the truth and who is lying? What is the reality? I
was captivated, and I think you will be too."
—*Readers' Favorite, 5-star review*

PULL

C.J. FINCH

Little Bird Books

for Matthew

BREAK.

SOMEWHERE IN THE BLACK swirling clouds of my fragmented mind, a memory was emerging.

Whose memory it would be, I didn't know.

Like looking through a clouded lens, the picture wasn't fully in focus yet. Just a growing diffuse light, accompanied by the muted sounds of echoing footsteps. And something else. A sense of dread knotting in the pit of my stomach, sharpening as the image took shape.

Now I could see, fully developed, two feet plodding down a beige-tiled hallway lined with cinderblock walls. Hands swung lightly at the corners of my vision, clad in familiar black leather gloves. My hands.

This was my memory.

I was in a police station, one I knew well, being led through a maze of hallways by an officer with a polite yet urgent smile. He fidgeted as he stopped and turned to face me, standing before a metal door with a plaque that read *Observation 1.*

"Right in here, sir."

I nodded and thanked him, then pulled open the door.

The small observation room was dimly lit, the acrid smell of burnt coffee and desperation hanging in the air, a broad one-way mirror on the wall peering into the room next door. There was currently only one man present, a detective I recognized by the name of Bill, sitting on the edge of a desk with his shoulders slumped and his head in his hands, deeply absorbed in his own helplessness. That is, until he looked up and saw me. "Alex, thank God!"

I kept my weight on my back foot, studying his face, waiting. He looked disheveled, the dark circles under his eyes creased by a long night of no results.

"This better not be about what I think it's about," I said.

He pointed through the glass into the interrogation room. "Look, you gotta help us," he said. "This perv, Drake, kidnapped three kids up in Albany. We didn't find them with him when we brought him in. Has them kept away somewhere." He fixed me with a pleading stare. "We need to figure out where they are. I need you to do your thing again, Alex. I need you to touch him."

I looked through the window at the man sitting at the table in the interrogation room. Stringy brown hair, stubble, dirt. A rat. Large and menacing, yet slight and brittle. He stared tight-lipped at the detective sitting across from him, an unhinged look in his eyes.

I wasn't going near that guy.

"No way."

"Alex."

"I told you before," I said sternly. "I'm not doing that again."

Bill raised his hand to reach for my shoulder. I flinched, edging back. He caught himself, remembering, and lowered his hand.

"We're not getting anywhere," he said. "If you don't help us, those kids are as good as dead. Please."

The words twisted in my gut like a knife. I turned my head back to the window. In the other room, the rat and the detective stared silently at each other, an unspoken barrier between them sealing the fates of young lives. One I knew I could break.

I gave a long sigh.

"I'll help," I said. "But I'm not touching him."

"So you'll profile him?" Bill asked, barely restraining himself from hugging me.

"Yes. Just a few questions." My voice was firm. "I want to make sure you heard me, Bill. I'm not touching him."

"Yes, I heard you. Thank you, Alex." Bill led me toward the door. "We'll take whatever help you can give."

When I walked into the interrogation room, the detective glanced up at me with a questioning look. Bill gave him a firm nod, and he scooted his chair, leaving me to take the seat directly across from the rat. Bill closed the door and stood nearby.

I settled my elbows on the table, careful to maintain a safe distance from the suspect, yet showing no sign of fear or hesitation. The rat and I locked eyes, studying each other carefully, the only sound ticking from the clock on the wall as the moments crawled by. The shadows on his face seemed a mile long under the dim, narrow light of the fluorescent above us. As I took in everything before me, I folded my arms down, resting my hands on the metal table. He looked down at them and smirked at the leather gloves.

He thought he saw a weak man. But I saw so much more. And he could tell, by the way I studied him, his mannerisms, his lip slowly abandoning his smile. A lifetime of collecting memories had given me a deep well of empathy, assigning thoughts and motives to the physical expressions that accompanied them. It was a skill that rivaled that of a veteran psychologist. A long, quiet minute went by, the rat and the puller studying each other. And then I spoke, softly.

"Someone hurt you when you were young, didn't they, Drake?"

He tried to stifle the slight contraction in his forehead, a second too late.

I kept my eye contact. "Was it your dad?"

The faintest twitch of an eyebrow.

"I see. It wasn't just you," I said, calmly. "He hit your mom, too, didn't he?"

The rat released an unnerving laugh, shifting in his chair. "I don't know what the hell you're talking about." His tone was forced. I didn't acknowledge and pressed on.

"It must have been terrifying. Growing up surrounded by violence. Nowhere safe to hide. Trauma like that, it does things to a person." I let my voice harden. "So now you do the same to the kids you take."

He grinned, his forehead tilting forward under sweat-matted strings of hair. "They bring you in to hit me with some psychology shit? I ain't got nothing to say."

I gave a small smile. "But you're saying everything, Drake."

He glared back at me, setting his teeth. He put up a tough front, that was for sure, but the subtleties of his eyes, his jaw, the strain in his voice, betrayed the man that lay beneath.

"There's a sadness in you. You try to hide it, be a tough guy. The tattoos, the hair." I gestured at him. "All of this. It's just a cover for the weakness you feel inside."

His jaw muscles flared, shifting under sweat and stubble.

"And the kids. They're just as helpless as you." I paused, letting the final picture sink in. "You see yourself in them. You relive your father's anger, his rage." I leaned in, locking his gaze. "But do you really want to be him?"

And there it was. I could see it in the corners of his eyes, the slightest waver.

"Do you really want to be your old man?"

The tension hung in the air. For the first time, he really looked at me, and I saw a human. Somewhere in that wrinkled, weathered face that had no doubt seen horrible things, I saw a soul. And he knew I saw him.

Finally, the rat released his breath. Looking away, he thought quietly for a moment, anxiously tapping his knuckles against the metal table. No one spoke a word, the detective sitting stock-still beside me, Bill holding his breath against the wall. Eventually, the rat said, "I'll take the plea."

The detective shifted excitedly in his chair. "I'm listening, Drake."

Drake looked up at me, solemn. "I *am* a better man."

"Where are the kids?" Bill said, stepping closer.

He kept his eyes on me. "725 Oxford Street, my old man's house. In the basement."

The detective jumped to his feet. Bill spun and opened the door, shouting to someone down the hallway to head to the cars. I leaned back in my chair, my work here finished, and yet I couldn't relax my gaze from the rat. My mind remained on edge, my ears still pricked, like a dog listening for movement behind a corner.

And then I saw it—the second tell. Again, in the corner of his eyes, the rat smiled.

Out of nowhere, his hands shot across the table and grasped my neck.

In an instant, I knew everything that lay within him. Everything he had ever seen, I saw. Across an eternity, shadows moved over frightened small bodies, chains rattled, light bounced off of blades. The smell of rotting flesh. Young eyes looking up with terror. And the most terrible sound, whimpering, crying, screaming, echoing in a swell. It surrounded me, swallowed me, threatened to drag me to hell. And running through my veins, an unhinged desire to snuff the light out of every living thing. There had been so many he'd taken, his malicious gaze reflecting in their eyes, the last glimmer of hope escaping as he laid claim to their lives.

And then the contact broke, and I fell back onto the floor, gasping for air. As the detectives slammed the rat onto the table, cackling loudly and thrashing wildly against them, I cradled my head in my hands, crying, howling. "No, no, noooo."

"Alex, what is it?" Bill yelled.

"No," I sputtered. "Not them."

"Alex!" Bill turned his head toward the open door. "We need a medic in here!"

"They're gone, gone, they're gone," I wailed. "He did it. They're gone."

The rat howled as footsteps approached, more hands to touch me. The room was spinning and I was in freefall, going down, down. The lights were dimming, the real world slipping away. Screams and whispers flooded my ears, pulling me under into the torrential current of fear and pain, as any last ounce of separation between myself and the memories of others collapsed.

And finally, my body gave out.

PART I.

NORMAL LIFE.

THE ALARM BROKE THE dream, like it always did. My eyes flut-tered open, staring at the ceiling, finding comfort in the familiar popcorn texture. The white glow of morning seeped in through the blinds, only for me, in the apartment all alone.

I rose from the bed, focusing on my balance, my head splitting. I stood at my desk, where I opened a leatherbound photo album. Inside, pictures of a young blond boy smiled back, holding hands with his parents, sharing ice cream with his brother. These memories were mine and only mine. I slowed my breathing as I allowed them to take the forefront, pushing away the memories of others. The fog was beginning to clear, the walls of the dam sealing back together.

At the vanity, I splashed cold water onto my face, my bare hands frigid in the exposed air. A tired young man with a frayed beard stared back with the soul of hundreds of years. I mean that quite literally. I closed my eyes, found my center, and exhaled.

As I stepped back into the main room of my studio apartment, I could feel the morning sun on my skin, hear a passing siren floors below outside. Next to the window, my goldfish watched me as it bobbed lazily in its bowl, the only sign of motion in my otherwise quiet home.

I was finally focused, in the present. I liked to think it was getting easier, but I wasn't sure. I rubbed a hand across my tired face, over my scrubby whiskers.

Time to face the day.

⋆⋆⋆

It was a chilly day in early November, my favorite time of year. Scarves and high collars were in, and people didn't mind my gloves so much. Fully enclosed in cloth and facial hair, my eyes and nose were the only parts of me exposed to the elements. New York weather suited me.

But I wouldn't be taking public transit. Not in a million years. In the protective shell of my electric car, I slithered through the morning traffic of Manhattan, separated from the thousands of hunched woolen coats marching to work on the teeming sidewalks. At the gleaming silver tower in Midtown, I thanked the valet and loaded into the empty elevator car. Level forty-five, Sentry Data Security.

Our receptionist greeted me with a smile when the door opened. "Morning, Mr. Hemsley."

I nodded. "Good morning, Sherri."

The west half of the office was a bunker of customer reps, some making sales, some setting up accounts, others delivering reports. The eastern hallways were much less busy, built mainly of top officer suites with broad spotless windows gazing out over the waking city. I walked down the hallway of Suite B, passing the four doors of my Chief Engineering team members, quiet and well-trained. I glanced in each one as my sneakers thumped down the thin gray carpet. Eric, Lucio, Priyanka. No Melanie today.

"Hey, boss," Eric said with a wave.

"Morning, Alex," said Priyanka, smiling from her desk.

I prided myself on the closeness of our team. In a professional sense, of course. Always positive, always supportive. But as I walked into my office at the end of the hall, I swiftly shut and locked the glass door behind me. There would be no buzzing about my desk, no office cooler talk. Perhaps amongst them, but never with me.

Alone in my office, the tension in my shoulders eased and I released a heavy exhale. Safe at last. My rectangle haven was quiet and sterile before me, the gray executive couches unoccupied against the wall, my wooden desk welcoming me to sit and work without disturbance for the rest of the day. Behind my chair, the city of Manhattan shone in brilliant daylight.

A loud knock behind me broke my peace and sent me stumbling forward. I turned around.

"Jesus, Drew," I muttered.

My brother grinned wildly through the glass as I retracted the lock. Dressed in a suit with a casual shirt, his blond hair messily styled and accompanied by a stubbled goatee, he was the picture of a fresh, young, bro entrepreneur. CEO of Sentry Data Security, Drew strode confidently into the room.

"What's hangin', bro?" he said, lightly bumping me with his elbow. He knew the gesture was harmless. I still flinched.

"Just got in. You're here early."

"You didn't hear?" he said, perching on the corner of my desk and immediately fiddling with something.

"Again, just got in."

"There was a breach at Pexler last night. Their knickers are in a tizzy this morning."

"I don't think that's the expression."

Drew ignored the comment. "Second breach in the industry this quarter. Want to make sure we've got ourselves shielded from this kind of thing."

"There it is," I said, teasing. "You're visiting me so early in the interest of the investors, not to wish your brother a good morning."

"I'm serious, Alex. This kind of thing could ruin us." Business bro was settling in.

"We're airtight, but I'll have the team do a round of checks today. We can put up another firewall but that could mean some clients have issues logging in on certain browsers, certain locations, until we get the wrinkles smoothed out. Do you really want that firestorm?"

Drew sighed. "You know I don't like talking about how the sausage is made."

"That's why they pay you the big bucks. To not have to talk about anything."

"Harsh, bro."

We smirked at each other.

"How long would it take you to perfect that firewall?" he asked.

I shrugged. "About a week."

Drew let out a long, dramatic sigh. "Do it. Fuck me, just do it. I'll regret it later."

I set my bag down and sat at my desk, starting my computer. Drew wandered over to the wall of windows, surveying the New York cityscape like a god perched in the clouds.

"Do we know what was taken at Pexler?" I asked.

Drew shrugged. "Data."

I sighed. "Yes, but what *kind* of data? Passwords, payment info, or... God, not actual asset identification?"

"They haven't disclosed it," he said. "But Alex, I'm counting on you to make sure nothing more damning than a credit card number leaves this place."

I stared at my boot-up screen, thinking of the sensitive information stored in our digital vaults. It was more than just consumer data and credit card numbers. There were medical records from hospital systems. Even classified informants, witness protection, secret identities. Sentry partnered with many police and legal departments across the country who needed a secure offsite server, offloading the burden of data security onto us.

"It's our one job," I said. "No one's information is leaving this place. The way the encryption is set up, it's impossible."

In a strange moment of wonder, Drew placed his finger on the glass and traced the path of a distant airplane, like a small schoolboy. Then he quickly spun around. "That's what I like to hear. And that's why you're my number one CTO who just happens to be"—he pointed with both hands—"my little brother."

"Glad to hear it wasn't all nepotism," I said, moving my mouse and starting up my software.

Drew could see I was ready to be left alone, so he showed himself to the door. "Oh, by the way," he said. "I have a social function later tonight, and I was wondering if you'd come along as my plus one?"

"I'm flattered, Drew, but I'm already taken."

Drew chuckled. "By who, your goldfish?"

I shot him a deadpan look.

"It's a dinner with a couple important people," he explained. "I need someone to come who I can trust."

"Don't you have an entire row of capable VPs to pick from?"

He lowered his voice. "It's… a little different."

I lifted an eyebrow. "What are you getting yourself into?"

"Just come. Real people, Alex. You remember real people?"

"Yes, I prefer to stay away from them."

Drew stepped through the door. "I'm sending a car at eight. Don't be late. And dress nice."

"I don't—"

Before I could object anymore, he slid the door shut, giving a wink through the glass and scampering off.

I sighed, slumped in my chair.

My brother and I could not be any more different. He was the fast talker, the charmer, the loose cannon. I was steadier, calmer, the listener. That I would be working for him, seeing him every day as I reported to his lavish Manhattan office, I would have never foreseen. But—I owed him.

Alone at last in the comfort of my office, the silence of the room deafening on my ears, I started running a protocol. Just me and my thoughts, by myself.

KIN.

Later in the afternoon, I got a call from Priyanka. She was distraught from the get-go, I could hear the pain in her voice as she uttered my name.

I called the team into the hallway and gently broke the news. Lucio put his arm around Priyanka's shoulder as she cried, all of us glancing at Melanie's office, dark and vacant.

"It needs flowers," Priyanka said, sniffling. "I'll bring flowers tomorrow."

As the team sunk closer together in a huddle, I backed farther away, until eventually I left for my office. I couldn't take part in any kind of grief.

I sat down at my desk and promptly called H.R. I'd never had an employee pass away before. This procedure was new to me. As the rep silently read through Melanie's file, I could feel corners of my mind trying to tug me away into shadows. I couldn't let it happen.

"We'll start closing her work account in a couple days," the rep on the phone said. "Someone on your team will need to deactivate her database credentials. I suggest you use your admin password to access her emails and migrate anything important."

I set down the phone and looked solemnly at the email login, then at the time. Four o'clock. An idle mind would kill me. I entered the admin password and a field of emails poured onto the screen.

Immediately I knew it was a bad idea. It wasn't the business ones, the information requests and reports. It was the personal ones, the small daily interactions with her coworkers. One email read, *Congrats on the wedding! You looked beautiful!* My chest began to sting. Another message read, *Thanks for your help moving this weekend. Couldn't have done it without you, Mel.* And another asked, *When are you and Miguel coming over for game night again?*

Only thirty seconds had gone by and I was completely overwhelmed. My hand shot out and jabbed the power button on the monitor, ending the parade of personal messages. I was breathing heavily, feeling claustrophobic, the tightness of all those memories closing in. I grabbed my coat and rushed through the door, not stopping to tell the team goodbye. Barely giving a glance to the receptionist as the elevator came.

I hurtled like a fireball out into the cold November air and took a hard right. The shoulders of bustling New Yorkers brushed against me, agitating me even more. I felt like I was going to drown in this sea of people. This big, breathing, terrible sea.

A block and a half later, I ducked in the black-paneled door at Knoxley's, a quaint English pub. I had only been a couple times before, rare outings to pick up lunch, but it was the closest place I could think of to find salvation in a drink.

The warmth and homeliness of Knoxley's enveloped me, and slowly I began to calm down. Each step up to the counter was a drop in my heart rate, soothing my nerves. The place wasn't very busy, only a couple tables occupied by workers early for happy hour. I took an open seat at the bar, letting my weight settle on the barstool, exhaling and centering.

"What can I get you, mate?" asked the bartender in a black V-neck shirt.

I looked at the drafts and picked something dark and heavy. I needed a weight to anchor me to reality.

"Coming right up."

The cold beer sweated against my warm black gloves. I carefully removed them to let my fingertips trace the condensation along the side of the glass. Slowly the alcohol brought me down back into myself. I was Alex, sitting at the bar at the end of a blustery Thursday. I would go home to my apartment on the Upper East Side. I would feed my goldfish, fix myself dinner, and go to sleep. In the haze, I briefly remembered the dinner Drew had arranged, groaning as I looked at my watch.

"Need anything else, mate?" the bartender asked.

"No, better not," I said. "I'll take the ticket, please."

It happened when he brought the bill a moment later, setting it down in front of the empty spot to my right. There was an old man sitting two chairs away from me, and we both gestured for the ticket. The way we stopped and withdrew our hands. The way our eyes looked up cautiously, as if a bomb were about to go off. We clocked the threat immediately, a feedback loop of death. He knew, and I knew.

His fingers shook, his eyes were nearly buried in the wrinkles of his face. And yet, despite the eons of life washed upon him, there was a calmness underneath.

"Been awhile since I met another puller," he said quietly, placing his hand back on his empty glass and staring down into the bottom. "You're quite young."

"Twenty-eight," I said.

A small noise escaped from the man's white beard. "You ever met another one before?"

"Yes," I said. "He was thirty. Committed suicide a few months later."

The old man nodded. "Long life doesn't exactly suit us, does it?"

"How many have you met?"

"Oh, seems I run into one every decade or so." He frowned grimly. "Knew a pusher once, too. That was nasty business."

I studied him, trying to disguise my awe, but I knew he saw it. He huddled low over the counter, wrapped in a fading black wool coat. He looked back at me next, glancing down at my gloves as I pulled them back onto my hands. "That's a smart idea. Wish I'd thought of that when I was younger."

"You don't wear anything?"

He shook his head. "I've learned to live with it."

My breath hung in my chest as I considered this, alcohol still warming my veins. "How?" I finally asked.

"You gotta know where to put 'em," he said. "The memories that aren't yours. Takes practice. I figured it was the only way I didn't go to an early grave."

I stared sadly at the empty glass in front of me. So hard I had tried to do this, over so many years. Ever since I was young, about five years old, and I'd touched my brother in a game of tag. "Why did you steal my toy?" I stopped to ask. Drew was speechless. How had I known? He had pocketed the toy while I was brushing my teeth that morning.

I hadn't mentioned my ability to anyone besides Drew. I was aware, even at that young age, just how crazy it sounded. It was like my own little secret, a lucky knack I had for figuring people out. It wasn't until I was in my teens that I heard rumors of other people like me. Like an urban legend, unverified and unstudied, there seemed to be a handful of us out there. Living under the radar, away from society's eager eye, like a bug scrambling away from a jar. And because of our affinity for secrecy, most people didn't know pullers existed.

School had been difficult as a kid. I learned early on not to ask too many questions, as we all lined up and held hands. I knew which classmates had the happy families; they were my favorite to stand next to. I knew which ones didn't, and thus to avoid.

Dating was another animal entirely. At first it had been thrilling, to know a girl so well that I could win her heart in a matter of minutes. Frankly, forming relationships with women had always been easy for me, because I had what so many other men lacked: empathy. With every soft touch, I saw every interaction that had made them who they were.

Unfortunately, that only became more terrifying as the years grew on. In beautiful, kind women, I saw the evilest things. Drunk fathers who clawed at them, handsome young men who hit them, trusted friends who raped them. Eventually, I stopped dating anyone. I couldn't stomach collecting any more painful experiences from people I cared for.

So instead, I threw myself into my work. I thought I'd enlist my help with the local police, where my ability made solving crimes almost instantaneous. It would make bearing this difficult burden worth it. But I only touched a handful of criminals before I realized I was losing weight, my face gaunt when I looked in the mirror at the end of the day. With my years of extreme observation and analysis of the human condition, I still managed to make a decent profiler without touching anyone. But we know how that ended. In a room with a rat.

I completely walled myself off after that point. The only thing that saved me was Drew. He's the only one who knew me anywhere near as well as I knew the rest of the world. His business was taking off and he wanted me to come to New York and work for him. He already had a tight engineering crew and needed someone to oversee them. I had the know-how; I'd accidentally pulled my college roommate back in the day, a computer engineering major, much to Drew's jealousy at the time. He told me I wouldn't have to answer to anybody, hell, wouldn't have to speak to anybody if I didn't want to. So I took the offer. I kept to myself, biding my time as a pencil pusher, or a key pusher, whatever you call it.

I still desired human connection; living the rest of my life without meaningful relationships sounded depressing. But the thought of pulling another person's memories again was taxing.

I looked over again at the old man next to me in wonder. How could a puller possibly live to be his age?

"I've tried to compartmentalize," I said. "It's been difficult."

"When's the last time you pulled?"

"A while ago."

He thought for a minute. "Next time you do, set yourself up a spot in your mind to put it. It's like pouring liquid into a cup." He raised the empty pint glass. "Put the spigot just right. It'll go into the right place."

He was so wise, I thought. I needed to listen to this man.

"My name's Alex," I said.

"Roger. I'd shake your hand, but uh…."

We smiled.

"You come here often, Roger?"

He nodded. "Every couple days. Just because I still pull doesn't mean I got anyone close to me. Besides the drink here."

"Ah, same. Well, except for my brother."

"A brother is a nice thing to have," he said, staring distantly into his glass. "Family. Hold onto it as long as you can."

As we sat in silence, I registered how much busier the place had become. I'd been so absorbed by this conversation, I hadn't noticed the noise grow louder. Chairs scraped as Manhattan's businesspeople poured in to discuss the workday with their friends, still clad in their suits and dresses. Roger and I gave an uneasy look behind us.

"Best I get going," I said, throwing a ten on the counter.

"I don't mind the crowd," Roger said, raising his finger to the bartender for another drink.

"I hope to see you again," I said.

"You know where to find me."

DINNER.

THE DRIVER CALLED AT eight to tell me the car had arrived. I shrugged on a sport coat and looked glumly at my unshaven face in the mirror. I wasn't even attempting to make a good first impression tonight, with whoever these people were.

The car sailed down through the arteries of Manhattan, a shining beacon darting next to the crowded sidewalks of winter coats. Somewhere on 65th, I was let out into a lobby and escorted to the top of a ten-story building, the open-air restaurant dotted with fire pits and heat lamps. In a private corner I saw Drew stand and wave me over. Four other guests sat at the table.

"Hey all, this is my brother, Alex," he said, introducing me. He gestured to the other end of the table. "These are my friends, Trey and Bex."

Two thirty-something New York socialites tipped their wine glasses and chirped, "Hello."

"And these are their friends, Analise and Jessie."

I could sense the care with which he spoke their names as I turned to look at the two young women sitting across from each other in the seats next to us. Whoever they were, they were the reason we were here tonight.

Analise was perhaps in her mid-twenties. Her bottle blonde hair was tied up in a bun, a stunning necklace laid over her collarbone. She tucked a loose tuft of hair behind her ear as she smiled sweetly at me. Jessie was older twenties, brown bangs draped along the side of her glasses as she looked up from her menu. For a brief second, she studied my face.

"Hello," they both said.

I took my seat between Jessie and Drew, and the waiter took our orders. I was barely hungry, but a bourbon would do, anything to get me through this. After he left, Analise turned in her chair to get a better look at the view from the rooftop.

"Wow," she said. "It's so beautiful. And look, you can see Pexler from here."

I stared questioningly at her. Pexler Technologies was our top competitor, nestled in a tall Manhattan office building about a mile from our own.

Drew didn't waste a moment. "Ah, yes, Pexler," he said, leaning in. "Tell me more about your brother's work."

I caught my jaw before it dropped, but I did not spare the daggers I sent staring at him. This was the reason we were here, to milk competitor information from this young woman, and he'd brought me along as some kind of wingman. I sensed the slightest smirk in the corner of Drew's lips. *Deal with it, bro. We're in.*

Analise sighed. "Gideon's life is work. You know, he's the CEO. He basically lives there. Literally, he lives in the same building."

"I hear he's quite the *visionary*," Drew said, hitting the word too hard. He leaned in on the table. "Tell me, does your brother outsource a lot of the marketing? Go all in-house?" He shrugged. "Just… curious."

"Oh, I don't know, I'm not really that involved in how he runs his business." She gave a small laugh, rubbing her arm with her hand anxiously. I could sense she was uneasy with Drew hovering over her.

"Probably a bit of a rough week for him, huh?" I said. "Sorry, I don't mean to bring it up, but I did hear about a… a breach." Out of the corner of my eye, I saw Drew's smile grow a little wider.

"Ugh," Analise said, gesturing with her wine glass. "Yes, yes. He's beside himself this week. Luckily nothing important got leaked, I'm told. And I mean, I'm not surprised. Gideon's very smart. He was top of his class at MIT."

"Smart cookie," Drew said, bouncing his eyebrows up and down idiotically.

My whiskey double arrived, and I promptly drowned myself in it.

"So what do you do, Drew?" Analise asked.

"Oh, uh…." I could see the smooth-talking business bro gears turning quickly. "I'm an analyst at an investment firm."

"Oh, ok. Which one?"

He struggled for a name. "Goldfarb… Fachs."

Absolute gibberish.

"Oh, I'm not familiar," said Analise. "Wait. Did you guys back Trinity Tech?"

Drew stared blankly. "Um."

On the other side of me, a low chuckle caught my ear. "These two are peas in a pod, aren't they?"

I looked at the woman next to me, Jessie, who had barely spoken yet.

I smiled. "Yeah. Nice to see Drew's finally met his match." I turned in my chair, leaving Drew and Analise to their exchange.

Jessie studied their conversation from afar, sipping calmly from her beer, then her eyes drifted over the lights of the city. "Nice night tonight. Not sure why I got dragged along to this, but boy did I need a drink." She gave a heavy sigh.

"Sounds like we're both medicating," I said, gesturing with my rocks glass.

"Oh yeah? What's done it for you?"

I swallowed. "Employee died."

"Oh," she said quietly. "Shit, yeah, that is bad. Need to talk about it?"

I didn't know how to answer. I couldn't remember the last time anyone had asked anything about my own emotions. I was always taking in everyone else's.

"No, that's okay," I said. "Wouldn't really help anything, I suppose."

She nodded. "I get that. Sometimes it's best to keep the dark stuff tucked away, try and stay positive."

I blinked, watching her take another sip from her beer, sitting in comfortable silence as she breathed in the cool night air.

"So what is it you do?" I asked, trying to spur conversation.

"I'm a CTO," she said, a hint of pride in her voice. "Chief Technical Officer at an up-and-coming tech company."

I nodded. "Oh, um, me too."

"Really?" she said, perking up. "Is it at Goldfarb Fachs?"

We both laughed.

"No," I said. "No, it's not."

"Well, where do you work, then?"

I glanced at Analise, who was caught in the middle of one of Drew's rambles. "I'm not sure I should say."

Jessie looked down at her beer, balancing it against the edge of the table, the corners of her lips easing down. I took another sip of my bourbon. To hell with discretion. If Drew lost his lead, so be it.

"Okay, I'll tell you," I said. "But can you keep it a secret until after we leave?"

Her smile returned. "Your secret's safe with me."

I kept my voice low. "I… actually work for one of Pexler's competitors. Sentry Data Security."

"Really?" Jessie said, her eyebrows rising. "See, I thought there was something fishy here. And your brother over there, he works there too, doesn't he?"

"Yes." I didn't elaborate on his title. "Please don't whisk Analise out of here."

She shook her head reassuringly. "Don't sweat it. Analise's interest in the company is about the same as her interest in quantum mechanics." It was a playful jab, but I could see care and familiarity in the glance that Jessie gave her. "No, she's too smart to get caught up in her brother's business."

"How do you know Analise?" I asked.

Jessie set down her empty beer and spun it, smiling to herself. "She's my sister." Then she turned to look at me, her eyes absolutely grinning. "I'm the CTO at Pexler."

Shit.

She burst into laughter. "Your face, my god! No, no, no. Don't worry. I won't run if you won't."

I laughed in relief. "Are you kidding? This is about the most normal conversation I've had in years, and it's with my arch nemesis."

Jessie clinked her empty beer bottle against my now empty whiskey glass. "Well, cheers to family rivalry."

Drew and Analise turned their attention to our comradery. "What's so funny?" Analise asked.

Jessie pointed at me. "Oh, turns out we both know the same guy at Goldfarb Fachs." She could barely finish the sentence, and I completely lost it.

It had been so long since I'd truly laughed.

★★★

THE AIR HAD CHILLED considerably over the past couple hours, making me pull my scarf close as we lined the sidewalk waiting for our cars, still buoyed by the blunt edge of drink.

Analise walked up to my side, smiling politely. "It was nice to meet you, Alex," she said in a sweet, cordial tone. "I hope this doesn't sound weird, but... you have a calmness about you. It's rare. And it's really comforting to be around."

"Thank you," I said. "It really was a pleasure meeting you tonight. And your sister." I turned and looked at Jessie, pacing a few yards away as she checked her phone.

Analise glanced at her. "Ah, yes. She can be a hard one to crack. Always so serious, so buried in her work. It was nice to hear her laugh tonight."

Something in my chest hung for a moment, as the silence passed between us.

"We should do this again," she said. "Your brother's certainly an *eccentric* man." She leaned into the word comically but also with a hint of admiration, which surprised me.

"Yeah, well, don't encourage him," I said.

"Have a good night, Alex." She nodded and walked away, her heels tapping lightly on the concrete. She reached out a hand as she approached Drew, busy rubbernecking at the incoming pack of vehicles, and rested it gently on the back of his shoulder, bringing him around with a goofy smile.

"Well, that was quite the evening," Jessie said from behind me, catching me off guard.

I held my coat tightly against me, my breath floating away in the chilly night air as I turned to face her. "I'm not so sure I can chalk our spy mission up to a success."

She watched Analise chatting excitedly with Drew. "Well, don't worry, I don't think little miss caught on. And I won't say anything to Gideon. He and I barely speak anyway."

I sensed a tension in that last statement. I ventured to ask, "Why not?"

She shrugged. "He's just got this macho thing. He's big Mr. CEO. It's like the fact that we're family doesn't even matter. But you and your brother seem like you have things figured out."

I looked at Drew, currently nudging Analise's arm as they watched a plane flying overhead.

"Yeah," I said. "We're pretty good."

"Good." Jessie perked up at an alert from her phone. "Well, my Uber's here. It was a pleasure dining with you, Mr. CTO." She extended her gloved hand.

I took hers in mine. "You too, Jessie."

She smiled. "Good night, Alex."

GHOST.

"You absolute idiot."

Drew disregarded my comment as he came chuckling into my office the next day.

"You really set us up on a blind dinner date with Analise and Jessie Pexler?" I said. "Are you fucking mad?"

Drew shrugged. "Hey, I thought it went well." The corner of his lip rose. "I actually think Analise is kind of into me."

"God spare her soul."

"Hey now, I'm not as clueless as I used to be. And what about you and the sister? You were real chummy."

"She's the fucking CTO at Pexler."

I turned my computer monitor so he could see the chief officer lineup on the Pexler website. A headshot of Jessie Pexler smiled back at him. His eyes widened in surprise.

"Yeah, dude," I said. "News flash, sisters can hold those roles too."

"Clearly I targeted the wrong one for information."

I raised an eyebrow. "I know why you picked Analise to interrogate."

Drew gave his best attempt at a wink.

"Do yourself a favor and never do that again." I shook my head. "Why are you still in my office?'

My brother parked himself in front of my window again. "How's the firewall coming along?"

"Just fine. But sounds like if Pexler didn't lose anything valuable, we have nothing to worry about."

"Unless Jessie's just a better programmer than you."

"Shut up."

Drew sighed and sat on the corner of my desk. "We should see them again, right?"

I glared at him. "NO."

"I bet I could ask Bex for Analise's number. She and Trey really did a solid for me last night."

"Dude, I don't know what you're expecting. Certainly not the inevitably of Gideon Pexler annihilating your balls at the next family picnic."

The phone on my desk rang. I picked it up. It was Eric.

Drew watched me as I listened in disbelief. "I'm sorry, what?"

***

ERIC AND DREW HUDDLED around my computer screen as I scanned the activity logs.

"There." Eric pointed. "Seven fifty-seven."

An entry for database login. Username: Melanie Abrerra.

"Doesn't make any sense," I muttered.

"Alex, what does this mean?" Drew asked, standing behind us.

"It means that someone with Melanie's login credentials accessed our database last night."

"Alex." With every utterance of my name, he grew further on edge. "What does this mean?"

"Someone must have snagged her info and logged in remotely," Eric said.

"No, wait." I pointed at the second line in the entry. "This is the IP address for the office. They logged in here."

Nobody said a word.

Abruptly, I picked up the phone and called the security desk. "Hi. We suspect some suspicious activity last night around seven fifty-seven PM. Can you do me a favor and check the camera footage for floor forty-five, Suite B and let me know who was here?"

I pressed the cradle button and called Priyanka, asking her to come to my office. A moment later she entered.

"Hi, Priyanka. I have a question for you. Have we deactivated Melanie's database credentials yet?"

"Yes," Priyanka said. "I moved them to deactivation status last night."

"What time?"

"Just before five o'clock."

I nodded, my eyes returning to the monitor. "Alright, thank you, Pri."

"Of course, deactivation isn't always instantaneous."

The room was dead silent.

"What do you mean?"

"Sometimes it can take a few hours for it to fully register in our system."

"So," I said carefully, "if I was looking at a database entry at seven fifty-seven last night in Melanie's name, that would be perfectly plausible to you?"

My stomach was dropping, dropping.

Priyanka stared back at me. "Except the part where she's dead. Yes."

Gone.

Drew pivoted and withdrew his cell, punching buttons rapid-fire. "Jake, get me someone from PR," he barked into the phone.

My mind was racing, my mouse barely keeping up as I expanded the activity log for the entry. I scrolled down to the log text, reading the actions. There were only a few lines.

"Wait, wait!" I said.

Drew turned, lowering his phone.

"Nothing happened."

"What?" Drew said.

"I said nothing happened."

"I heard you," he said, returning to the desk. "What the fuck does that mean?"

"They just logged in and logged out."

Drew glanced at the log lines. "How can that fucking be?"

"They didn't take anything in the database," Eric said, bewildered. "It would have logged if anything was changed, transferred, downloaded."

"There was an attempt," I said, finishing the log lines, "to access a top-level client. But that requires an admin password." I shared a look with Drew. He and I were the only people in the company with top admin access. "Confirmed, nothing was taken."

Just then the phone rang, scaring the piss out of me. I punched the speaker button. "Yes."

"Alex Hemsley?"

"Yes."

"Sir, this is the security desk. I can confirm I see a young woman in Suite B around seven-fifty last night, leaving at eight oh-five."

Drew, Eric, Priyanka, and I all stared at each other.

"A young woman?" I asked, my voice breaking.

"Yep. I've seen her here before. She had her badge and everything."

"Her badge?" I phrased this carefully. "She was no longer employed as of yesterday afternoon."

"Well, sometimes those security badges can take a few hours to deactivate—"

Drew slammed his fist on the desk.

"What the hell do we pay this place for if we can't even manage who comes in and out?" he snarled into the phone.

***

Ten minutes later we were standing in the security office, watching footage of Melanie Abrerra entering the dark suite, accessing her old office, and logging on to the computer. Her motions were as casual as if it had been just another Monday morning. We couldn't see her screen, but she was only there for a few minutes. Then she turned everything off and left.

My arms were covered in goosebumps.

"Fucking ghost," Drew whispered.

"Clearly she's not dead," I said.

"*Clearly* we need to vet these people working for us."

I shook my head. "But she's been on our team for almost a year. I trusted her. We all did. Even if she's still alive, why would she have come back into the office?"

We pondered this for a moment. The security guy said, "Maybe she just came back to collect her things? Running from a bad boyfriend or something, had to be discreet."

Drew shook his head dismissively.

"Well, whatever it is," I said, "it's not a crisis. Nothing was taken." I turned to the security agent. "This doesn't leave this room."

"And for the love of God," Drew said, "fix the timeout on the security badges."

***

Things were calmer when I returned upstairs. Drew had blown off to his office in a muttering fit of rage, but the Engineering team was quietly collecting itself, puzzled over what had just happened.

Priyanka set a chamomile tea on my desk for me as I stared into my gloved palms.

"Are you sure it was her?" she asked.

"One hundred percent," I said.

"I don't understand. The call yesterday, from Melanie's husband. He was in tears. Said it was a medical event, something she's been fighting the past few weeks." She swallowed, her voice containing a tinge of hurt. "I honestly had no idea."

"Has anyone tried to get ahold of him today?"

"The call just goes to voicemail. So does hers."

I sighed and took the small cup in my hands, the warmth emanating through the black leather.

"Are you reporting it to the police?" Priyanka asked.

"We'll file a report for the break-in, minus the part about the database login. We'll leave Melanie's name out for now. We're not necessarily looking to press charges if there's no ill intent. We don't want this to get any kind of attention from the press."

I stared deep into my tea. I hadn't touched anyone for a year, but now I wished I'd pulled Melanie, to see what kind of person she was.

"You knew Melanie, right?" I said.

"You and I both did."

I nodded. "So am I right in my assessment that she would never do anything malicious to harm the company?" I paused. "To harm us?"

Priyanka held my gaze for a moment, then confidently nodded. "Yes."

"Okay." I sighed. "Okay, then."

FLOAT.

I tried a sensory deprivation tank once. It nearly killed me. With nothing to dampen them, all those voices came out of nowhere.

So instead, I took solace in floating in my indoor apartment pool at odd hours when I could be undisturbed. Saturday morning at seven AM, I drifted under the dancing light with my waterproof headphones on, listening to Rachmaninoff.

I'd barely slept the night before. My mind was racing, trying to find the missing variable to an unsolvable puzzle. Finally I'd given up for now, pushed those thoughts away as my toes dipped in and out of the water.

I thought about the first time I'd ever used my ability to help someone. It was a lost toddler at the waterpark, so scared he couldn't talk. I was only ten, but I knew to take his small hands into mine, like some kind of sacred guardian.

When I make physical contact with someone, instantly I absorb everything. It happens with everyone I touch, there is no choice. It's as if time freezes, and I become a sort of audience member, watching someone else's memories as a third party. Eventually, I learned how to maneuver in them, to skip ahead to the important ones. Learning this control was a necessary reflex, to not get lost in the memories and the emotions that came with them. But they're all still in me, stored away like photocopies in a filing cabinet, reviewable at any time.

Memories are finicky things. Sometimes I can see through the fog and find details that were left behind. It was what made me invaluable at the police department years ago, snagging clues from troubled victims, finding evidence left by careless assailants.

For the lost little boy, there wasn't much to dig through. But I could see a young woman cradling him lovingly in her arms. He loved her so much, she was his world. There was a man too, a bit distant, but he was present at dinners and tossed a baseball with the boy once. There was a mailbox in front of their house, but the boy could not read, so I could not make out the name printed on the side. Then one day, another woman brought a little girl over to play. When the mother answered the door, the woman called her Alice.

In his most recent memories, the boy had come to the water-park with his mother. He was very excited. She waited in line to get ice cream, and he was supposed to stay by her side, but he ran to the pool, dodging between kneecaps. I did not hear her calling after him. She did not see him leave.

When I emerged from the pull, the boy was still looking at me as he had when I'd taken his hands. I led the boy to the concession area and looked for his mother. Eventually I saw her, staring out into the pool, scanning over the dozens of bodies. "Alice?" I said. She turned around, and mother and son were reunited. The look on her face was one of my happier memories. It was a place I liked to go.

Now, twenty-eight and floating uselessly in a pool, I turned and submerged myself under the surface. Bubbles trickled up over my face as angsty piano filled my ears. I was retired now. Retired into a meaningless office job, coming home to a meaningless existence. It was all I could handle anymore.

But what good was life if I couldn't have happiness? Surely I could find it somehow without pulling disturbed memories from criminals or troubled kids. A comfort that existed without the inherited wounds of a lover.

This was the variable I could not find. This was another unsolvable equation.

★★★

"Tell me more about your brother," the old man said, sipping from his beer.

I figured I'd find him on a Sunday afternoon, the crowd thin as young regulars were still out at brunch sipping mimosas to cure their hangovers.

"He's a piece of work," I said. "But I can trust him. We have each other's backs."

"Older? Younger?"

"Older."

"So he looks out for you."

"Yes," I said. "He's the one who called me when I was having a hard time, asked me to come work for him here."

"He got any kids?"

"No. Can't say I could picture that." I took another sip from my beer.

Roger chuckled. "Fatherhood has a habit of finding the least likely of figures." I sensed a sadness in his voice.

"Did you want kids?" I asked.

"Oh, I… did." He paused. "I had a daughter."

The care with which he spoke the last word touched my heart. But I was sure my surprise was plastered across my face. "Sorry, but how did you…?"

"Well," Roger chuckled. "The act was not exactly hard. Surely you…?"

"Oh, well, yeah. It's been a long time, but yeah."

Roger nodded. "Okay, so. I was seeing her mother, but it didn't last long. It never does, you know. But I was there when she was born, came to see her every weekend until she was about twelve. It's easier, with children."

I nodded back at him. "Fewer memories."

"And most of them happy. For those first few years, anyway." He sighed. "But she grew up, became her own person. We haven't spoken in a very long time."

I looked at my beer, thinking about what he'd just told me. "Would you say it's worth it?"

Roger beamed. "For those first twelve years, absolutely." He could see the relief this gave me. "You'll find your way, young man. You'll find someone somewhere to hold on to. Even if it's not forever. Just having something, for some time. That'll be enough."

★★★

THAT NIGHT, AS I lay sleeping in my bed, my mind drifted across memories as it often did. Mine and all the others', no barriers. Memory bleed, I called it.

I was walking with a little girl, and she felt like my own, her warm little hand in mine. We were going to get ice cream just down the block. The summer sun blossomed on her pink skin. She turned and smiled up at me, missing two teeth.

I recognized her, her name was Emily. She walked hand in hand with her father down the sidewalk between a beautiful green park and a moderately busy thoroughfare, cars passing by in clusters. I followed them, watching warily from behind.

"One scoop or two?" her father asked at the ice cream truck parked at the curb.

"Two."

"Of course." He turned back to the man at the window. "Two please."

Emily's father handed over his payment and the cone was placed in his hand. He turned, calling, "Baby." But she wasn't next to him anymore. He surveyed the empty sidewalk, and then lifted his gaze further. She was picking up a penny at the side of the road.

"For good luck, Daddy," she cooed.

He flashed his daughter a loving smile.

And then the car came out of nowhere.

Screeching tires echoed mercilessly in my ears as I shot up in bed, gasping for air. "Jesus Christ," I muttered. My heart was racing. I reached blindly for the photo album, knocking it off the desk onto the floor. When I leaned forward to grab it, my head spun.

I tried to calm my breathing and leaned back against the headboard, my body striped by the blue night light coming in through the blinds. My fish fluttered in its bowl, as if watching with concern.

You're all right, I told myself wearily. *You're gonna be all right.*

I muttered it enough times that it became a tired trance, and as my breathing slowed, my heavy eyes began to close. Sliding down back onto my pillow, my mind slipped away to another memory.

TRUST.

I walked into the office Monday with my mind a little clearer. Drew was in a meeting, but I left a coffee and donut from his favorite cafe on his desk. As I walked down Suite B, I stopped at Priyanka's doorway and thanked her for her help the other day, the two of us sharing a meaningful glance. I thanked Eric as well and suggested the team go out to lunch together.

Settling in at my desk, I turned on Market Watch and called up the industry newsletter for the day. As expected, nothing about an attempted break-in at Sentry. There was an article about the breach at Pexler Technologies, with a statement from Gideon Pexler clarifying that no sensitive data had been stolen. I nodded, feeling distant relief for Jessie and her team.

I bit into my donut and began opening the small pile of mail on my desk. Mostly junk mail from service providers, marketing vouchers from their competitors. Trash. Then my hand rested on a plain white envelope with a slight bulge in the middle. There was more than paper inside. I lifted the envelope to examine it. No return address. Just my name and office, and a stamp.

I froze. Should I even open it? My mind shot back decades to anthrax scares. Was that still a thing people did? It didn't feel like powder. It was a solid rectangle, perhaps plastic. I shook my head—*don't be ridiculous*—and slid my finger under the fold, still holding it slightly away from me. Separating the edges, I peeked inside at a small flash drive.

I stepped into the hallway and spoke loudly so the team could hear. "Did anyone leave this envelope on my desk?" Everyone peeked out their doors and shook their heads no.

I sat back at my desk and studied the drive. *Just throw it away,* I thought. Then my mind flashed to Melanie sitting at her computer the other night. What if it was from her? What if she was trying to communicate something?

I wasn't about to insert the drive on a company computer, so I decided to sacrifice my personal laptop instead. I set the machine on my desk and attached the flash drive, holding my breath. In the disk lineup, an icon appeared with the name for the drive.

A gift.

Warily, I opened the contents of the drive.

My stomach dropped. I thought I might vomit my coffee. Files of unencrypted names, addresses, social security numbers, and passport photos poured across my screen.

This is it, I thought. *We've been hacked. For sure.*

But upon closer look, the layout of the files appeared different from ours. Text fields were altered and arranged in a different orientation. I scanned the names in bold at the top of each entry. None of them were familiar, though I thought I recognized some from old criminal reports back in the day.

These were not our files, I concluded.

I inspected the long strings of filenames more closely.

Holy fuck.

These were from Pexler.

★★★

"ALEX," DREW SAID. "I don't think my heart can take any more surprises."

"None of it is ours," I said, scrolling through the list of names as he watched. "It's all Pexler."

Drew glanced across the room at the door, checking again that it was locked.

"Okay," he said, "but what the fuck is a drive full of sensitive Pexler data doing on our doorstep?"

"I don't know any more than you," I said, pushing the envelope toward him.

"Whoa, whoa, anthrax alert!" Drew took a few steps back.

"There's nothing else running on this drive. No hidden files. No malware."

"Could it be from Melanie?"

"I don't know," I said. "Why would she have a drive of Pexler files?"

"Why the hell is a dead woman walking around alive?"

"This was definitely mailed," I said, examining the postmark on the stamp. "And it wasn't sitting here on Friday."

"Okay, okay, so here's my next question." Drew parked in front of my desk. "What the hell do we do with it?"

"What do you mean what do we *do* with it? We tell Jessie there was a leak."

"No." Drew shook his head hard, his arms flying in front of him. "No fucking way we tell them."

"It's the right thing to do."

Drew put his hand up by his ear. "Uh, hi, hello, Jessie. Hello, Analise. I know you recently had a breach attempt. We're your biggest competitor, but here you go, here's a truckload of your most sensitive data that just fell into our lap. P.S. It *definitely* wasn't us who stole it. You believe us right?"

"They need to know this data was accessed. There could be copies of this drive. They could've been mailed to every competitor this morning." I leaned forward on my desk. "Drew, the names on this drive belong to real people. Their lives are at risk if this data was shared with anyone else."

Drew sighed dramatically, throwing his hands to his sides. "I didn't get into this business for the morals."

"Listen," I said. "I don't think we should have this conversation over the phone. You said Bex has Analise's number. Text her and ask if Jessie will meet with me today. I'll give her the drive and explain what happened. I think they'll trust us. And ultimately, they'll thank us."

★★★

THERE WERE A FEW other occupied tables in the small restaurant, the lunch rush having just passed. The sun was already starting to slip toward the west, gleaming off the polished round tabletops. I sat hunched in my coat and scarf, sipping water and trying to steady myself. Across the restaurant, I could see Jessie approaching.

"Well, well," she said. "To what do I owe the pleasure?"

"I wish it was under better circumstances."

Jessie's face flashed concern.

"Here," I said, gesturing to the empty chair across from me. "Have a seat."

Water had already been delivered to the table and the waiter dismissed. Nothing more would be needed, and I did not want us to be interrupted.

I lowered my voice. "I have something to tell you. I know it sounds crazy, but I hope you'll believe me."

I slid the envelope onto the table. Jessie frowned at it. Quietly I explained how it had come into my possession, how I had launched the drive and seen the contents, and more importantly, how I had no idea where it had come from.

Jessie stared at the envelope, then looked up at me. I was surprised to see not concern, but amusement. "Alex, you can't be serious?"

I blinked.

"You're joking, right?"

"I'm afraid not," I said, still sullen.

Frowning, Jessie lifted the envelope and slid the thumb drive into her palm.

"What exactly did you find on it?" she asked. "Usernames and encrypted passwords?"

"No," I said. "I didn't. I'm afraid it looks like... more sensitive information. Unencrypted."

"Alex," she said. "I'll share some insider information with you. We weren't lying when we said nothing sensitive was stolen in the breach last week. So if what you say is true, then whatever's on here doesn't make any sense."

"Maybe it's not even real then," I said, suddenly feeling dumb. "That'd be great if it wasn't even really a threat."

"Bogus files," Jessie said. She shot me a suspicious look. "Are you trying to throw me off my game here?"

My face flushed. "No, no, not at all. I just wanted to tell you first. In case it was legitimate, before you found out from another source. I swear I just received this in the mail. I don't have anything to do with what's on there."

She continued to stare at me.

"You have to believe me," I said.

I couldn't read her, my head was swimming. Was I an idiot? Did she trust me? I could sense a contemplation swimming in her brown eyes. But growing underneath, I saw trust. She closed her hand around the flash drive. "Well, either way, thank you for bringing this to me."

I thought I would sense terror or shame, but it was clear she was much more confident at her job than I was, and probably more capable. There was a sense of conviction. I could see her already formulating the next steps in her head. She was brilliant.

"I'll figure this out," she said, looking up reassuringly. "In the meantime, don't forget to look after yourself. We're not the only ones being targeted right now."

I'm not sure what was displayed on my face at that moment. Perhaps admiration. She studied my face, a sense of mutual appreciation blossoming, hanging there between us. Then she reached out a hand. "You have an eyelash."

Quickly I shot back to avoid her touch, in a sharp, rigid motion. She looked surprised, and I'm sure I looked petrified. We were frozen there like that, and embarrassment poured all across my body.

"Sorry," I said. "It's—"

"No, no, I shouldn't have... overstepped." She lowered her hand back to the envelope in her lap and cleared her throat. "Anyway, I need to go see to this flash drive."

Together we rose and exited the restaurant, stepping onto the sun-bathed sidewalk. We turned to face each other.

"Thank you again," she said. "Truly."

"Well, hopefully it's nothing," I said. "Some kind of prank."

"Yeah, I'll let you know." She pulled out her phone. "Here, give me your number."

Her fingernails tapped against the phone screen.

"Oh, and Analise keeps mentioning your brother," she said, looking up with a smirk. "Maybe we'll meet up again under happier circumstances."

"I hope so," I said.

Jessie smiled, brushing the hair from her face as a November breeze passed by. "Take care, Alex."

We nodded at each other and departed. I was walking the three blocks south to Sentry when my phone pinged. It was a text from a new number.

It's Jess :)

DREAMS.

It wasn't the police station this time, or a sunny walk to the ice cream truck. It was Jenny Starling's last day at summer camp. She and her friends were playing hide and seek. It was as if I was standing there with them, watching them scatter as a twelve-year-old boy with glasses crouched in the grass and counted. The heat was blistering, sweat dripping down their skin, the sun beating down hard as it does in Tennessee August.

I followed Jenny as she stomped across the grass, cicadas buzzing in our ears. The children laughed as one by one they ducked away behind a tree or bush. The lowering sun cast long shadows across the grass, giving one or two of them away.

Jenny ran the farthest, all the way to the arts and crafts cabin. She rounded the corner and flattened herself against the doorway, snug in the darkened alcove. I stood behind a nearby tree as if I was hiding myself. Hiding from the memory.

Jenny was so far away from the others. There were no sounds of other children. But there were approaching footsteps.

Run. I always think it, plead it.

A camp counselor, the quiet one that people whispered about. It's his face Jenny doesn't expect to see when he steps into the alcove. Something hits me in my core when I see the look on her face when she looks up.

I know what happens next. I can feel everything she's about to feel, the pain, the vomit, the loss of innocence, the betrayal of trust.

I didn't need to see it for the terror to rip me from sleep.

Shooting straight up, I fell out of bed and retched on the floor. I collapsed onto my side, sweating and panting, letting the tears stream down my face.

Quickly I pulled myself up to my desk, grappling for the photo album and tearing it open to the first few pages. Drew and I on a carnival ride. Our first fishing trip. Playing cards at our grandparents' house.

My breathing steadied as my own sense of self returned and Jenny faded away.

But that itself was also hopeless.

★★★

"The dreams. Yes, I used to have the dreams quite a bit."

"You don't anymore?"

"Not for ten years or so." Roger tapped his glass against his head. "It's the spigot."

"The spigot," I said, tasting the words. He had mentioned this the first time we met. "Okay. So you channel other people's memories into their own sections?"

"Yes," Roger said.

"How?"

The old man nodded. "Well, like any skill it takes practice. My advice would be to try taking some new memories from someone safe. What about your brother? When's the last time you pulled him?"

"Several years ago," I said, then shook my head. "That's a violation of trust."

"Alright. Someone else you know with a happy childhood?"

I cycled through the small handful of people I knew in my head. Eric, Priyanka, Lucio. Jessie.

"Hard to find one of those these days," I said jokingly.

The old man waved his hand. "Young folks. So dramatic. Try pulling a war veteran."

I held my tongue and pivoted.

"So that brings up another question," I said. "The violation of trust. If I want to make a new friend, or date someone. Does that ever bother you, knowing exactly what they know?"

The old man gave a slight shrug.

"For instance, someone who works at a rival company," I continued, running my thumb along the edge of the counter. "Being around them means I might pull them at some point. I don't feel right knowing their proprietary information."

Roger took a swig of his stout. "I believe there are people who would literally pay millions of dollars to be in your very shoes."

I sighed, feeling hopeless. The old man sensed this.

"You are going to have this information in your memories whether you like it or not," he said. "There is no way to filter a pull. Believe me, I've tried." He shifted in his chair. "But haven't you had memories of your own that you've chosen not to revisit?"

I thought about this carefully.

"Maybe something embarrassing or hurtful that you've blocked out. Can you not try the same thing?"

"I guess so."

Roger shrugged. "Regardless, I don't think this is as big a deal as you make it to be."

I chuckled. "I appreciate your bluntness."

"It's the nature of relationships. We reveal things to others that we didn't necessarily plan to share. And we just tuck those things away. We know they're there, but we pay them no mind."

His words warmed me along with the alcohol, the lights above the bar glimmering in my hazy vision. Among the distorted glare in my eyes, Roger's face looked younger in the light, and for a moment I could picture him as a middle-aged man, a caring father doling out words of wisdom to a child. He was already more of a father to me than my own. My simple-minded father who always found me to be too much of a sissy.

I shook my head to clear the thoughts, which caught a glance from Roger.

"You just did it, didn't you?" he asked. "I saw you go somewhere, and you didn't like it. So you put it out of your mind."

I smiled and nodded. "You're exactly right."

★★★

MY PHONE PINGED AS I left the bar. It was a text from Drew.

Got a setup with the hotties again.

I frowned.

In English please?

The phone rang. I sighed and answered it.

"Tomorrow night, bro," Drew buzzed into my ear. "You, me, and a couple of Pexlers."

"Jesus, Drew, they have names."

"Hey, did you see this bust on Ackheim?"

My mind spun. Ackheim was another tech database firm. "No. What's up?"

"Another breach. They're pretty tight-lipped. CEO has yet to be heard from. I'm guessing it's pretty bad. Hey, did you ever hear anything from what's-her-face about the drive?"

I sighed. "You mean Jessie?"

No response.

"No," I continued, "I haven't."

"That's a little sus, don't you think? You probably did her a big favor."

"It could mean anything, Drew. Including nothing."

"Either that or the police are about to come arrest your ass tomorrow," Drew said, laughing.

"No, no," I said reassuringly. "I could tell she believed me."

"Oh yeah? Did you look into each other's eyes and recite the CTO Creed of Honor?"

"Be honest," I said. "How high are you right now?"

"Very."

"Uh huh." I glanced eastward, picturing him cartwheeling in his penthouse. "You need anything?"

"Come over tomorrow after work, we'll get ready together."

"Aren't you a little old to be needing someone to dress you?"

My ear was assaulted by an uncontrollable cackle. "Good one, bro."

He hung up.

Slowly I inhaled the cold night air, feeling the people on the sidewalk rush past me. I held it in my lungs as I watched exposed hands dance by, hanging at people's sides, holding phones to their ears, being gestured in conversation. If I removed my glove, I could touch any one of them and add another stream to my collection. I could try the spigot.

But it was a risky move. I released the air from my lungs, continuing the journey back to the office to retrieve my car.

In my head, wildly, I thought of sitting next to Jessie at dinner tomorrow evening. Laughing and carrying on. Then I pictured her leaning forward to brush an eyelash from my cheek. The touch of someone smart and warm. I didn't move away.

FAVORS.

Wednesday afternoon and still nothing from my newest contact.

I picked up my phone and hovered my thumb over the text app. Then quickly set it back down.

The office phone on my desk rang.

"Hey, boss! How are you?"

"I'm fine, Lucio," I said. "Thanks for asking."

"Great. Just wanted to let you know I've updated the credential system to execute deactivation requests immediately."

"Wonderful. Thank you so much."

I hung up and turned to my monitor where I tabbed through the security logs from the night before. A new daily ritual for me.

No access requests. Nothing in or out. Everything business as usual.

I looked up at my glass door and thought a second. Then I rose and entered the hallway, walking to the first door on my right.

Melanie's office was still unoccupied. I hadn't had the heart yet to ask HR to start looking for a replacement. Her old items were still sitting on her desk, including a wedding photo of Melanie and her husband, Miguel. It was as if she never left, and again I felt the sting of betrayal and confusion.

I saw Priyanka watching me from across the hall.

"Still haven't been able to reach her?" I asked.

She shook her head. "No."

"What about social media?" I asked.

"Nothing. It really is like she's dead."

A chill ran down my spine. "Shame we can't get these things back to her."

"I was thinking about dropping them off," she said. "See if she's still at her old address."

"Not a bad idea," I said. "Let me know how that goes."

"Will do."

I returned to my desk and prepared myself for the call to HR. *Time to move on*, I thought.

But something was nagging at the back of my head.

I turned back to the monitor and called up the email portal, logging into Melanie's account. Maybe I'd find some information buried in here to shed light on the situation. The messages flooded the screen once more. *Spigot*, I thought. Into a cup they'd go, and away they'd be tucked.

There were several new emails at the top, received earlier this week, still unread. One of them caught my eye.

I frowned at the sender address.

afriend@ackheimcorp.com

The subject: *Database asset transfer*

There was an attachment. A moderately sized CSV file.

Immediately I forwarded it to my personal email and pulled up my laptop. There I opened the file. About six hundred rows of data spilled before my eyes. Fully unencrypted information concerning identities, witness protection numbers, passports, addresses.

I pushed myself away from my desk.

"What the actual fuck is happening."

★★★

"Someone's pranking us," Drew said, shaking his head furiously at the screen.

"I don't know," I said. "Why send it to Melanie's email?"

"Maybe it's her!" he said, his voice elevating. "Do we screen for shitheads in this department?"

"Relax," I said. "Let's just think about this. There's no risk for us right now."

Drew pointed at the laptop. "Did you open that on a company computer?"

"Of course not."

"Do you think it could be malware?"

"It's just a CSV file."

"What does that mean?"

"Just a simple spreadsheet. Plaintext rows and numbers."

Drew stared at me blankly.

"No, it's not malware," I said.

I lifted the receiver from the phone on my desk. "Eric, you haven't received any strange emails this week, have you?"

"Um, no. Should I have?"

"No, thank you."

I called Priyanka and Lucio. No strange emails for them as well.

"You know what you should do," Drew said after I hung up. "You should ask Jessie about this tonight."

"Absolutely not."

"Maybe she got one too?"

"I'm not about to reveal to anyone that this happened."

"Well, then...." Drew shifted nervously. "Maybe...."

I waited. "Maybe what?"

The corner of his mouth lifted in a small smile. "Do your thing?"

I stared at him, frowning. "I'm sorry?"

"You know." Drew gestured with his hands. "Touch her or whatever. See what she knows."

Flabbergasted, I drew away from him. "No way am I pulling a competitor for information."

Drew sighed dramatically. "*Jesus wept.* Why can't you just do this for me?" He was starting to yell.

"What's it matter?" I growled back.

"It matters a great deal. It's my fucking company! *Our* company! Support your brother, come on!" He paced furiously in front of the window.

"I'm already supporting you by making sure we don't find ourselves in this same boat as everyone else."

"It doesn't have to be about the leaks, just give me anything!" He turned back to me, furious. "Why the hell do you think I'm arranging these little dates, huh?"

I stared at him, speechless.

"Just fucking mind-read one of them and let's have a leg up on Pexler!" he exclaimed. "Use your ability to our advantage!"

The harsh sting of betrayal hit me in my chest. I stood up and pointed a finger at him. "Fuck off." Storming across the room and ripping open my door, I added, "Fuck *right* off!"

★★★

THE OLD MAN WASN'T at the tavern today. I sat quietly at the bar, shoulders slumped, staring at the grain in the dark wooden counter. I thought about how I'd sat there and told him about my brother and how strong of a connection we had. What a fucking joke.

"It's a bourbon today," I said to the bartender.

The alcohol burned my sadness into anger. My photo album at home held all the good memories with my brother. But currently on rotation in my mind were the bad ones, spinning reel to reel. His rude comments to my college girlfriends. His arrest on my twenty-first birthday for public intoxication. My bailing him out the following year for his DUI, still drunk. My embarrassment around him anytime we were in public, for the absolute swine he was.

I considered texting Jessie that the event tonight was off. She and Analise shouldn't come. Blame it on Drew somehow. I hiccupped as I reached for excuses.

But then I thought better. I thought about how much I'd been looking forward to tonight. To seeing Jessie again. Clearly I couldn't rely on my brother for companionship. Not if he was willing to exploit me for his own personal gain.

Sliding the empty glass back across the counter and laying down a twenty, I rose and left the tavern. The afternoon was just beginning to fade into evening, the sun painting the sky in shades of pink.

I had to take some kind of step forward. And I wasn't going to let this be taken from me.

GOOD COMPANY.

A LIGHT DRIZZLE HAD begun to fall from the sky as I arrived outside the restaurant. My phone pinged and I looked down at an incoming text, the first from Jessie.

Drew says you're not coming?

I texted back, *I just pulled up.*

Oh, good. I was worried I'd be doomed to third wheel status.

Ha. Be there in a sec.

Wet tires rolled across the pavement behind me as I ascended a large flight of concrete steps. We were down in the Financial District somewhere. The Hudson slinked lazily by in the distance, shimmering in the mist.

A highly polished maître d' led me to my party upstairs in the coveted lounge, sparsely sat and overlooking the lights on the riverbank. Staff in crisp white shirts and jade green vests diligently ran drinks and food among the big round tables where customers laughed politely in that way that only wealth creates.

Our table was over by the window. Drew was dressed in a tan suit, not exactly flattering against his blond hair. Analise wore a sleek navy dress, leaning in to listen to Drew who was sitting back in his chair, always the one to demand an audience.

Jessie looked up first as I crossed the room. She wore a red blouse under a white blazer, her brown hair resting on her shoulders. She was studying me as usual behind her black glasses, but this was no surprise. Having gone home and showered, trimmed my beard, and pulled back my hair smoothly in a bun, I felt myself walking taller tonight. Taller than I had in years.

Even Drew and Analise's eyes lingered briefly on me as I took my seat, willfully shedding my long jacket and setting it on the seatback. I couldn't remember the last time I wore a crisp button-up shirt to a public outing. The cool air against my neck only made the night feel more thrilling.

"Drew," I said grimly, giving a light nod in his direction. Then I smiled at his date. "Analise, so nice to see you again. And—"

"Mr. CTO," Jessie said, smiling. "So glad you haven't abandoned me."

"I wouldn't dream of it."

***

By the time the first round of food arrived, I could feel Drew's persistent glare burning into me like a fire. I was doing my best to ignore him, like a parent refusing to acknowledge a petulant toddler.

"I'm gonna take a pic," Analise said, turning around and angling her phone to get the entire table into frame. "Everyone lean in."

Jessie and I hunched over the table, brushing shoulders. Analise threw up a peace sign and winked, snapping the photo. "Perfect," she sang.

Drew still looked displeased. He placed his napkin in his lap without speaking a word.

As I raised my glass of bourbon to my lips, I saw Analise's eyes land on my black leather gloves.

"I hope you don't mind," she said. "Can I ask you something?"

"Of course," I said.

"Is there a reason you wear those?" she said, gesturing to the gloves. "Cold hands?"

I smiled, not offended. I always had an answer ready for this. "I got some bad burns on my hands when I was a kid," I lied, setting down my glass. "I prefer to wear these in public so as not to disturb anyone."

"Oh," Analise said, looking sad. "I'm sure it can't be that bad!"

"It's actually quite hideous," Drew said sourly. I shot him a look.

"Drew!" Analise hissed, taken aback.

Drew kept his eyes down on his soup, sipping nonchalantly from his spoon, then changed the subject. "So Jessie, everything all good with the data breach?"

The corners of Jessie's mouth pulled back slightly as she tried to hide a grimace. This wasn't something she wanted to talk about tonight.

"Yes," she said. "Like we told the press, nothing important was stolen."

"But the drive," Drew said, sipping his chowder, never once smiling. "Was it fake then?"

Jessie's pleasant smile was faltering. She thought he was being a prick, and she was right.

"Drew," I snapped under my breath.

"Got something to say, little bro?" Drew asked, finally looking at me. The look on his face dared me to raise the stakes.

"Not now," I said.

Analise laughed nervously. "Let's talk about something more interesting."

"You know what I find interesting," Jessie said, no longer smiling as she stirred her soup. "Pexler and Ackheim have been recent targets, but Sentry doesn't seem to be having any trouble at all."

The recording of Melanie flashed through my head. Drew and I shared a fleeting glance. Neither of us said a word.

"That's a little suspicious, don't you think?" Jessie looked up at Drew, welcoming a response.

Drew shrugged. "Sounds like a lack of competency."

Immediately I shot back in my chair and stood, glaring down at my brother as everyone else looked up in shock.

"You're crossing a line," I said, my voice rising.

Drew shrugged again, the picture of arrogance. "I guess we'll never know if I'm right though, huh?"

Jessie frowned at Drew. "What the hell is that supposed to mean?"

Voices began to overlap. Analise desperately waved her hands over the table. "Guys, guys! Stop this!" But already nearby patrons were beginning to stare.

I jabbed a finger at the empty double bourbon sitting in front of Drew. "Sounds like you need to cut yourself off. I've seen what happens when you have too many."

Drew's face reddened as he shook his head back and forth. I could see his lungs filling with a queue of abhorrent words.

I was aware of the attention we were drawing and how badly this was going. Whatever my intentions had been for the night, clearly they weren't going to happen. I dropped my napkin on the table and left before we could descend into chaos any further.

As I walked away, I was surprised to hear a set of footsteps behind me. Jessie had risen and left the table as well. "I'll come with you," she said. Behind her, Analise was trying to calm Drew down as he laid his face in his hands.

★★★

We left the lounge upstairs and descended to the main floor, where tables were beginning to clear out as dinner was coming to an end. Jessie touched my back and pointed to a few empty seats at the bar.

"I'm so sorry," I said immediately as we sat down. "There's no excuse for him, there's no excuse for me, there's—"

"Relax," she said, touching my sleeve again. "It's okay. You're fine. And as for your brother, I've dealt with a lot of arrogant men. It's part of the job." She signaled the bartender to bring us a couple beers.

I sighed, staring at my lap, feeling shame pour over me, pulsing with the bourbon. The beer was set with a clink before me.

"Honestly, I'm kind of glad to get away from those two." Jessie took a swig of her own beer. "I only tagged along because you were coming."

I looked up at her in bashful shock. She laughed.

"Don't look so surprised!" she said with a shrug. "Finding good company is hard these days."

"Tell me about it."

A moment of silence passed before Jessie spoke again. "Everything okay with you and your brother?"

"We're just not seeing eye to eye right now."

"Wow, that's the most diplomatic summary of a fight I've ever heard."

I sighed. "It'll all boil over. I'm…." I hesitated before I continued. "I'm thinking about going in a new direction with my life."

"Oh, okay, wow." Jessie took another drink. "Big words. What direction?"

"I don't know," I said, shaking my head and laughing. "I don't really know what I mean by that."

Jessie nodded slowly, thinking for a moment. "Can I ask you something? Something that's been on my mind for a while?"

"Shoot."

She placed her beer on the counter and set her hands on her knees, lowering her voice. "Do you think what we're doing is good?"

I blinked. "I'm sorry?"

"Our jobs. Our employers. What we're actively doing. Protecting the identities of people who probably did some bad things in the past."

I thought carefully. "Well, it's not like that's our entire database."

"True. But they're in there, right? I mean, it's no secret Sentry and Pexler both host information from major police and legal departments across the country. Ackheim too. I've seen some names in our database that I recognize from headlines."

I nodded, taking another drink. "I understand what you mean. That's a really good question." My eyes drifted to the wall behind the bar, focusing on something much farther away. "You know, I used to work with the police. It used to be my job to help catch the bad ones. I mean, some truly *awful* people. You do what you can, and know when you've hit your limit."

"Wow," Jessie said. "I never pegged you as a former cop."

"Not a cop exactly." I shifted my weight in my chair. "But, even after all that, I don't feel personal responsibility for my brother's business. You just can't save everyone." I could hear the hollowness of my own voice, the sadness plucking at my throat.

"I suppose," she said. She thought silently to herself, then shrugged. "Anyway, just something I think about from time to time. And I don't know, maybe in a 'new direction in my life' kind of way, as you say." She tilted her bottle toward mine. "Here's to not having a clue what we're doing with our lives." I clinked mine against hers with a smile.

As we each sipped from our beers, I registered how quiet it had gotten, the finely dressed patrons slowly trickling from their tables to the door. It must be getting late. Time passed so easily, it seemed, with this conversation partner.

Jessie lowered her beer back to her lap. "I'm sorry I didn't text you," she said.

"Oh, it's fine, I wasn't expecting…." I trailed off as she continued.

"There was, shall I say, a surprising discovery involving that flash drive." She looked grimly at the counter. "I didn't necessarily want to discuss it over the phone or anything." She waved a hand.

"And it's nothing major anyway. I just… want to say thanks again for bringing it to my attention."

I watched her face carefully, trying to decode what she'd just told me, when suddenly she pulled her phone from her pocket.

"Looks like sis is ready to go home," she said.

"My brother's charm has worn off at last."

★★★

WE GATHERED OUR COATS and stepped outside, where the drizzle had turned into a slow, light snow. The restaurant had mostly emptied at that point, its guests long gone in their cars, leaving the entire block to ourselves. Lining the steps, dormant green bushes shivered against the dreary cold night.

Jessie and I descended the steps slowly, our companions lagging behind as Drew helped Analise with her coat.

"We should do this again," Jessie said. "Without the airheads next time. Ever been to Sculpture Park?"

"No, I haven't."

"I'll send you a link. It's nice even in the winter."

We reached the landing separating the flight of stairs. Up top, I could hear Drew apologizing to Analise as they started their goodbyes.

"Well, I look forward to it," I said, turning to face Jessie.

I was stuck in time, considering whether or not to touch her. She seemed like a genuinely good person, with no apparent demons. But if I decided to do it, how would I? Would it be an overstep to remove a glove and tuck a tuft of hair behind her ear?

As the seconds ticked by, I could feel myself retreating from the task. Which was why I was relieved, and then thrilled, to feel her take a step closer. Smiling, she looked up into my eyes.

I braced myself. I prepared my mind, just as I'd been told.

She closed her eyes, and I could feel the warmth of her skin as it closed the space between us.

Please be all right inside, I thought. *Please be good.*

Her lips touched delicately against my cheek, and the world around me went silent.

PULL.

"Sissy. Help me."

A small girl, no more than four, held up a plastic doll to another girl with darker hair, about seven. The latter was constructing an elaborate Lego display, sitting at a table in a large white room.

The older sister turned in her chair and pointed to the doll's back. "See the Velcro? That's how you remove it." She fiddled with the little pink shirt with her small fingers.

The younger one smiled, a small tongue poking out between her lips as she breathed in excitement. She looked up at the display her sister was constructing. "Whatcha building?"

"It's the Louvre," the older girl said. "It's a museum in France. Where the Mona Lisa is."

"It's a triangle," the little one said curiously.

"Yes. It's the strongest shape there is."

I was standing in the corner of the room, having just realized where I was. Somewhere in a memory.

I don't need to index everything right now, I thought to myself. I bowed my head as the room dissolved and let the stream of memories pass over me like water. Science fairs, soccer games, piano lessons. A caring, elegant mother. An absent father, always busy with work. When he wasn't working, he was overseeing the education of his eldest by three years, an awkward, quiet boy with thick glasses. He didn't interact much with his daughters.

It was all instant knowledge to me. And if I focused hard enough, I could push most of it aside, like a swimmer struggling for the surface. But as any human being knows, there are key moments that make a person. Defining interactions that set a cornerstone in the foundation of character. These were the memories that drew me in the strongest. One spooled out before me as I opened my eyes to watch.

"Chris, where are you taking him?" the mother called from the kitchen.

A man with graying hair and glasses shrugged on his coat, his spectacled preteen son in tow. "I'm taking Gideon to the NASA seminar tonight at Harvard. A colleague's reserved a spot for us."

The brown-haired girl peeked around the corner.

"Why don't you take Jessica as well?" the mother said from the other room. She had observed her eldest daughter's keen intellect for science and numbers.

"Father and son only, I'm afraid," the man said. He smiled at his boy and placed a hand on his shoulder. He was to be his protégé.

The girl saw it all, and jealousy sparked within. But this did not make her bitter. Rather, as the scene dissolved and I progressed through time again, this jealousy fueled her passions even more. She worked harder at her studies. Her grades rivaled that of the son, both top of their class. She watched from the wings to see if her father would notice.

Once the brother left for college, it was sure to be her chance to win her father's affection. But then the mother became ill, and it fell on the brown-haired girl to care for her sister. She heard nothing from her brother at MIT, who couldn't be bothered to care about anyone beyond himself.

In front of me, the tear-soaked image of a woman lying in a hospital bed took shape. She wore a knit cap over her balding head, and sitting in the chair next to her was her oldest daughter, stroking her hand. The girl's brown eyes were fixed desperately on her mother, willing her to wake, to smile, to laugh. The heart monitor beeped slowly, echoing as the months marched on, and the room evaporated into a haze.

Another memory unfolded. Now sixteen, the girl was arriving home after a late evening in the school computer lab where she'd been experimenting with creating a new program. Her father was angry at something from work and smelled of drink, muttering as he paced in the den.

Her younger sister was listening to music in the other room, and the father yelled for her to turn it down. She didn't hear. She was on the phone laughing with a friend. The father took several long strides into the room and raised his voice, beginning to swear.

The brown-haired girl listened in horror as items were kicked and shoved aside. When she rounded the corner, she saw her father towering over the little girl, who let out a whimper.

The spark inside the older girl returned, but it wasn't jealousy this time. It was rage.

She sprang into the room and planted herself before their father.

"Leave her *alone*," she said, staring into his eyes.

The man raised his fist, an instinct fueled by alcohol.

"If you touch her, I swear to God I'll call the police," the girl hissed.

"Oh, yeah?" the father said, slurring his words. "Is that what you want? To end up in a foster home?"

"Is that what *you* want?" the girl said. "To lose your children in addition to your wife? How about your job?"

The man struggled for words, blinking furiously at his daughter.

"If you ever threaten her again," the girl snarled, "I'll make sure your life is a living hell."

The man shook his head angrily, but said no more. He turned and left the room, muttering under his breath.

The girl knelt beside her younger sister, who still sat on the floor with her hands over her face.

"Are you okay, sis?" Jessie took her sister's hands in her own.

Analise looked up at her with tear-filled eyes. Then she threw herself into her sister, who wrapped her arms tightly around her shoulders.

From now on, she would be a fighter. A protector. She wouldn't try to please anybody, because there was nobody important enough in this world to please. Not even her father.

She whispered this to her mother the night before she died. One week later, Jessie left for college at Northwestern on full scholarship. Analise went with her. Those first few years they were barely able to cover their rent, unaided by their father's wealth. But things got better.

The rest flowed quickly over me. Her brother's invitation, years later, for her to come work at his company did not hold much weight within the context of her life. She believed it to be a half-hearted offer, perhaps out of guilt. I closed my eyes and tuned out the remaining three months spent as CTO at Pexler, deliberately shielding myself from any insider knowledge. It seemed to be working.

The pull was finished, and the memories melted away. I felt a warm glow in my heart for the girl I'd watched grow. The fighter, the protector. The spark in her eyes as she stared down her father. The love in her eyes as she hugged her sister.

She's good, I thought with a hopefulness that almost made me cry. *She's a good person.*

This could actually work.

★★★

It had been so long, but that familiar feeling of waking up from a dream fizzled over me. How comforting it was to open my eyes and be looking down into Jessie's. She smiled warmly at me as she took a step backwards.

"Good night, Alex."

I didn't want to let those brown eyes go. Those eyes that contained that same spark I'd seen in her memories. She turned and walked down the lower flight of stairs. *I'll see her again*, I thought with a wave of excitement.

Analise walked past me after her sister. The little blonde girl, all grown up. We gave each other a small nod as she joined Jessie at the empty curb, the concrete at their feet sparkling in the snowy mist. Silently, the younger sister tucked her hand into the elbow of the eldest. A gentle quietness fell upon the block like a featherlight veil, shielding us from the cold city night.

Then I remembered the douchebag of the evening. I turned around and looked up the steps. There he was, frowning with his hands on his hips, staring out toward the river.

Maybe I was still moved by the protector. *I shouldn't leave him here in this state.*

"Alright, Drew," I called up the steps. "Let's get you a car and get you home."

Suddenly Drew's head snapped left, his attention drawn by something on the street. The sound of screeching tires echoed off the concrete steps. I spun around, puzzled by the commotion.

Bouncing headlights flashed across my eyes. It took me a second to blink the light away, and realize that a black SUV had pulled up onto the sidewalk at the bottom of the stairs. Its great metal doors with tinted windows were flung open. Two men, dressed in black and donning ski masks, leapt out of the car.

My heart stopped as I looked down at the sidewalk.

"*Jessie!*" I yelled.

"Don't fucking move!" a third man boomed, sliding from the car with a large rifle in his arms and pointing it at me.

Jessie and Analise turned, their faces stunned, struggling to grasp what exactly was unfolding before them. Then Jessie grabbed her sister's arm and began to move. Unfortunately, the other two men were already off to a running start, and in a matter of seconds they had their arms wrapped around the women, pulling them to a halt.

"Someone help!" I called out to the empty block, with not a soul to hear to me.

I stepped forward onto the stairs. The man with the gun fired a warning bullet toward my feet. "I said stay *back!*"

"*Jesus, fuck,*" I heard Drew mutter somewhere behind me.

Analise screamed as one of the men dragged her toward the car. Jessie, on the other hand, grunted and tossed her head as she stepped on her captor's foot and wriggled free. The man kept a hold on her wrist.

"Someone call the police!" she shouted. The man sank a punch into the side of her head.

"*Hey!*" I bellowed.

But Jessie raised her hand and returned the blow, right into the man's stomach. He lost his grip and for a second she was free, but he quickly recovered and lunged after her, grabbing her coat.

At the car, Analise's captor was loading her into the backseat. The man with the large gun turned his head to his struggling colleague. "Wrap it up!" he yelled. I took a few steps forward, but he snapped his attention back to me. My pulse racing, I sized him up, wondering if I could overpower him and take the gun. He was only ten feet away from me.

The other man grunted as he leaned back and lifted Jessie's feet off the ground, backing up with her toward the car, his arms locked around hers. She was able to land a kick to his knees, and he dropped her to the ground, still clutching her forearm. Then she looked down, and I could see her clock something. She reached toward the man's waist.

"No!" the man grunted. There was a fast movement of hands and the sound of metal.

My breath caught in my throat. "Hey, hey, be caref—!"

A shot rang out, echoing across the empty street.

I flinched, ducking my head.

All had become eerily silent. Jessie and the man stood with their hands tangled together in front of them. They appeared stunned. Slowly, Jessie released her grip and the man stepped back. In his hand was a pistol.

On her blouse, a dark crimson began to spread across her stomach.

"*Jessie!*" I yelled, my voice breaking.

Her aggressor turned and ran for the car. Ignoring the gunman, I took off running down the stairs toward her.

Jessie dropped to her knees, clearly in shock. She looked down at her stomach and let out a rasping exhale, before collapsing back onto the concrete.

"Jessie, no!" I cried. "No, no, no." I knelt down next to her and laid a gloved hand on her cheek, before remembering what needed to be done. I pressed both my hands against her stomach, where a massive amount of blood had pooled, soaking into her shirt.

Don't die on me. Please.

But I could already see on her face that she was fading fast. Behind me, I barely registered the sound of car doors closing, the engine roaring like a lion as the SUV sped off past us into the night.

"Please," I whispered to her, begging. "Please don't go."

Moments passed as I listened desperately for the sound of a siren, snow drifting silently around us. Her brown eyes looked straight up into the night sky as her breathing slowed into nothing. Tears fell from my face into the mess of blood below. I could tell, better than anyone.

She was gone.

PART II.

HOLLOW.

I LAY IN MY bed, unmoving, watching the blue city lights dance against the wall as they shone through the sleet on my window. Slipping in and out of sleep, flashes of the night before tangled messily with memories that weren't my own.

I hadn't eaten, hadn't moved since I returned home that morning. It had been a long night in the NYPD station, sitting next to Drew under fluorescent lights as we waited for the cogs of the justice system to slowly turn. I'd waited hunched over, my elbows on my knees, my stomach sick. My hands scrubbed raw. Drew just stared down the hallway expressionless. We said nothing. One at a time, we entered the detective's room for an official statement, then we left the station at four in the morning.

Please let it be a dream, I thought every time I woke. But every time, it wasn't.

As I drifted back to sleep, I saw a young teenage girl with a backpack, her brown hair pulled back, walking along a sidewalk. Somewhere behind her, someone yelled for her attention. She stopped and turned to look. Her eyes met mine and we stood locked in each other's gaze, knowing and resigned.

I'm so sorry.

★★★

Jessie stood on the upper level of the Brooklyn Bridge, looking out over the foggy river. Her first day in NYC. All around her people jogged, walked, talked. She held a bagel in her hand, a coffee in the other. A real New Yorker.

It's a nice change from Chicago, she thought as she sipped her coffee, watching the East River drift between banks of glittering buildings. She looked down at her watch. Time for work.

In a large metal building on the north border of Midtown, Jessie crossed the marble lobby floor toward a large bank of elevators, stepping inside one and swiping her security badge. Pexler Technologies was on the twelfth floor, overlooking Central Park. How strange to see such an expanse of green in the middle of a metropolis, she thought.

Her office was in a hallway with several others. Carter, her Chief of Security. Ciaran, her Head of Engineering. Tian, her IT Lead. They smiled and greeted her kindly as she arrived. On her desk was a note from her brother, the only communication she would receive from him that day. *Welcome, Jessie.*

The world shifted beneath me, the office melting away. Jessie stayed looking at the note, but she grew young again. Staring at her brother's chicken-scratch handwriting. An old clock ticked softly down the hall.

Took the laptop to Dad's work.

Jessie sighed. She was surprised he'd left a note at all. She picked up her bag and headed to the door. The school computer lab would be open for another few hours.

"Ana, let's go," she called.

"Ready." Analise skipped up to her side, dressed in gymnast tights and a tank top, a purple bag draped over her shoulder.

"Don't you want to grab a jacket?"

The younger girl looked out the window. "Nah, it's nice outside."

"It *looks* nice. But looks can be deceiving."

Analise reached for the door and stepped over the threshold. "Sometimes you have to let the sun in, sis."

The girls set out on the six blocks to the school. Ever since their mother had gone to the hospital, Jessie had become a glorified escort for her sister. It didn't bother her much. There was plenty to do in books and computers while waiting for gym practice to finish.

A gust pushed brown, dried leaves down the concrete. Jessie pulled her jacket tighter, but Analise eased her shoulders back and basked in the waxing sunlight.

The usual foot traffic was fairly light on this route to the school. A few neighbors would walk by, dogs pulling ladies, kids with their heads bowed under their headphones. Today an unkempt man with shaggy hair and a pale trench coat approached. Jessie eyed him cautiously.

"Let's cross over here," Jessie said, steering them toward the crosswalk.

She could feel the man's eyes on them as they diverted their path. *Don't be scared*, she told herself as they proceeded to pass the man on the opposite side of the street. She felt herself ease once he was out of sight.

But a moment later Jessie checked behind her to find the man had reappeared, following fifty feet behind on their side of the street. Analise turned and looked as well. The older sister reached for the hand of the youngest.

"Don't be scared," she said. "He can't do anything."

But in her mind, she was surveying the neighborhood around them and noting her options should an emergency arise. She glanced back down at her sister, walking quietly. The face of Jenny Starling looked back up.

No, that wasn't right.

Jessie looked behind her again as the sunny fall day dissolved into cold city night. Manhattan, leaving Pexler to grab a coffee across the street. She had sensed someone nearby as she approached the crosswalk to wait. Sure enough, a figure stood in the shadows of the building, studying her. She couldn't see their face, but they looked vaguely familiar. The sudden white of the walk sign shone through the haze, and Jessie made note not to rush or appear afraid. She turned and took calm, steady strides.

In the cafe she scrolled through her phone messages as she waited for her coffee. Her thumb rested again on a new contact, not for the first time this week. She wondered if she should text him with some kind of update. If he could be trusted. If he even wanted to know.

Jessie began to type the words.

The flash drive was—

And stopped. Her thumbs hovered over the keyboard before swiftly erasing the draft. It seemed weird to text the details, like some kind of novel.

She typed out the start of another message.

Hey.

She paused, thinking. Willing the word to morph into something interesting.

I watched the blinking cursor beat time. Then I looked up from the phone screen and the cafe was gone. I was sitting in a dark room, the smell ripe. The bed sculpted around me like a protective shell.

Hey, Drew had texted.

I stared at the blaring screen light.

How are you?

The silence was crushing. The staleness of the room hurt my head. I felt dirty and unwell. I hadn't eaten, slept, in days.

Mom's worried about you, you know.

Who was this imposter who spoke in whole sentences? I scratched at my overgrown beard, and realized my hand was shaking.

The phone began to ring, and Drew's picture flashed across the screen, some dumb photo from college. I knew what this was, even before answering. It was a lifeline. Did I want to be saved?

I pressed the accept button and held the phone to my ear.

The voice was not Drew's.

"I am a better man."

Suddenly hands grasped my neck. The sound of screaming children echoed in my ears. I turned to look for help from anything or anyone. Roger was sitting there next to me. He lifted his beer and nodded.

"Spigot."

But I was overwhelmed. I couldn't possibly compartmentalize under such an attack. I was sinking, sinking in the pool, struggling for the surface and desperate for air. My chest tightened, my throat squeezed.

I was in a car as it slid across the highway. Licked by a fire as it burned my face. Winced from the searing pain as a knife split the skin of my shoulder. The world was coming down on me.

And then a gunshot shattered everything.

The world now silent, I was kneeling before Jessie as she lay bleeding on the sidewalk. Tears slid down my cheeks as her breathing slowed, and then she whispered into the night air.

"Are you okay, sis?"

I heard the car doors close behind me, louder than before. This time I turned to look as the car drove by, the silhouettes of hunched figures behind the tinted windows. And Analise was one of them.

When I turned back to Jessie we were standing, the snow falling slowly all around us. She was looking at me with her warm brown eyes, wearing her knowing smile.

Find her.

WHEN DREW ANSWERED THE door, we didn't say a word. His eyes were heavy with dark circles as they looked into mine. We were both exhausted, physically and emotionally. Maybe that's why we regarded each other with some kind of relief. Whatever tension had been there the night before had expired. I was glad to see him.

"You okay?"

Drew gave a small nod. "Barely functioning. I couldn't sleep until I knocked myself out with some pills this afternoon."

I walked into the apartment as Drew gestured to a pizza box on the living room table. "I haven't eaten all day. This is for both of us. Dig in."

I sat on the couch and flipped open the pizza lid. Reluctantly, I pulled a slice from the box, cheese snapping. I still wasn't hungry, but I was starting to feel my body's desperation for energy.

Outside the window of Drew's corner apartment, the city sky had gone dark. An entire day had passed at what seemed a snail's pace. Now it seemed like wasted time.

Drew placed a hand on my shoulder. "Hey, I'm sorry. About Jessie."

I shook my head, pushing back emotion. "It's Analise we need to worry about now. What did the cops say to you when you went in?"

"The same thing they told you, I imagine. No witnesses, at least none who stuck around. Restaurant said the cameras weren't recording. It's all pretty convenient, don't you think?"

I shrugged. "I don't remember anything else around us after the kidnappers showed up. There could have been tapdancing monkeys and I wouldn't have noticed."

I glanced over at Drew's hands, gripping his plate. He'd had a good vantage point at the top of the stairs.

"Anything you remember from where you were standing?" I asked.

Drew shrugged. "It all happened so fast. I don't think I saw anything you didn't." He looked at me. "You pulled her just before, didn't you?"

"Yes," I said quietly.

"Did you see any clues? Anyone who'd want to hurt them?"

"Not that Jessie knew of. Even then, we can't be sure their attackers knew who they were. That restaurant has some wealthy clientele. They could have just been looking to grab whoever came out."

Drew sat uncharacteristically quiet for a moment. He'd been quite subdued, but so far I'd chalked that up to exhaustion. Then he closed his eyes and exhaled. "I have something I need to show you."

I froze as he pulled his phone from his pocket. He tapped the screen and opened his text messages, then handed it to me. "It's from Analise's phone."

My stomach dropped.

I looked at the text thread between Drew, Analise, and one other number, contact unknown. The messages were time-stamped from four o'clock today.

The first message was a picture. Of Analise.

She was tied to a chair in a dark room, wearing the same navy dress from the night before. Her terrified eyes pleaded through the camera lens.

The message read:

We have Analise. We do not want money. If you want to save her, you will send us the unencrypted information on your top-level classified assets. We know the names. We will know if what you send us is not what was requested.

A lump formed in my throat and my hands began to shake as I read the final message.

No cops or she dies.

***

IN THE BATHROOM I splashed cold water on my face, having just voided the only bites of food I'd taken in twenty-four hours. I looked at myself in the mirror. I could practically see myself shaking, my nerves dancing around inside me on an empty stomach.

I took a deep breath to steady myself, then returned to Drew, sitting on the couch with his head in his hands.

"We have some choices to make," I said. "First one. Are we going to call the detectives and give them this information?"

"You read the text, didn't you? They said no cops." He got to his feet and began to pace. "And with a demand for our data? I'm not about to share this with anyone."

"Second one, then. Do we hand over the data to the kidnappers?"

Drew stopped and gazed out the window. The lights of Manhattan glittered faintly on a blanket of darkness. "No. Not yet anyway."

"Okay," I said. "Then I strongly suggest we rethink the answer to choice number one."

"I'm sorry," he said, still facing away from me with his hands clasped behind his back. "But I can't put my company in jeopardy."

"Drew," I hissed incredulously. "Analise's life is in danger." The little blonde girl from Jessie's memories flashed through my head. "We have to do something with this information."

He said nothing, silently turning the situation over in his mind before his reflection in the window.

"I'm sorry, but I can't just sit here. We can't let her get hurt." I swallowed dryly, pushing against a lump in my throat. "We owe it to Jessie."

A harsh silence fell over the room. Drew's cell phone sat on the table before me, the text thread staring me down like a ticking time bomb.

Finally, Drew spun around. "If that's the case, then we try to figure this out ourselves."

"Drew. This is not a movie. We are not superheroes."

He looked at me, genuinely, with a sense of wonder that surprised me. "But you, you practically are."

"No—"

"No, really, you are!"

"We have nothing to go on, Drew," I said sternly. "I can't pull clues out of thin air."

"Just think a little more," he said encouragingly. "Let's just look at this a little longer. Please."

I sighed, rubbing my tired face with the palm of my hand. "Let me see that message again."

Drew picked up his phone and handed it to me. Something was bothering me, but I couldn't quite put my finger on it. I studied the texts and the picture carefully.

"I did a search online for the third number," Drew said. "Even paid for one of those reverse phone lookup things. But it's unlisted."

The third number.

As I read the digits left to right, they all fell into place.

"This… this is Gideon Pexler's number."

Drew and I looked at each other, dumbfounded.

"I recognize it from Jessie's memories. This is her brother's number."

Drew swiveled on his heel. "Holy shit."

"This ransom was sent to both CEOs. Pexler and Sentry." Again, we locked eyes. "They want data from both."

Drew pointed. "He never responded."

"Yeah, neither did you. What do you think he's going to do?"

Drew covered his eyes and released an anxious whine. "Gideon Pexler is one of the most reclusive men in the world. I'm talking underground bunker vibes. No way that man sticks his neck out to the police."

"And the data?"

"Hell if I know, man."

I thought for a moment. "I understand them kidnapping Gideon's sisters and demanding ransom for Pexler data. But why drag us into it?"

Drew sighed, taking his phone back. "I did some of my own memory searching while you were on your way here. Digital ones." He tilted his screen so I could see as he scrolled through a series of pictures. "Analise's Instagram. Remember that picture she took at the restaurant? Well, here it is."

His thumb rested on an awkward shot of the four of us. Drew and Analise took up the bulk of the foreground. Behind Analise, Jessie and I were barely in the photo at all, our faces split by the edge of the frame. The photo had been posted almost immediately after it was taken, around eight fifteen, and tagged with the name of the restaurant.

"That's how they knew," Drew said decidedly. "That's how they knew we were there."

The sliver of Jessie's face behind Analise's head caught my throat. I looked away.

"And here's a photo of us at the lounge last week," Drew continued, scrolling down. "Before you showed up. These freaks could see we were hanging out."

"Anyone like or comment on either of those posts?" I asked.

"Yeah, only like a thousand people."

"Oh, great. See if any of their accounts is labeled 'bad guys.'"

I scanned the rolodex in my head. Jessie didn't have an online account for us to check. Like me, she hadn't been a fan of social media.

There was one place left I hadn't examined.

I held out my hand, palm up. Drew looked at me.

"Give me your hand," I said.

"No."

Ever since we were little, there'd been an unwritten rule against pulling. Of course, that didn't stop me from occasionally breaking it when we were in spats as teenagers. But as mature adults, we'd resumed respect for the rule. It would be an invasion of privacy and trust, and with an honest, open relationship, unnecessary. I hadn't pulled him for three years.

But now things were different.

"You're the only other witness. You may have seen something I didn't."

"I said no."

"Drew. If we're really going to do this, you have to help me. You have to let me do my thing."

"You can pull me later." Drew began pacing and texting furiously. "I'm arranging for a car to pick us up first thing tomorrow and take us to Pexler. We're going to have a meeting with Gideon."

"You know how to get a hold of him?"

"I have his number, don't I? Plus, if he doesn't want to meet, don't you have an idea of how to track him down?"

Jessie did. I nodded. "Okay. We'll go in the morning."

"Eight o'clock."

One more thought sprang through my head, a beacon from Jessie's memories.

"There's another thing I want to do at Pexler tomorrow," I said. "There's an insurance policy I want to find."

Drew looked up.

The plastic rectangle settled in my mind.

"The flash drive."

ENEMY.

The Pexler building stood tall, a towering monolith in the gray morning light. Swarms of office workers in suits and skirts flocked through the lobby doors, their reflections dancing along the dark tinted windows, moving hastily in a way that people do when they know there's only eight hours left till the weekend. But the hurrying legs and coats felt more like a churning sea, dizzying my eyes as I surveyed the task before us.

Drew stepped up beside me, his car pulling away from the curb behind us. "No word from Gideon."

"That's okay," I said. "He lives here. He'll be here."

I led us into the lobby, its polished marble floor sprawling across a vast atrium. The taps of high heels and leather shoes dotted the air, the smell of perfume pricked my nose. It was a larger, more impressive version of the Sentry building. I could feel Drew stiffen next to me as he tried to act indifferent. I couldn't have cared less.

A line of elevators spanned the far wall where workers were filing in, security badges in hand. We had no badge, but I had a plan. I had seen in Jessie's memories every step to entering this place, every face, every routine.

I pulled out my phone and pretended to read a text as we lingered near the elevators. For a few moments I scanned the people coming and going before me. Then I saw a lady with a familiar face approach the elevators.

"Excuse me," I said politely. "Are you going up to Pexler?"

"Oh, yes," she said, looking at me curiously.

"I have a meeting with Hilary Vale," I improvised, "but they didn't give my name to security." I gestured to the guard perched at her kiosk near the entrance.

The lady smiled. "Of course, I can take you up. Right this way." She hailed an elevator and we filed inside, where she swiped her security badge. Floor twelve, going up.

"Is Jessie Pexler in today?" I asked the woman.

"Jessie? I'm not sure. Sometimes her team works remote."

So news of the incident Wednesday had not made the rounds. No announcement had been made about the loss of one of their own.

The doors opened on the twelfth floor, and a sprawling modern reception area unfolded before us. Big metal letters were affixed to the opposite wall, spelling out the Pexler name. Three young, posh receptionists sat at a long rosewood desk, diligently fielding phone calls. Beyond the clusters of plush maroon chairs, a wall of windows overlooked the green trees of Central Park. I couldn't help but turn to Drew and let out a small whistle. He jabbed me discreetly with his elbow.

"Hilary's office is this way," the woman said, leading us toward a hallway to the right.

"Actually, we're a few minutes early, so I'm just going to pop by Jessie's office and see if she's there to say hi."

"Oh, okay. Have a good day." The woman gave a small wave and continued on.

"Where's Gideon's office?" Drew whispered, turning away from the receptionists.

"One sec," I said. "Just stay here."

"Why can't I come with you?"

"Two strange men wandering around an office looks a bit suspicious. Plus, you're a bit more recognizable than I am. Text Gideon again. Tell him we're here."

I peeled off to the left, down a red carpeted hallway lined with doors and frosted glass panels. Silhouettes sat at their desks chattering on the phone, while others paced before their windows overlooking Central Park. A living, breathing office with no clue something terrible had seized hold of their company. I continued down the hallway as it veered right, passing two men squabbling over an expense report, followed by what looked like a construction worker in overalls, leaving from an open door with a roll of plastic extending into an unfinished hallway lined with the shells of offices. They were renovating the suites one by one, a reward for such a prosperous year.

At the end of the main hallway, I arrived at a large door with a bronze plaque on the wall next to it that read *Engineering*. The door was propped open, as it often was during business hours when people were coming and going. I stepped through the doorway into the suite.

It was like I had been there hundreds of times before. I knew the names on the doors well. Ciaran. Tian. Except Jeff, Jeff was new. Something stirred in Jessie's memories. In my head, I could hear distant voices yelling in a heated argument. Her previous Chief of Security had left on bad terms.

At the end of the hall, Jessie's door was closed and presumably locked, bearing a nameplate that read, *Jessica Pexler, Chief Technology Officer*. But Jeff's door just next to it was open, his shadow resting against the doorway. As I stepped in front of his office, a tired-looking man with spectacles looked up at me with surprise. I studied his face carefully. He looked irritated, but not grieving.

He cocked an eyebrow. "Can I help you?"

"Hi," I said, offering a friendly wave. "I'm Jessie's friend. She's across town and asked me to come by and pick something up for her."

He shot a disapproving glance at my gloved hands. "You have her security badge?"

"No. But she said someone could let me in. Would you mind?"

Jeff eyed me suspiciously, thinking it over. "What's your name?"

"Alex Collins," I lied.

He hesitated, looking me up and down. I could tell he wasn't convinced yet, so I reached for something else.

"She said to tell you it's for the Friedman-Harper account." I smiled. "So you'd know I'm not some stranger."

Jeff sighed. Begrudgingly accepting my story, he rose and approached Jessie's door, extending the laminated badge around his neck. Above the doorknob was a flat sensor, which emitted a digital chirp, and a small LED flashed green. "Okay, Alex. I'll wait here till you're done."

I stepped through the door, feeling Jeff watching me from behind.

There was an eerie stillness to the room that lay beyond. The shades had been pulled. The cleaning crew had swept the carpet in perfect rows, the trash emptied, the desk removed of any dust. Jessie had been a very organized person. There were no papers strewn about. Everything about her had been deliberate, confident. On her desk was a photo of her and Analise. Next to it, I recognized a photo of her mother.

I could feel Jeff's gaze hardening from the doorway. "What exactly are you picking up?" he asked.

Move with purpose, I told myself, turning toward the column of desk drawers.

"Just a flash drive," I answered.

Jessie had left the drive here Wednesday. I pulled open the center drawer and lifted the pen tray to find a tiny key, which I knew would unlock the top right compartment. I inserted the key into the drawer, pulled it open, and sure enough, there it was. That familiar black rectangle, sitting on a scattering of letters. The flash drive containing the unencrypted lives of Pexler's most confidential clients. Exactly what the kidnappers were asking for.

And If Gideon didn't come through with the Pexler data, at least now *we* could.

I evaluated what else was in the desk. There was one more thing that might come in handy. With a quick glance, I saw that Jeff was leaning into his office, answering a call. I reached into the back of the security drawer, and my fingers landed on the duplicate security badge for Jessica Pexler. I slid it, along with the thumb drive, into my pocket.

I looked back at Jeff's partially obscured frame, his voice carrying from the other room. Pausing, I considered my options. I needed to collect as many viewpoints of Jessie's life as I could, and his could provide more insight into the internal Pexler office. Slowly I began to peel back the edge of my glove.

"Got it. Be right there." He stepped urgently out of his office. "I've got to go. Just, close the door when you're done." He stomped hurriedly down the hallway. I sighed, fixing the glove back over my palm.

As I stepped out of Jessie's office and closed the door, I noticed that Jeff had left his own door cracked open. *Some Chief of Security*, I thought. I edged it open a little further. On his desk by the door were two computer monitors, and on the screens were several windows of what appeared to be camera footage. One of them read, *file not found*.

A couple workers passed the open doorway of the Engineering suite, laughing loudly. I stood back from Jeff's doorway, watching them nervously as they walked by without a glance. I needed to get going. Drew was wandering around the lobby without me.

With the badge in my pocket, I moved quickly down the hallway, feeling a heightened sense of stealth.

★★★

DREW WAS PACING IN the reception area when I returned.

"Jesus, about time," he whispered. "Did you get it?"

"Yes. Any word from Gideon?"

"No. I texted him again, still didn't answer."

"Okay." I grinned as I flashed the security badge. "We'll go to him."

Drew regarded the badge with mischievous excitement, one side of his lip turning up in a smile. I jabbed the button for the elevator.

We had the car to ourselves. Once the doors closed, I swiped Jessie's badge on the sensor. Instead of returning to the lobby, we were now able to select any floors that Jessie had clearance for. I pressed the button for number fifty, at the very top. The elevator sailed smoothly upward, the momentum under my feet invigorating, as I pulled the flash drive from my pocket and showed it to Drew.

"I thought the drive was fake?" he said.

I shook my head.

"So they *did* lose sensitive data in the hack?"

I shook my head again, conveying what I saw in Jessie's memories. "She was telling the truth. The hack they announced didn't contain any sensitive information. What's on the drive is from a separate incident. It wasn't an external hack."

"What do you mean? How did someone get a hold of Pexler data without chipping through their security?"

"Because it was someone from the inside."

Drew's eyes widened. "Like Melanie."

I nodded. "Here, it was their last Chief of Security. Carter Young. Looks like he downloaded the files while he was at work." *Kind of stupid really*, I thought, shaking my head. "He was caught and they fired him, the day before the kidnapping."

"Is he the one who mailed you the flash drive then?"

"I have no idea."

The elevator pinged, making us both jump. I straightened and took a deep breath. Remembering the task ahead, I pulled the gloves from my hands and shoved them in my pockets. My bare hands were cold hanging at my sides. If anything, it put me more on edge.

The elevator doors opened.

BROTHER.

I watched the memory of Jessie walk hurriedly out the doors into the dark atrium beyond, her long cardigan billowing behind her.

"Gideon! We need to talk!" she called, her voice echoing back from the large, empty hall. He hadn't answered her. Hopefully we would have better luck.

A shadowed lobby, sprawling with white tiles and curved walls, unfolded before us. In the center was a large assortment of shrubs, the only organic presence in an otherwise cold and sterile environment. It felt like an unattended, post-apocalyptic train station, waiting for passengers that would never come.

"Where the fuck are we?" Drew whispered.

"Gideon's home. He converted the top floor office space into his living and work quarters so he could be close to his business."

"Well there's a new level of work obsession for you."

I stepped from the elevator, my footsteps echoing in the large chamber. A vaulted ceiling with shuttered windows reflected the sounds of our intrusion as we moved forward. I pointed across the room to a large metal door, bulky and foreboding like a spaceship portal.

"That's the only way in," I said.

Next to the door was a complex security panel with screens and scanners Jessie had never had access to. A white camera perched over the doorframe, capturing a wide view of the empty atrium.

"Remind me to upgrade my home security," Drew said.

We stopped in front of the metal door, looking for some version of a doorbell. There was no way to page, no button to press. I looked up at the camera, stationary and unyielding, its red light blinking slowly with a patience I did not have. I knocked twice on the door, the eerie metallic sound bouncing around the space behind us. Nothing moved.

"Do you think he's home?" Drew asked.

"He's always home," I said. I knocked again, harder this time.

A polished recording of a female voice played over a hidden speaker. "Please leave deliveries outside the door."

"Enough of this shit," I muttered. I stepped back, square in the camera's view, and began to shout. "Gideon! I know you're in there! We need to talk about Analise!"

More seconds passed in silence. Drew fidgeted nervously beside me. Then we heard a sound above us. The small mechanical whir of the camera lens, adjusting us into focus.

"We're the other number on the ransom thread," I told the camera. "We were there the night it happened."

A small click, and a tinny male voice asked, "Name?"

I paused. "I'm Alex, and this is Drew. Hemsley."

Drew shifted his weight again, looking away. He didn't like begging for a meeting on his competitor's doorstep.

Another moment passed in silence. I wondered if revealing our full names had been a mistake, though I wasn't sure how we'd discuss the matter otherwise. Then the sensor panel by the door emitted a series of electronic chirps, and a heavy metallic latch moved inside the frame. The door drifted open a few inches.

The tinny voice said, "You may come in."

"Way to open the pod bay doors," Drew whispered nervously.

Beyond the door was a warmly lit room, a large den of sorts, dotted with small table lamps among sleek, modern furniture. Much more comforting than the lobby outside. A grand piano sat tucked in the far corner. A classical music recording played quietly in the distance.

The only unusual presence here was a pair of metal railings running wall to wall that barred us from entering more than six feet into the room. In between the railings was a tranquil koi pond, dividing guest from occupant, a lazy waterfall trickling peacefully near the wall. To our right was the only way forward: a closed wooden door, which I assumed we would not be able, or welcome, to access.

Drew and I ambled up to the railing, silently taking in our surroundings. I had yet to see a living person on this floor.

"Hello?" I called out.

Soft, carpeted footsteps approached at the opposite end of the room. And then a middle-aged man with black hair and glasses, in a tight black t-shirt across a fit torso, rounded the corner.

"Good evening," he said in a calm, deep voice.

I recognized him at once.

So did Drew. "Gideon."

The man nodded. "Andrew." He stopped at the opposite railing, six feet across the water from us. My eyes dropped to his hands, clasped together. Clad in black leather gloves. Already I could sense a stiffness, a distance about him. There was no urgency or worry. He was neither pleased nor irritated. He did not smile.

"May we come in?" I asked.

"I prefer not," he said plainly. "Now, to what do I owe the pleasure?"

Drew and I were taken aback. The fact that it was not clear why we were there was perplexing.

"The text thread," Drew said, holding up his phone. "I assume you saw it?"

Gideon sighed. "Ah, yes. I did see."

Drew stammered, "So… so we're here to discuss it."

Gideon nodded, still emotionless. It puzzled me. It reminded me of the suspects I used to interview at the precinct, disconnected from the rest of the world.

He finally opened his mouth to speak. "So it is, then, that a demand has been made on both of our companies' most prized assets."

"It appears so," I said.

"And do you feel she is worth it?"

We blinked in silence.

"Come again?" Drew said.

"Is my sister worth your most valuable assets?" Gideon sighed. "It's a very simple question."

"I—" Drew stammered.

"Have you called the police?" I cut in.

"No. Nor do I intend to." Gideon looked down at his gloved hands, rubbing his thumbs together. "Messrs. Hemsley, this would not be the first time my sister has tried to meddle in my affairs."

"I'm sorry," I said, trying to shed my disbelief. "Are you telling me you think she's... involved in this somehow?"

"Please do not mistake me for a fool. It would not require much effort on her part to stage a photo, and to bribe the both of us for her convenient reappearance in exchange for money."

"But we were there!" Drew said, the trauma from that night edging into his voice. "We saw the whole thing! They took her in the car and drove away!"

Gideon shrugged. "If that's so, then perhaps it's something she deserves."

I was starting to see red. "How can you say that?" I hissed.

Drew took a step forward. "Look. We just want to get on the same page here. Are you sending them your data?"

"No," Gideon said flatly.

"Okay. Then neither are we, for the time being."

He said nothing.

"Are you going to do... anything?" I asked.

"No."

His indifference tore at my heart. *Sociopath.*

"Anything else I can assist you gentlemen with?" Gideon asked.

Drew stood speechless as I glared silently at the man.

"Good. I believe you can leave now."

Drew and I looked at each other, defeated. This was not how we had planned for this to go. Without saying anything, Drew turned to the door. I looked back at the man, searching for some kind of connection, anything I could draw from him.

"And Jessie? What about her?"

Gideon stared at me, unmoving.

I could hear my voice beginning to sharpen. "Do you have anything to say about what happened to her? Or are you just as indifferent about that as well?"

"Mr. Hemsley," he finally said, his voice monotone. "I have no idea what you're talking about."

"She died right in front of me!" My voice was shaking, my eyes began to water. "Surely the police contacted you."

"I am not very easy to get a hold of, by design." Gideon looked down at the koi pond, the light reflecting off the water and dancing eerily on his angular face. "As for our promising young CTO, the news of her passing is unfortunate. Though truth be told, her presence in my life was barely consequential, and our scarce interactions brought me great unease. Indeed, perhaps it's for the best that we all move on." His dark eyes rose back up to mine. "You should too."

There were no words I could throw at him to suffice the boiling resentment I felt for his apathy. He was emotionally detached, selfish, narcissistic, a sociopath through and through.

And just like that, Gideon turned and walked away. Our visit was seemingly over.

I could not move, could not think. Memories, images, laughter poured before my eyes from Jessie's life. Her brother's isolation from his sisters, how he barely acknowledged them, far too self-interested to see his sibling's brilliance well into their adulthood.

The ground beneath my feet began to feel unsteady. The walls danced before my eyes as I worried I might go unconscious. Drew glanced at me, his face moving from confusion to worry. He reached out and placed his hand behind my shoulder.

"Come on," he instructed. "Let's go."

I was barely able to walk as the memories and emotions flooded over me. Out into the white atrium we stumbled, crossing to the elevator doors. Drew stabbed the button repeatedly. My body was coated with sweat, soaking into my clothes. The ding of the arriving car echoed distantly in my head.

"He's just putting up a front," Drew said, trying to calm me down once we were in the elevator. "Covering up the grief inside. No one's that careless."

You haven't seen the people I have, I thought.

I pictured Gideon again, staring expressionless in the news of his sister's death. And then I blinked and I saw the rat, laughing maniacally. All the same.

"Look, we're gonna find her," Drew said. "We're gonna do better than Gideon ever could."

"How?" I whispered between hyperventilated breaths. "Where do we even look?"

Drew frowned, struggling for words.

In my mind, a young Jessie looked away from her Legos toward her baby sister.

Find her.

As the elevator car began to slow, I turned and stared into my brother's eyes. Eyes that had seen the same terrible thing that night.

He looked confused. "Wha—?"

I reached with my bare right hand and closed it around his wrist.

***

From the top of the stairs, I watched the black SUV pull up onto the curb. I watched the men emerge in their ski masks, the front two reaching for the women, the third pointing his rifle toward me. My heart ached as the whole thing unfolded again beat by beat, yet I couldn't let myself look away.

Please let there be something here, I thought. I couldn't put myself through this again for nothing.

But Drew seemed to have seen the same thing I had, just in a seat farther back. He watched on in stupefied horror, shamefully debating if he should run back inside the restaurant. I looked disdainfully at myself on the landing, frozen before the gunman. *Move, you idiots! Do something!*

I could feel tears beginning to roll down my cheeks. Jessie struggled with her captor, reaching clumsily for his waist. I knew it was coming, but it still hurt, the gunshot burning my ears and singeing my nerves. And then I was watching myself watching her die, dropping to my knees on the sidewalk, Jessie's shirt soaked with red, my gloved hands fumbling hopelessly to apply pressure.

Suddenly, the perspective changed. It was no longer clear what I was doing down by Jessie's dying body. Instead, Drew was watching the men load into the car, Analise shrieking for help as the back door was closed. I could see her struggling desperately behind the darkened windows, hear her voice continuing to scream. I hadn't heard any of it as I'd tended to Jessie, clouded out by the urgency of her condition.

Drew felt panic as the car drove away, the gunned engine echoing in his ears. He couldn't move, couldn't think. But he could still see, Camera A was still recording. And through the fog of terror, I could just make out the edges of a small plate of text.

Stop everything.

The commotion halted. Slowly I descended the stairs, walking through suspended snow, a cloud of fumes, the glow of red light. I knelt down behind the stationary SUV, no longer a menacing vessel beyond capture.

"My god, Drew," I whispered, staring at the letters and numbers before me. "You did it."

But as this memory was ending, something else was echoing behind me, tucked away in a memory further back. It rivaled the triumph I felt. No, this was something dark, a shadow in my brother's mind.

It pulled at me, like a black hole. The street outside the restaurant began to fade away, like dark oil paints swirling together. I squinted, looking further back, almost a year ago, into a bright rectangle of white.

I stood in Drew's penthouse bedroom. He was slouched over in his king size four-poster bed. On the nightstand beside him lay a light dusting of white powder. Head-numbing dance music played from his speaker across the room.

Should I do it? he thought.

He stared down at his phone. The empty text field beckoned him.

It wouldn't be honest. In fact, it would be exploitation. What kind of brother would he be?

Aaaaah just do it.

I watched over Drew's shoulder as his thumbs clumsily typed out the first message.

Hey.

As he texted, Drew's mind raced with possibilities. His special-abled brother meeting with competitors, shaking their hands, covertly absorbing their company secrets.

How are you?

The pit of my stomach dropped, as he pictured his stock price rising.

Mom's worried about you, you know.

★★★

I WAS BACK IN the elevator with Drew, the car finally settling, the door opening. We were looking into each other's eyes. Before the pull, I had prepared to see betrayal.

Instead, I saw shame.

"Alex," Drew whispered.

My throat was catching, my eyes were filling with tears. The hurt I felt was tremendous. It only deepened the guilt on Drew's face.

"Alex, I'm so sorry."

I turned and stormed out of the elevator, leaving him behind as I crossed the bustling ground floor lobby. Blinking back the tears, I yanked my gloves back onto my hands.

To think that I had placed so much importance on our relationship, that I had admired my brother so much for reaching out to help me. But he hadn't wanted to help me, he'd wanted me to help him.

Stepping out onto the crowded sidewalk, the cold winter air stung the tears sliding down my cheeks.

To hell with him. To hell with everybody.

Normally I would have glided skillfully between the bobbing shoulders of New Yorkers. Today I brushed past them carelessly. Let them hit me. Who cared anymore.

Jessie's brown eyes passed through my mind, smiling at me. *Finding good company is hard these days.* I thought of her own pathetic brother. Icy, walled off, an absolute prick. If there was anything clear from this morning, it was that I was on my own.

I brushed aside the hurt and focused on the task at hand. Once more the letters and numbers formed in my head, navy digits against an orange background, plucked from Drew's memories. What security cameras had failed to capture, I had retrieved.

A license plate.

This was my lead, the next step to finding Analise.

SEEK.

I stared at my phone perched on the edge of the table. I was sitting in a coffee shop, unusually slow for a Friday morning. I didn't necessarily want anyone in earshot for what I was about to do. On my phone screen was a number for an old contact, one I hadn't spoken to in over a year.

You have to do it.

I sighed heavily. Then I picked up the phone, hit the green call button, and pressed it against my ear. The line began to ring.

A click. "Hello?" a man's voice said. "Alex, is it really you?"

"Yeah, Bill."

"Jesus." His voice passed from astounded to relieved. "How ya been? It's been so long."

"Yeah. Listen, I need a favor. Do you still work at your PD?"

"Yes," he said with a hint of sourness. "Bit of a shakeup after you left. I worked the desk for six months, but I'm back in detectives now."

"Great. I have a license plate number I need looked up, for a private matter. Can you check the database and tell me who the owner is?"

A beat of silence. "Listen, Alex, I'm really not supposed to do something like that for someone outside of a case."

"I'm well aware." I turned my head away from the barista at the counter, speaking lower. "Look, this is urgent. I'm helping someone who's in danger."

"I'd love to help but I can't, Alex."

"Bill."

"I'm sorry, Alex. I really can't."

My grip on the phone tightened in frustration. From between clenched teeth, I finally spoke the words burning in my mind.

"You *owe* me."

A heavy silence sat on the line, like a thick wool blanket threatening to snap a thread. I waited patiently for his guilt to process. Finally, I heard Bill sigh. "What's the number?"

***

I wasn't sure what I had been expecting. Perhaps that the SUV had been stolen; it was a rookie move not to remove the plates after all. Or that it belonged to some mysterious corporation.

What I was not expecting was to be standing in the lobby of a luxury car rental service, surrounded by potted ferns and white loveseats, the scent especially musky. Framed posters of sportscars and glossy SUVs lined the walls. The man behind the counter was gruff, with a sharp goatee and stocky build wrapped in a suit and tie. He looked up at me and clocked the stringy man in a thick coat standing before him, unshaven with dark circles under his eyes, not exactly his usual clientele, and decided not to smile.

I really didn't want to pull him.

"Can I help you?" he grunted.

"Yes," I said, trying to keep my voice firm. "I'd like to rent an SUV."

The man pushed a paper with a list of models and prices toward me. "Here's our day rates. Any particular model you're looking for?"

I pointed at the one that matched the vehicle description tied to the license plate.

"Great. Let me give you this paperwork—"

"How many of these do you have?" I pressed.

The man clicked lazily on his computer. "Looks like we have four available."

"Doesn't seem like a lot to have on hand."

He looked up at me with the most bored, *I-don't-give-a-fuck* look I'd ever seen.

"Actually, look, I'll cut the crap." I reached for a pen and scribbled the plate number on the list of cars. "I'm looking for the prick who hit my bumper the other night and barely missed my kid. Did this car come from here?"

Now the man looked surprised. "Oh." He pulled the paper toward him, sounding nervous. "I'm sorry, but we're not liable for actions by our drivers. You'll have to take it up with their insurance."

"Great. I'll need his name." I tapped the paper impatiently.

"Okay, sure, let me get that for you." The man clicked a few times on his computer, starting up a nearby printer. He took the freshly printed paper and handed it to me. "Here's his contact info and insurance carrier. I'm so sorry for the inconvenience, sir."

I looked at the copy of the intake form and driver's license in my hand, name and address laid clearly next to a picture of an unassuming, balding man. *Pete Brown.* Such a simple name, it didn't seem real. Maybe he was the driver. Or more likely, he'd had the car stolen from him. Nothing left to do but locate him and find out.

"Strange that car was in an accident," the man said just as I turned to go. "There wasn't a scratch on it when it was returned."

I turned back to him, dumbfounded. "I'm sorry? You *have* the car?"

"Yeah." The man nodded. "It was returned the next morning."

My gut was screaming, *call the police.* But that wasn't an option. *No cops or she dies.*

"Anything unusual inside?" I asked.

The man shrugged. "Nothing of note from the cleaning crew."

Cleaning crew, right.

"Thanks." I pushed against the glass door and gladly left the smell of simmering cologne behind.

***

THE PHONE NUMBER ON the paper for one Pete Brown didn't ring. Instead all I heard was, *The number you are trying to reach is no longer in service.* Bum number, I thought. He'd obviously put down a fake one.

I sat quietly in the back of the taxi, lost in thought as it made its way slowly across the island. Outside the window, my eyes fell on a flock of commuters leaving the stairs of a subway station. I hadn't taken public transit once since I'd moved to the city. So many people crowded together, hands gripping bars, bodies knocking into each other as the train hurtled down the tracks. It would've been a straight shot to get to my next destination, short and quick under the compact street traffic.

My phone vibrated in my lap as a voicemail from Drew came in. I immediately dismissed the notification and continued to scour the internet hopelessly for anything on a Pete Brown from Manhattan. But the name was so generic, it was impossible to narrow anything down.

The taxi slowed as we reached the address. I looked out the window and up at a big square building made of auburn brick, dotted with the double windows of rows of condominium units. I removed my gloves and tucked them into my coat pockets, then stepped from the car.

A green awning, flapping agitatedly in the wind, signaled the entrance to the building, double white doors with chipping paint. I pulled on the brass handles, but the doors were locked. I stepped over to the callbox and squinted at the fading text behind yellowing glass.

Pete Brown, Unit 325. I dialed the number and pressed *Call*, then held my breath, waiting for it to ring. But the box emitted a click, and then once more I heard a familiar automated voice blaring unintelligibly through the aging speaker, "*Zha nammer yuer drying oo reezh izh no longer in zhervizh.*"

Huh. The callbox would have likely been set to forward calls to his cell phone. I looked again at the phone number on the piece of paper in my hand. Maybe it was his real number after all.

I hit *End* and stepped back, considering my options. Then I studied the list again, and dialed 324, the next unit over. This time the box emitted a strangled ring. After the second one, someone answered.

"Hello," I said loudly into the box. "I'm here to visit Pete Brown in 325, but he isn't picking up. Can you buzz me in?"

"*Whazh?*" a distorted voice barked from the speaker.

"I said, I'm here to see Pete Brown in 325. Can you—"

The door buzzed and I could hear the latch withdraw. I tugged open the white door and slipped inside.

The lobby was small and unremarkable, covered in a beige glazed tile and complete with a drooping shrub in the corner by the mailboxes. I blinked confusedly at myself in the wall-length mirrors, obviously placed to make the walk-in seem larger. To my right was an elevator, the arrows completely worn away from the buttons next to it. I stepped inside the cab and summoned myself to the third floor.

It certainly wasn't anything fancy, I thought as I walked down the carpeted corridor, watching the numbers on the doors climb. But it also wasn't lowbrow, not the kind of rundown shabbiness you might expect a kidnapper to be hiding in. In fact, the building smelled rather stale, and the tacky bronze sconces on the wall suggested an older, stuffier kind of life.

I rapped on the door labeled 325 and waited, listening carefully for signs of life inside. A minute passed, and I knocked again. "Pete?" I called. "Is there a Pete Brown here?" My ears fought through the distant sounds of the traffic outside, straining to catch any kind of footstep. But there was no movement.

Instead, the door to the right opened with a slow squeal.

"You're looking for Pete?" a middle-aged man said from the doorway of 324. "Was that you who buzzed me from the callbox? I can barely understand anyone through that thing."

"Yes," I said, giving a small, polite smile. "Thank you for letting me in. Do you know if Pete's home?"

The man shook his head. "I don't think so. He and his wife and the girls left yesterday morning. Looked like they were going on vacation."

I tilted my head. "Wife and girls?"

"Yeah. Two daughters." The man hesitated, looking me over. "I… assumed you knew Pete?" His trust was withdrawing.

"Oh, he, uh, is a client of mine," I fibbed quickly. "He left something at my shop, and I told him I'd bring it by this week."

"Ah." The man nodded reluctantly but didn't press further.

I studied him carefully, his sweater and glasses, his brown goatee, his soft-spoken voice. "Do you know Pete very well?" I asked. "He seems like a nice guy."

"Oh, yeah, Pete's great," the man said, smiling. "Lovely family too."

"And you saw them leave?"

"Yes." The man looked concerned again. "You sound like a cop."

I gave a small laugh. "I'll try not to take that as an insult." Then an apologetic shrug. "Sorry if I'm being too nosy."

The man relaxed once more. He appreciated when I acted easygoing, I could tell. Right now, he seemed receptive to our conversation, but I knew there was only so much interrogating I could do before he grew suspicious. It was time to try something else.

"Well, I suppose I'll have to try him again sometime later," I said, looking back at the door to 325.

The man next door shrugged. "You could always leave the item with me. I could give it to him when he gets back."

"Oh, uh," I stammered. "Well, it's a credit card. And no offense, I just don't know you." I flashed an apologetic smile.

The man shook his head. "Totally get it. If you want, our leasing office is down in the basement. You could leave it with them, maybe they could put it in his mailbox or something."

"That's very helpful, thank you. I'm sorry, what was your name?" I stepped closer to him, heavily aware of my bare hand hanging at my side.

"Kevin."

"It was nice to meet you, Kevin. I'm Alex."

Engaged in amicable conversation, it felt appropriate to extend my arm and offer a handshake.

The man stepped forward, compelled by formality. "Pleasure to meet you, Alex."

And he shook my hand.

Spigot.

FLEE.

A SMALL BOY LOOKED down solemnly at a young woman laid peacefully in a casket.

"Why did God take her?" he asked the man holding his hand.

"It wasn't God. It was cancer."

"But God can do miracles. Why didn't he save her?"

The man stood in silence, the bags heavy under his eyes, his voice tired and cracking. He released his son's hand and pulled him close. "I don't know, Kev."

I was watching from the first row of the chapel, a chorus of sniffling behind me. But I needed to be elsewhere. I took a breath and turned away from the funeral service, focusing on the information I was after. First, I needed to see what Pete was doing on Wednesday night, the night of the ambush. The colors blurred and rushed beside me, passing by years of teasing, bullying, and eventual social isolation, then settled abruptly into a cozy living room, quiet except for the hum of evening news.

The man named Kevin was reclined on the couch, his laptop teetering on his legs as he typed a new chapter for his latest romantic novel. He had published a few already under a female pseudonym, and it had helped support his mortgage while he continued his hobby. For this reason, he was home around the clock, entire days spent in his pajamas as the world passed by outside his door. He was quite familiar with the comings and goings of his neighbors. Near the window was a pair of binoculars sitting on a chair, next to a notebook filled with times and schedules scribbled in blue ink.

There was not much to overhear Wednesday evening. The Brown girls and their mother chattered occasionally next door, but Kevin didn't hear the door open until well after Pete's usual return time. Normally it was six o'clock. Tonight it was ten thirty. *Late night for Pete*, Kevin thought.

He walked up to his door and pressed his ear against the wood. A murmur from Mrs. Brown, very similar to a "Where were you?" Inquisitive, concerned, but not mad. And the male voice that responded was calm and tired.

Kevin placed his hand on the handle and turned it slowly, pressing the door open just a crack. Down the hall, Pete's wife cooed, comforting her husband and saying something about a long day. Their door closed and that was that. Kevin returned to the couch, but I stood listening for the next half hour, the only sound the muted note of conversation drifting from next door. Eventually, it faded away.

Okay, I thought, *let's see the next morning.* Time progressed almost twelve hours later.

Kevin stood yawning at his kitchen counter, waiting for the toaster to release his slice of rye, when he started to hear a commotion next door. There was scuffling, something heavy being moved around, and the excited chatter of the girls. *What're they up to this morning?* Wasn't it a school day? The time on the microwave read nine thirty.

Ten minutes later, the door of 325 opened and the sound of rolling suitcases rumbled through the subfloor. Kevin set his laptop on the couch beside him and stepped up to the door, opening it quietly and peeking out into the hall. He caught the last glimpse of Mrs. Brown with her daughter passing beyond the corner.

Kevin, being a naturally inquisitive human, walked discretely down the hallway, pacing himself to round the corner just as he could hear the sound of the elevator closing. At the end of the hall were wide windows that looked out over the street. From there, he saw the family of four spill out onto the sidewalk, the sun reflecting off of Pete's balding head. Pete's mannerisms were casual, not agitated or tense. Mrs. Brown was smiling, and the girls spoke animatedly.

Moments later, Pete's hand rose into the air, waving at an approaching vehicle. A large taxi pulled up to the curb, and the driver began to assist the family with their luggage. They piled in, closing the four doors one by one, like the collapsing wings of a yellow bug, and the vehicle drove away.

Huh, Kevin thought. *I guess they'll be gone for a bit. Early Thanksgiving trip, most likely.* God, it had been forever since he'd travelled.

I was standing beside Kevin at the window, surveying the sidewalk and the departing car, when my eyes fell on a shadow nearby. A slight figure in a dark sweatshirt was leaving a shaded section of the sidewalk, about twenty feet away. I hadn't noticed any movement there before. Had they been watching as well?

Kevin pulled his phone from his sweatpants pocket, dialed a contact, and looked over his shoulder as he held it up to his ear. "Yep, I've got one for you," he said in a hushed voice. "325 just left, for a few days at least."

I watched in abhorrence as the blanks began to fill. Kevin was indeed a nosy neighbor, and it paid off well for him. He had a friend whose specialty was picking locks. When Kevin observed a departing neighbor, he would inform his friend, who would then come by in the middle of the night and swipe the kind of items that were not easily recognized as missing: a few video games, a couple earrings, some leather shoes. He would return with a finder's fee for Kevin, as per their agreement to keep the calls coming.

Figures, I thought, shaking my head.

Okay, we're done here.

***

I stared at Kevin back in the present, standing in the hallway, his hand still grasping mine. My smile fell. He clocked this, and immediately his fell too. No wonder he'd warmed up to me when I'd acted nonchalant; he'd been worried I was onto him. But it was of no importance to me right now.

I turned and stepped away in silence, walking back to the elevator, brow furrowed in thought. Down the hall behind me, I heard the door of 324 close, but I knew that nosy bastard would be at the window shortly to watch me leave. I stepped into the elevator and glanced at the panel, my finger hovering over *L* for Lobby. Underneath was an *O* for Office. I pressed it.

The basement foyer was a similar size to the lobby above, the same beige tile, but this time no mailboxes. There was a door to the garage across from the elevator, and next to it, a small glass door labeled *Office*. A young man was sitting at a desk inside, working at a computer. I stepped up to the door and gave a small knock. The young man looked up, his face forming a polite smile, then rose and hurried to the door.

"Can I help you?" he asked, standing in the open doorway.

A story began to form in my head as I plucked a name from Kevin's memories. "Hi, I'm Alex. My mom lives here. Ellen King, in 322. She's just told me she thought she saw someone trying to break into her car Wednesday night."

The man's eyes widened in shock. "Oh, gosh!"

"Now she says her purse is missing, and she thinks it might have been taken from the car that night." I tightened my lip, settling into a type of haughty concern. "Do you have surveillance in the garage?"

"Yes, we do."

"Mind if I take a look?"

The young man was certainly agreeable. I stood behind him as he sat at his desk and navigated the security footage. "What time on Wednesday night?" he asked.

"About ten thirty." I watched as he scrubbed through the grayscale video, scanning the occasional car that came or went. And then I saw it, the black SUV.

I couldn't believe it. He'd actually driven it home.

"I think this is it," I said, pointing to the large black vehicle. "She mentioned a strange car. This isn't usually parked here, is it?"

The man shrugged. "I can't really keep track of all the cars. But I recognize that man, he lives here." He pointed to Pete getting out of the SUV. We watched as he walked casually toward the garage exit. "Well, *lived* here."

I turned toward the man. "What do you mean?"

"They sold their place just yesterday. Bit weird. Priced it real low, sold for cash. Movers come tomorrow. Had no idea they were looking to sell."

So it wasn't a vacation. They'd been leaving for good.

Fleeing.

"Do you know where they've moved to?" I asked.

He shook his head. "They didn't say."

I pondered if I should pull his memories too. Pick up any overlooked details in the conversation.

"Was it a phone call?" I asked. "Did they call you to tell you they'd sold?"

"No, we only found out through the broker. They called our other manager on duty. Didn't hear anything at all from Mr. Brown."

I looked back at the screen. "Can you do me a favor? Can you scrub ahead to when that car leaves?"

The man hesitated. "Um, sure, I guess. Why?"

"My mom gets confused sometimes. Maybe it was in the morning."

The man scrubbed ahead, the SUV sitting patiently in its parking spot, the time ticking away in the upper right corner. At around seven in the morning, Pete stepped back into frame, walking to the vehicle, his balding head bobbing in the harsh fluorescent light.

I studied his stature and form. He wasn't very tall and had a bit of a hunch to his shoulders. He definitely wasn't the gunman who'd held me off with the large rifle; I would've recognized those hard cold eyes anywhere. But the other two kidnappers hadn't been exactly tall or menacing. His silhouette could've matched the man who'd grabbed Analise, the one who'd driven the car away.

In the video, Pete raised his hand to stifle a yawn, with no sign of urgency in his step, completely relaxed as he climbed back into the driver's seat and drove the car out of the garage.

And there he goes to return the car, I thought. When would he come back?

"Do you have a camera on the outside of the building?" I said. "I wonder if someone may have snuck in when the garage door was open."

"Of course." The man clicked another window, and a new camera angle appeared on the screen. I could just see the back of the SUV driving away, the familiar letters and numbers on the license plate growing smaller and smaller.

"Keep going," I said. I knew Pete would be coming back.

The man was scrubbing ahead, both of us watching the pixels closely, him staring at the garage door and me watching for any sign of Pete's return. The numbers of the morning time scrolled quickly in the corner, until suddenly the screen went black.

The man leaned forward, studying the screen. "Hm. That's odd."

"What happened?"

"Looks like there's a missing video file." He pressed his finger against the screen. "See, it saves it in fifteen-minute increments, but the one for eight AM is missing. We have seven forty-five to eight, and then it jumps ahead to eight fifteen."

I stared in disbelief. "So there's just… no recording. For that exact fifteen minutes?"

"No, I'm afraid not." The man shook his head. "Gosh. We better look into that."

I did the math in my head. The missing footage was about an hour after Pete had left. It was possible it contained a record of his return. Which bugged me.

"Can you keep scrubbing ahead please?" I pressed.

The video continued, with no sign of Pete until two hours later, when he and his family emerged onto the sidewalk pulling their large suitcases. I could see him more closely here, his un-creased face, his smile toward his family, the long thoughtful look he gave the building behind them. It was odd. He didn't look like a man who was running.

"Do me a favor, call me if you recover the missing fifteen minutes of video." I leaned down to write my number on a stray Post-it.

"Oh, sure. Or you can stop by next time you visit your mom."

Right.

I let the door swing closed behind me as I veered toward the stairs nearby, trying to sift through the details in my head, turning the puzzle pieces and failing to make them fit. I had been hesitant to believe a seemingly average Joe like Pete could be involved in a murder-kidnapping. But after learning he'd dumped his assets and left town, all signs pointed to him playing some kind of part.

I pictured his easygoing face, the simple yawn as he returned the car like it was a routine task. The slow ease with which he raised his hand to flag down the taxi to take him and his family away.

If you were involved in a kidnapping scheme, why rent a get-away car in your own name? Why leave the plate on? Why park it at your home, where your family lives, where your children live, after you've committed murder? Why bother taking the getaway car back?

I stood outside the white double doors, staring at the front sidewalk.

More importantly, where was I going to look next?

VANISH.

I DECIDED TO TAKE a long walk back to Sentry, the hectic sounds of a Friday afternoon like a static canvas of noise on which I tried to connect the dots in my head. The dreary clouds were starting to part, and an encouraging beam of sunshine was pouring onto the streets of Midtown. But still I pulled my coat close as I walked among the crowd, my gloved hand clutching my lapels closed over my chest.

My phone buzzed again in my pocket. I checked the screen, knowing it would be Drew, and had the fleeting urge to answer and tell him about the mystery of Pete Brown, our enigmatic getaway driver. But Drew wasn't going to be a source of help to me. His narcissism would only slow me down.

The trail concerning Pete had come to an end, at least for now. What other aspects of the kidnapping, the murder, the ransom, had I not observed yet? If Pete was as uninvested and unmotivated as he seemed, what was the real driving force behind this scheme?

The kidnappers wanted data. I thought of the breach attempts in the news over the past couple weeks, at Pexler, at Ackheim. Could it all be connected? I shook my head, dismissing the thought. A remote, external hack wasn't anywhere close to the same M.O. of a murder-kidnapping.

But still, the text from the kidnappers rolled through my head again.

If you want to save her, you will send us the unencrypted information on your top-level classified assets. We know the names. We will know if what you send us is not what was requested.

I'd forgotten a company in the list of breach attempts. I'd forgotten Sentry.

Our own Melanie Abrerra had tried to access our VIP clients and failed. And now here we were, faced with a demand for top-level client data.

I checked my watch as I crossed Eighth Avenue, picking up my pace. The day had passed so quickly chasing loose ends. But I had another potential lead in mind, and if I hurried, I could gather some intel for a clearer picture.

★★★

WHEN THE DOORS OPENED to the Sentry lobby on the forty-fifth floor, Sherri was just gathering her things and putting on her coat. "Oh, Mr. Hemsley! I haven't seen you for a couple days."

"Hi, Sherri. I've, uh, had some early international calls, so I've been working from home."

She smiled and waved her hand. "Was just strange not to see you come in, that's all. You're doing okay?"

I was breathing heavy from my fast walk, sweating in my coat, tired from little sleep and exhausted by emotional trauma.

"Yes, I'm all good."

Most of the office had clocked out for the weekend. Only a few voices drifted from the hallways as I headed toward the Engineering wing. The nearby clock on the wall read four fifty. It wasn't unusual for our workers to head out a little early on a Friday if their work was finished.

My footsteps thudded into Suite B, where the last signs of daylight painted the walls in purple hues. My eyes scanned down the hall. Melanie's door was opened, of course. Eric's and Lucio's closed. In the fourth doorway, a shadow moved from within the room.

Priyanka was still here.

I tapped lightly on her door frame. She turned in her chair away from her computer.

"Alex!" she said, looking delightfully surprised. "It's good to see you! We've been wondering if you're okay."

"Yes, I'm doing fine." I glanced at the watch on my wrist. "What's got you staying late?"

She looked back at the computer monitor, her voice falling. "I'm just filling in on some of Melanie's duties"

"Oh, right. Sorry. I'll get that job posting up first thing next week."

"Thank you." Priyanka dropped her eyes down to her hands, folded in front of the keyboard. She was still somber over her coworker's departure.

My eyes fell on a couple boxes sitting stacked next to her desk, Melanie's name written in Sharpie along the side. "Thank you for packing up her things," I said.

"Oh." She turned to look at them. "I actually went by Melanie's place after work yesterday to drop them off, but no one was there. It looked empty, so I didn't want to leave her stuff out on the curb. I brought these back here until we figure out where she is, in case she does come by."

"That's very nice of you."

"Thanks." She turned and looked defeatedly into Melanie's office across the hall. "I looked through her stuff again for any information where she might have gone. I just don't understand why she would leave without saying anything."

She sighed, lowering her face into her hands. A small sniffle emerged from behind her fingers.

"Hey, hey." I sat in the spare chair by the door, leaning forward in an effort to comfort her. "I miss her too," I said. "And I'm still struggling to find an answer. For all of us, her strange, sudden departure was jarring. But for someone close to her, like you, I can't imagine how hard this must be."

Priyanka smiled. "Thank you, Alex." Her eyes began to mist as she looked at her lap and nodded. "It's been... weird. None of it makes any sense."

"If you need to take any time, that's fine."

She wiped the corner of her eye. "Thank you."

Priyanka and I had a positive professional relationship. We were about the same age, and got along well. I wouldn't normally make physical contact with my employees, but there was something I'd been wanting to see, that I needed to see now that the stakes had been raised.

I leaned forward. "If you need anyone to talk to," I said, extending my hand toward her upper arm, "I'm here."

Carefully, as a friend, I set my hand comfortingly on her sleeve, my pinky extending just below the hem.

***

SOMEWHERE IN CANADA, a small girl looked up at her mother, pulling at her shirt. "Mum, when will the samosas be ready?"

Her mother looked down at her and responded in Hindi. It didn't matter that I didn't know the language, Priyanka's memory provided the exact translation.

But I didn't want to stick around, wading into personal moments. I skated over twenty-eight years of school lessons, sleepovers, graduations, even a failed engagement. Then I found myself once again in Suite B, standing in the corner of Priyanka's office.

"Hi there."

Priyanka turned her head to see the young woman smiling in her doorway.

"I'm Melanie. You must be Priyanka?"

"Yes." Priyanka leaned forward to shake Melanie's hand. It reassured her to see such a warm face on her first day.

"Nice to have another woman around here," Melanie said in a low voice. "Did they set you up okay with login credentials?"

"Yes."

"Parking, security badge?"

"Um, yes." Priyanka nodded as she sorted through all her new employment items in her head. "I believe so."

"Good. Well, just let me know if you have any questions. I'm right over here across the hall." She waved over her shoulder toward her office.

"Thanks. Melanie." The two women shared warm smiles.

I'd known they were friends, but I had never seen just how involved they were in each other's lives outside of work. They would get dinner together sometimes during the week, and often dinner led to karaoke bars. Stifling their laughter as they sent gifs about how tired and hungover they were from their desks, yet still accountable and trusting of the other's work. Melanie assessing Priyanka's potential dates on Tinder at lunch, her fork suspended and swiping through the air. "Nah, nah, that one looks like a ferret."

Priyanka had even been a bridesmaid in Melanie's wedding several months ago. Dressed in a brilliant scarlet dress, she watched on proudly as Melanie said her vows to her husband. She admired their partnership.

It was all these heartwarming memories that made Melanie's sudden departure so hard on Priyanka.

I was standing back in her office again, last Thursday afternoon. She glanced across the hall at Melanie's closed door, wondering where her friend was. Priyanka pulled her phone into her lap and stared at a missed call notification from Melanie that morning. She hadn't even heard it ring. No voicemail, no text. Hopefully everything was okay.

And then she jumped with a start, her phone vibrating in her hand. *Miguel Abrerra.* Immediately, her stomach turned. I watched carefully as she raised the phone to her ear, swallowing her fear as she opened her dry mouth to speak.

"Hey, Miguel. How are you?"

A sniffle on the other end. "Not well," said a man's voice.

I listened closely.

"Is… is everything okay?" Priyanka asked.

"I'm so sorry, Pri." His voice cracked. "She passed away this morning."

A hand flew to her mouth. "What?"

Tears began to glide down her face.

"She's had heart issues, they've been worse over the past few weeks, and she just… I woke up this morning and she was just gone."

Priyanka inhaled a shaky gasp. "I'm so sorry, Miguel."

For a moment, the line was quiet except for the unspoken anguish laced in the heavy breathing coming from Miguel's end. She could hear him trying to pull himself together.

"I know you were close," he said. "We're thinking Sunday for the funeral, I'll let you know where. But I just… wanted you to know so you could sort it out with work."

"Of course. I'll let them know. Do you need anything?"

"The neighbors brought by some food. My family will be here later tonight. I'll be okay."

"Okay," Priyanka whispered. "Take care of yourself."

"You, too."

The office melted away as she buried her face in her hands. I felt the pain spreading through her, wrenching her heart. But carefully I pulled myself away before I could get sucked in.

I fast forwarded to yesterday evening, where Priyanka was pulling up in her car to a small brownstone in Brooklyn, the home of her friend who apparently wasn't dead after all. She'd been there a dozen times before for game nights, girls' nights,

Melanie's bridal shower. The home was usually so warm and welcoming. Tonight, it stood cold and foreign, the windows darkened and still, the mystery of Melanie's actions weighing on its eaves.

Priyanka stepped from her car and approached the door. There was no stir of a cat in the window, no TV playing, no kitchen smells. She knocked on the door. Nothing.

She began to lean over the railing and peer into the living room window. Then from a neighboring lot, someone coughed. It startled Priyanka, and when she looked up, she saw an old woman craning her neck out the window next door to watch her, scowling. She knew the look. Priyanka stepped away from the glass and returned to the sidewalk.

As she surveyed the house front one last time, something caught in the back of her throat. "Mel, where are you?" she whispered, fighting back tears. She turned and walked back to the car, as the night around me faded away.

I returned to the present, sitting across from Priyanka in her office. Slowly I removed my hand, unfaltering in my attempt to comfort her. She wiped a tear from her face. "Well, I should probably finish up and get home," she said.

I looked at her like I did after every pull. Like she was an entirely new person. I knew everything about her. Her passion for her skill, her dedication for her job, her care for the ones around her. I nodded and stepped to her doorway.

"Take care, Pri," I said.

"You too."

***

I SAT IN MY office as the full dark of evening enveloped me through my windows, the only light coming from the small lamp on my desk. I stared at my own reflection in my sleeping computer monitor, rotating the Pexler flash drive in my fingers.

My mind worked through everything I had learned today. Gideon. The getaway car. Pete. Melanie. Drew would have loved to be spewing possibilities with me now, but I was still letting his calls go to voicemail.

Priyanka's most recent memories with Melanie danced through my head. Lunches, brunches, happy hour. They'd even gone to a midnight showing of *Monty Python and the Holy Grail* two weeks ago. I could see better who Melanie was through Priyanka's memories, even if they were rose-colored lenses. In what world would she have attempted to deliver her company's information to another party? She walked willingly into a room with video surveillance to commit a felony after office hours.

I locked eyes with my reflection in the monitor, then sat forward, wiggling the mouse. I navigated to my email and looked up a message from building security. They had sent me a copy of the video recording for the break-in. I watched again as Melanie's ghostly form walked casually into her office, sat at her computer for just a few minutes, then picked up her purse and left. It was the second time today I watched someone act unusual on camera.

In our database history, I pulled up the access log from the night Melanie had logged in. I scrolled through the text until I found the name of the client she had been looking for, a particular police department.

I gave a wary look at the empty office around me. The hum of the heater blended with the sounds of rush hour to stifle the eerie silence. Feeling paranoid, I stood and walked to my door, closed it, and turned the lock. I examined the room again, making sure no one else was here lurking in the shadows, confirming I had indeed lost my mind.

I returned to my desk and pulled up the restricted top-level Sentry accounts. I entered my admin password, and a short list appeared on the screen. The police department in question blared at me in white pixels.

In the account were the declassified names and addresses of several informants, people whose lives were in our hands. Their families' lives as well. I paused on one name in particular that sounded vaguely familiar. *Thomas Portmeau.* Where had I seen that name before? Probably on a police report back when I worked at the precinct.

Something else stirred in the back of my mind.

I logged out of the database and went back to my email. I searched for the word *Ackheim.*

There it was. Melanie's mysterious gift from a friend. The email I had forwarded from her deactivated account, with a complete CSV file attached. The rows spilled out on the screen again as I scanned the names, a couple more I vaguely recognized. My eyes narrowed at the sender address.

afriend@ackheimcorp.com

It just didn't make any sense. Melanie was almost surely a good person, a regular employee with no ill intent. But somehow, she'd been caught on camera trying to steal our company's assets, and now here I was looking at a competitor's data in her email.

I checked my watch. Outside the sky was completely dark, the city lights illuminating the bustling streets of Friday night. It would take a while by car, especially at this time in the evening, but I needed to go to Brooklyn. If I couldn't find Pete, maybe I could at least find Melanie.

BROOKLYN.

I WAS WAITING IN traffic around Greenpoint when another voice-mail from Drew came in. I dismissed the notification and returned to the social media profile I was perusing. Melanie Abrerra, employee of Sentry Data Security. Current city, Brooklyn. Hometown, Providence. A steady stream of pictures of outings with friends right up until the day she supposedly died. After that, nothing. And no moving tributes from loved ones of the newly deceased.

I clicked the names of friends tagged in her recent photos. Melanie was absent from any of their posts from the past week. None of their faces were familiar to me, except Priyanka's. My heart ached as my thumb rested on a photo of the two of them smiling at Melanie's wedding. The bond between them was evident. A bond I'd observed in other people, but rarely in my own life.

A wave of immense sympathy washed over me for Priyanka. She had already been outnumbered and unwelcomed by so many in her field. Bossy young men who dismissed her, talked down to her, even some women from privileged families who couldn't connect with her. But Melanie had been cut from the same cloth, and in her Priyanka found her first true friend in her line of work.

Was it any wonder that they had both been hired by me this past year? I could see past the bloated confidence of over-eager young men, dozens of them marching in for interviews, some of them even daring to sneak a sniveling glance at my gloved hands.

Melanie and Priyanka were solid in their skills and kind in their actions. They weren't just good at what they did, they were good people.

I stared down at my covered palms, guilty at how quickly it had taken me to attain a moderate level of programming knowledge. I hadn't even intended to pull my college roommate, he was just rather handsy after a couple rum and cokes. Drew had been jealous when I revealed that the intellectual assets of anyone I pulled copied over instantly into my own skillset; I now knew everything they did, after all. Drew had been paying out the nose for a programmer to build the base of his tech startup. He begged me to help, but that was when I was about to set out on my own crusade. Back when I was bright-eyed, and not so jaded.

Back when it mattered if I helped people or not.

***

THE NEIGHBORHOOD WAS DARK and silent when I pulled up. A quiet middle class block, the occasional couple strolling in their jackets, tucking up their hoods as a light drizzle began to fall. Rain bothered me a lot less than people. I pulled my scarf tight and stepped out of the car.

Melanie's house stood before me, exactly as it had in Priyanka's memories last night. There were no lights in the windows, no stirring inside. I went up to the door and knocked out of formality. I also wanted to lure the eyes of any neighborhood peepers.

"Melanie?" I called. "It's me, Alex." I tried the door handle, but it was locked. "I just want to check that you're okay."

I looked down and saw a brass mail slot. It was loose when I prodded it with my finger. Crouching down, I lifted the flap and peered inside. From the dim light of a nearby streetlamp, I could see a smattering of white rectangles on the floor. Mail that was piling up.

"Hello?" I called through the slot. The sound didn't echo like an empty house. I could see the silhouettes of furniture sitting in the living room. A plant towered in front of a window at the back of the house.

It sure didn't seem like they'd packed up and left. More like they'd dropped everything and vanished.

"Excuse me?"

I stood and turned to the voice that had called from my right. An elderly woman leaned out of her doorway on the steps next door.

"Can I help you?" she asked.

"I'm looking for Melanie Abrerra," I said. "Have you seen her lately?"

"Who are you?" she said, squinting. A hooded man with a beard was not the most welcome stranger, I imagined.

"I'm her boss, Alex. She hasn't been at work the past week. We're getting worried about her, that's all."

She studied me, crossing her arms. It occurred to me that this was the source of the coughing Priyanka heard that had prompted her to leave.

In my head, I viewed the interior of Melanie's house over the past year through Priyanka's eyes, plucking a detail to share.

"They have a cat. Figaro." I glanced at the door. "Do you know if anyone's been feeding him?"

This struck a chord with the old lady, and she relaxed her stature.

"Come over here so we don't have to shout for everyone to hear," she said. I looked over my shoulder, eyeing a single figure approaching on the sidewalk from the east.

I left the Abrerras' threshold and stepped up to the elderly woman's. The faint buzz of local news sounded through the open door, drifting outside with the smell of cookies and cat litter.

"Figaro's all right," the elderly lady said. "I've been leaving him scraps. Don't know why they left him outside."

"So you haven't seen them?" I asked.

She shook her head and lowered her voice with an irritated look. "Don't speak so loud. We don't need to invite any opportunists. Whole city's gone to shit." She gestured toward her door. "Come inside."

I stepped into a dimly lit hallway, dark red walls illuminated by a faint antique lamp. To the left was a living room, two threadbare recliners sitting before an old box television where a man was giving the weather report. The old woman lowered herself into one of the chairs, muting the TV and sipping her tea. I perched on the other.

"When did you see them leave?"

"Took off late in the night last week. Thursday, I think? Just got in the car with a couple bags and left."

Thursday night had been the night of the break-in at Sentry. Had they left directly afterward?

"Has anyone come by since then?" I asked.

"I might have seen one or two come and go. It's hard to remember at my age." She gave a small tut. "Must not know they're on vacation."

I nodded. "Right. Vacation."

"Can I offer you some cookies?"

"No, thank you. Can you try to remember who came by? And when?"

She sipped her tea again, her eyes watching the extended forecast. "Well, there was a visitor here yesterday evening. Didn't really look like she belonged in the neighborhood though. I managed to scare her off." Her lips lifted in a small, proud smile.

"Uh huh." Slowly I unrolled my glove. "Have you heard from Melanie or Miguel at all since they left?"

"Oh, no. Why would they want to call an old lady while they're off having a good time?" She frowned. "But it is strange, usually they leave a key and ask me to feed Figaro while they're gone. They didn't do that this time."

I mulled the details over in my head. Unexpected departure, leaving things behind in a rush. It was starting to sound eerily familiar.

"I'm afraid I have to go," I said as I stood. "Can I leave my phone number with you? In case you hear from them?"

"Oh, sure, love. But I'm sure everything's fine."

I pulled a business card from my wallet and set it on her table.

"My name is Alex," I said. I extended my hand. "What was yours?"

She seemed surprised by the formality, in a delighted way. "Oh. Clarice."

Clarice reached out and pressed her cold, wrinkled hand into mine.

***

Pulling an elderly person is always interesting.

First, there are decades on decades of memories, some of them spanning back to a time you've only seen depicted in movies and history books. The traditions of the early twentieth century are always... uncomfortable, for me to witness.

And second, in the later years, there develops a type of fog. Like looking through a pair of old glasses. Things don't seem quite as sharp as they did before.

I watched Clarice as she stood at the window last Thursday morning, sipping her English Breakfast and observing the daily routines of her neighbors. Her orange tabby Clyde sat tall on the windowsill at her side.

Melanie and Miguel both stepped from their house next door and walked in the direction of the subway. They did this every day. Both of their jobs were in the city.

But this was puzzling to me, because that would be the morning that Melanie didn't come in to work, and Miguel would call to report her untimely death. Instead, I watched them hold hands and share a laugh as they rounded the far corner.

The day flashed before my eyes. The sun was beginning to set, and workers would be arriving home to their families. No Melanie and Miguel yet. Sometimes they stayed late in the city with their friends. *Oh, to be young*, Clarice thought.

And sure enough they did arrive home well after dark. But it was hard to know the time from Clarice's memory. The night all blurred together, her clarity softening after sundown. I looked at the local news playing on the TV. The weather report had long passed, and they were on the sports segment. Sports review started at ten, of course, in Clarice's recollection.

But not long after, she heard the sound of a car idling at the curb just outside. Miguel had pulled the car up, and Melanie was loading a few bags. There was no quickness or urgency. It was as Clarice had assumed, like they were simply going on a trip.

Light poured out the open doorway behind her as Melanie loaded up the final bag. Figaro the cat padded outside and down the steps, scurrying away down the sidewalk for a night hunt. *Strange that she would leave the door open like that*, Clarice thought.

Melanie returned to the doorway, turned out the inside light, and closed and locked the front door. She looked up at the facade and gave a final sigh.

Like she's saying goodbye, I thought.

Then she returned to the car, and the Abrerras drove off into the night.

The following week passed before me. Postal deliveries continued. Even a package was left outside, which left unclaimed had vanished by the next morning. Figaro meowed at the back door. *Poor hungry kitty*. Clarice fed him some of Clyde's canned tuna.

To Clarice's recollection, no visitors came knocking until last night, around six o'clock when a young Indian woman showed up at their door. Clarice watched from her window. The woman didn't seem to be doing anything inappropriate, except she was hanging around too long. So Clarice gave a cough from her open window, and the young woman left.

But I could see there was more.

Hours later, after the weather report had ended, Clarice heard knocking at the Abrerras' door once more. The thuds brought Clarice to her feet to watch out the window. The person had their knee on the living room windowsill next door, their palms pressed against the glass, trying to force it up. My eyebrows rose as I clocked the shadowy visitor. A lean, short figure in a sweatshirt, hood pulled up tight.

Clarice picked up her old cordless phone and dialed the police. Forced entry attempt. *Be there right away, ma'am.* She cracked open her door and watched as the stranger knelt on the Abrerras' doorstep and tried to pick the lock. Clarice was too nervous to leave the safety of her home and confront the stranger head on, so instead she cleared her throat as a warning.

The hooded stranger turned and looked at her, their face shadowed by the night. Clarice worried she had been too eager, that she should shut the door and just wait for the police to arrive. But then the stranger rose to their feet, descended the steps, and walked hurriedly in the other direction. Their gait was unfamiliar, but perhaps feminine. I watched from Clarice's doorstep as this unknown variable disappeared into the darkness.

And then this young man showed up tonight, bearded with his hood and the rain. She thought to call the cops again, but he seemed like he knew the Abrerras. His shouting had interrupted her in the middle of something.

★★★

I snapped back to reality and looked toward the kitchen.

"Sorry, I think I smell something burning," I said.

"Oh?" peeped Clarice. But I was already walking into the next room.

The empty kettle was sitting on the open flame of the gas stove, a discolored tea towel propped against the handle. Clarice had been pouring her tea when she'd heard me shouting next door, interrupting her routine. I turned the knob and extinguished the flame.

"All settled," I said, coming back to the living room.

Clarice sighed frustratingly. "Thank you, dear. It's no fun getting old."

I gave a soft smile back.

"Stay safe, Clarice. Good night."

FIGMENTS.

I ate a late dinner back in Manhattan, alone in a red leather booth at an old-school diner. It was Friday night, so the only people there were teenagers who couldn't club or drink. A rowdy pack of brats howled in the far corner, but I was too absorbed in the events of the day to pay them any mind.

What was troubling me was that I, as someone who had for years excelled at accurately reading human behavior, could not begin to explain what I had seen in the memories I'd gathered today.

It had been a little uncanny when I'd seen it with Pete's family, his casual demeanor with the getaway car, with his family leaving town. But I'd seen that same lack of urgency in Melanie, that exact same song and dance of leaving with a smile on one's face, despite having had a crack at committing a felony, and vanishing without a trace.

To see that in two separate instances, with two unrelated parties… frankly, I wondered if I was going mad. I held up my hands in front of me, fingers spread. Could it be possible I was losing my ability? It sent a rush of panic through my body. But then I sighed and thought, *Would that be so bad?*

I stared at my phone on the table. Nine missed calls, five voicemails. A million texts. It was nearly ten o'clock, almost twelve hours since I'd last seen Drew. I flicked open the latest text and read it begrudgingly.

Please just tell me you're okay.

With murderers on the loose, I supposed it wasn't an unreasonable request.

I'm fine, I typed and sent.

But that was all I would give. I pushed the phone away and pulled a faded twenty from my wallet, laying it next to my plate. It was time to go home. I was exhausted from a long day of schlepping around the city on very little sleep. Besides, there was nothing more for me to do until I figured out a next step.

I just hoped Analise was okay, wherever she was.

I looked up toward the front door, about to rise from the booth and leave, when I saw someone standing outside the window staring right at me.

A slight figure in a sweatshirt, the hues red or purple, their features hidden in the shadow of their hood.

The hairs stood up on the back of my neck.

Immediately, they turned and walked away. I stood and rushed to the door, turning right after them.

"Hey!" I yelled.

But the sidewalk was packed, the droves of Manhattanites and tourists swarming up and down the concrete. Over their shoulders, I could see the top of a hood bobbing in and out of view, getting farther and farther ahead of me as I shimmied between coats, bumping elbows, feeling the breath of strangers dangerously close to my face.

I stopped at the street corner, pivoting as I observed the three options to turn, with no sight of the hooded figure. I'd lost them.

There was still one option left.

I sighed and closed my eyes, unrolling my right glove. I hadn't done this in years. It could be dangerous. But I was going to have to start taking bigger risks. From somewhere within, a long-lost surge of courage burst through my veins.

Slowly, I extended my hand to brush the knuckles of a passing pedestrian, a man in a bulky down coat.

Had he seen the person in the sweatshirt?

I focused hard, separating a lifetime of memories from the ones that were necessary to me. I skated vaguely over thoughts of an ex-wife, a younger girlfriend, a lost brother. They passed in periphery, as I observed the dark city street he had just walked down moments ago. Was there a small, hooded stranger he'd passed?

No. There was nothing.

I looked around as the masses continued shifting. There was a woman passing nearby who had just crossed the street. I reached out and tapped her wrist, ignoring her glance as though it had been a simple accident.

There was deep pain about her mother, somewhere in the void. But as for the past few moments, no red-hued sweatshirt.

An older woman crossed from the final direction, wearing a long extravagant coat and thick scarf, her fingers studded with rings. Carefully I touched her pinky, making sure to look away when she snapped a scowling glance toward me.

My mind was like a muscle, getting stronger and stronger with each pull. I treaded carefully on thin ice above a looming pool of memories. But if I did not look down into the vast black water, I could stay focused on the snowbank ahead. And unfortunately, there was no slight, sweatshirt-clad figure on that bank.

They'd slipped away. Easy to do with this many people. But something told me they'd be back.

I turned and walked toward my car, resigned and headed home. Every few steps I gave a nervous check over my shoulder, goosebumps rising on my arms. I didn't like feeling I was being watched; it was normally the other way around.

But I didn't see them again.

★★★

Somewhere in the depths of sleep that night, I was riding the elevator up to Gideon Pexler's bunker. I crossed the atrium and looked up at the camera above the metal door. The little red light blinked sleepily, a slumbering guard towering over me.

"Please," I said. "It's about Analise."

My cries echoed wildly in the cavernous void. No matter how much I pleaded, it would not let me pass.

I closed my eyes and thought of Gideon, picturing him just beyond those walls, living his life like a snake confined to a cage. Drinking fine wine while listening to Wagner. Playing his piano in front of a window overlooking the Manhattan skyscape. Or sleeping soundly in his bed, his body resting in a dark, quiet room.

If I could just reach him. If I could just see what he knew. I extended a hand toward the sleeping figure, my fingertips grazing the skin of his neck.

He reacted violently, throwing his arms and kicking his legs, wrestling my arm away. He turned on a light, and when I stepped back and looked at him, I realized—it wasn't Gideon.

An old mustached man scowled at me. "Marie!" he spat. "What the hell are you doing?"

But I wanted him to die. He'd served his purpose. He needed to go.

I pulled something metal and sharp from the pocket of my velvet robe, clutched in a hand of glittering rings. The man's eyes widened.

"What are you...? No. No!"

I covered my face with my hands as the blade when down. But what hit my arm did not slice my skin. It bruised. It was the blow of a fist.

I was knocked back a few steps, my arms raised before my face. When I lowered them, I was looking into a face of rage, framed on a middle-aged woman.

"You absolute whore!" she screamed. "I give you two children, she gives you a blowjob, and you decide to leave me for her? How long do you really think it's going to last?"

She threw another hand and I blocked again, mildly scared but otherwise wishing she would leave so the young woman hiding in the closet would be safe.

"I hope you rot in hell." The words were dripping with hatred, slicing into a vulnerability not felt in years. The man suddenly felt small as a child, and for one fleeting moment he wished his wife would stay and comfort him.

But with an agitated motion she grasped the door, stepped through, and slammed it shut, the wooden frame cracking like a gunshot that rang for years of guilt, splinters shattering, almost like glass.

And suddenly—I was looking down through Drew's hands at a glass figurine in pieces on the floor. I'd howled drunkenly as I smashed it, and the room around me erupted into a mix of cheers and jeers. I was in someone's penthouse, at a large party. The cocaine flowed through my blood, my pupils dilating.

"You *imbecile!*"

Drew turned, frightened by the unexpected intensity of the voice behind him.

A clean-cut man with gray hair in a gray suit jabbed his finger into Drew's chest. "Come into my home and destroy my prized possessions? What a poor display of character, Mr. Hemsley."

The drug-fueled grin on Drew's face began to fade.

"You wanted our investment? You should have thought about that first before this grand display of foolery."

The man walked away, and Drew stood before me, staring at the floor. I was so angry at him, for this—though really I was feeling his own anger at himself—but also for betraying me, for tricking me into thinking he cared.

I grabbed his shoulders and shook him as hard as I could, squeezing my eyes shut, and with a great breath, I yelled into his face.

The room around me froze. It was quiet enough to hear a pin drop. I relaxed my hands on Drew's shoulders and my breathing began to slow.

Enough.

I turned and looked at all the faces staring at me.

"Enough!" I screamed.

I couldn't take the crossover anymore, the memory bleed. I put all these people, donned in their suits and dresses, into a box, and I put it all away. Slowly they faded from my mind's eye.

Now. Something mine.

A faint glow painted the sky. The sun was coming up. I was sitting on a bench, and I was five. My mother sat next to me.

"Isn't it beautiful, Alex?" she whispered, holding a mug of coffee between her hands.

I nodded as we watched the morning begin, alone in the neighborhood park. She placed her warm hand on my shoulder. Serenity pooled in my chest.

If I squinted, I could make out something in the distance, rising slowly in the horizon as if it were coming closer. They looked like spires, even skyscrapers, settled across a body of water.

I looked down at my hands. They were no longer those of a child, but an adult man. The sun basked my face with a kind radiance. I breathed in the wet air, cleansing my lungs and calming my mind.

At last, I was at peace.

A soft hand pressed into the one on my right, ungloved. I looked at the woman sitting next to me.

It was Jessie.

She smiled warmly at me with her brown eyes.

This would've been our next date. I felt a catch in my throat, and for the first time in ages, I didn't want to leave this dream.

The wind gently blew her brown hair from her shoulders, the sun painting her face in a golden glow.

Just then there was a noise nearby, and a shadow cast upon our bench. Both of us looked up at the person walking by. A slight figure in a burgundy sweatshirt, hunched over, walking briskly. Our heads followed left to right as we stared, puzzled.

I looked to Jessie.

The figure in the sweatshirt. The vanishing families. *Does it mean something?* I asked her.

Slowly, Jessie leaned forward, her lips near my ear.

She whispered.

Find her.

DECEIVER.

I woke Saturday morning to the bitter greeting of reality. The sunlight was gone, the room cast dark by the gray clouds hovering over the city. Slowly I moved my fingers along the edge of the bed, feeling the individual threads under each blooming ridge of skin.

I had to figure out the next step. I had dragged myself all over town yesterday collecting mysterious clues, like scrambled codes without a cipher, meaningless in their current context. How much time would we have before the kidnappers grew impatient?

I brewed some coffee and sat at my desk, staring into the fine wood fibers as though the answer might pop out of the surface after long enough. I was scanning through everything I'd gathered, looking for holes.

This Pexler employee, Carter Young. The one who'd been let go after stealing unauthorized company data, a disgruntled team member under Jessie's own watch. He was a pending question I'd liked to answer. But how to reach him?

My eyes lingered on my laptop. I'd worked so hard to keep Jessie's professional life separated in my mind. But I supposed it didn't do much good anymore. Resigned, I pried open the screen and let Jessie's memories take the lead.

At the Pexler employee portal, her password danced from my fingertips. My index finger led the way to the employee database, authorized only for executive level and HR personnel. And when

I typed in the name Carter Young, the text displayed in firm, solid letters a phone number and address.

I picked up my phone, took a breath, and dialed the number.

Ring one, ring two, ring three. A voicemail kicked in, and the firm voice of a man instructed me to leave a message. I guess I didn't often answer unknown calls at ten AM on a Saturday morning either. I thought carefully about the words I was about to say as the recorder beeped.

"Hi, Carter," I said. "My name is Alex. I'd like to talk to you about your departure from Pexler Technologies." I ran my knuckle along the edge of my desk, thinking quickly on my feet. "I understand your termination was sudden and retaliatory. I'm hoping you can help me with a difficult situation. I may be able to help you in return."

A phone call would be less helpful than a pull, which would mean speaking in person.

"I'd love to meet with you and chat," I continued. "Totally confidential. Please give me a call or text if you'd be open to meeting somewhere today."

I ended the call with a sigh, staring at my phone for the next few moments as though willing a return call to come. But it didn't.

I scratched sleepily at the whiskers on my cheeks, then slumped forward onto my elbows, hanging my head over my coffee. In front of me, my goldfish floated lazily in its bowl, making bubbles in its idle state.

I tried to picture Pete and Melanie as members of a high stakes criminal ring, sneaking into offices, kidnapping family members, wielding guns. I'd seen some unusual perpetrators in my time. Docile relatives, caring lovers, with a whole different identity lurking underneath, waiting for the flip of a switch. This version was a possibility. It could be that Pete and Melanie were so steady and practiced in their skills, they held no anxieties about slipping out of town without being caught.

That was the easy answer. But it didn't satisfy me.

I raised my head and gazed pensively at my fish, its bulbous black eyes staring back, a feedback loop asking the same difficult question.

If only I could've pulled them, I thought. If only I could've seen their intentions. I would've seen... what exactly? Money being handed to them? People under blackmail or bribery weren't usually so calm.

The fish's scales rippled under its wavering fins. It's a myth, you know, about goldfish having tiny memories. They're just as capable as any other animal when it comes to food and survival. A three-second memory, I thought with a chuckle. Imagine a pull that contained only three seconds, everything before that overwritten. And a clueless fish, happily skating back to the next flake of food until it consumed too much, its insides overexpanded, unknowing of the consequences of its actions. Or so the urban myth goes.

I pressed my fingertip against the glass, the fish edging forward as if to give an appreciative tap for my thoughts.

And somewhere, way back in my mind, something began to nag at me. Something said once in a passing comment. I stared at the flattened tip of my finger next to the floating fish.

It could mean anything. It could mean nothing.

But the more I pondered it, the more I gave it weight, the greater it edged urgently into the forefront of my thoughts.

I looked at the time on my laptop screen. By the time I made the drive, Knoxley's would be open. Maybe I would find him there, maybe I wouldn't. And maybe I was completely misguided about the concept now occupying my mind. But I needed to keep moving forward, investigating every possibility.

My phone buzzed as another text from Drew rolled in.

We need to talk.

No shit, I thought. Try harder.

I gave a final tap on the fishbowl and reached for my coat.

***

I'D MADE IT THROUGH a round before Roger showed up. I flagged the bartender down to bring him a pint as he gingerly settled on the stool next over. The crowd was sparse, the softened sunlight glinting off the empty polished tables by the window.

"Don't normally see you here so early," he said, still wearing his jacket and scarf as he slowly warmed from the winter air. "I hope everything is all right?"

God, where to begin. The events of the past few days sped through my mind: the death of my friend, the kidnapping of her sister, the bizarre behavior I'd witnessed. But instead of relaying the entire story to him, I thought I'd just get right to the point.

"You mentioned something once, when we first met," I said. "And I need you to tell me more about it."

The old man frowned with confusion, but nodded. "Okay. What is it?"

I stared at my drink, carefully parsing the words before I turned to face him.

"What is... a *pusher*?"

The silence hung in the space between us. The old man's eyes locked on mine, but inside, he went somewhere else for a good long minute. He sighed heavily.

"Ah yes. Nasty business, pushers. Can't say I've ever heard of a good one."

"What... what exactly do they do?"

Roger took a large drink of his beer, letting the alcohol warm his senses. Then he set the glass down and turned directly to me. "They do the opposite of what you and I do. They *push* memories." He held up his hand. "By touch, just like us."

"So like... they can show their own memories to other people?"

"Yes. That's right."

I nodded slowly. "Okay. I get it. But how is that a bad thing necessarily? Seems like it could be helpful."

"Well, the thing is," he continued, "the memories don't have to be true."

"What do you mean?"

"They'll make stuff up if they need to. They have a reputation for being deceivers. Use their power on people as a means to an end."

The old man could see I was struggling to grasp the concept.

"Here's an example." He settled closer, lowering his voice. "You came in here today to see me. But what if, on the way in, that man over there by the door"—he gestured with his head—"reached out and touched your wrist." Roger gently tapped the base of his own hand. "And suddenly, you remembered, as sure as ever, that that man was your closest friend. And he's sick and broke from hospital bills, and he's just told you he's about to end up on the street. You open your wallet and immediately give that man every dollar you have."

I stared at the man laughing with a friend by the door, a total stranger.

"Or," he continued, "maybe the pusher wants someone to forget something that happened. Maybe they've wronged someone, and they'd rather cover it up than seek forgiveness. So, they replace the real memories with something fabricated, something happier and nicer.

Replacing memories with something fabricated. I hung on every word.

"Or maybe they want to hurt someone," Roger added. "So they push a memory that causes them great pain."

I struggled to stretch my comprehension of reality to accept what Roger was telling me. If we lived in a world that had pullers, then there could certainly be pushers. Someone sending tailored memories into unsuspecting people.

"What if," I said, "a pusher needed someone to do something for them, in their place. They could just give them new memories to make someone *think* they need to do that thing?"

"Absolutely."

Jesus Christ.

Somewhere over my shoulder, someone released a cackle. Someone with no burdens, at least not right now, enjoying a pint with a friend. It was convivial, and yet it made me start, like a bite on my nerves. I cast a wary glance at a group of patrons coming in the door, at a trio by the window, at a young man sitting silently in the corner.

I turned back to Roger, queuing the next question. "Would a person know that they've been pushed?"

He shook his head. "Not a normal person, no. But pullers like you and me, we can tell. I've seen pushed memories before in a person's mind. We're masters of memory." He tapped his finger to his graying temple. "We know what a true, emotional memory looks like, rather than something fake and flimsy."

"And it's just permanent, those memories?" I asked.

"Sure," Roger said. "As long as the person never wises up to the notion they're fake."

I thought of Melanie and of Pete, leaving with their families for new lives. "Or if they're overwritten again by more memories?"

"I don't see why not."

The more I thought about it, the more the pieces seemed to fall into place. And the more it made my skin crawl.

"You said they're known to be deceivers," I said. "So there are just... no good pushers?"

Roger shrugged. "Wouldn't know of the good ones, would we? I only know the ones that broke laws, hurt people, wound up in jail. And most of them *do* end up in jail."

I thought of the old precinct, the indifferent souls sitting behind the bars, grinning as I peered over them. How some of them had been so eager to let me in to their madness. Had any of them been pushers?

"And you said you've actually met one?" I asked.

Again the old man's eyes were distant in thought. He nodded, the weight of the memory heavy on him. "Yes. It wasn't pleasant. Of course, I knew immediately I was pushed. But it was nothing compared to what I've seen in others."

I dared to press. "What have you seen that was so bad?"

Roger placed his hand on his beer, clearing his throat. "That, I'm afraid, is not appropriate for table talk." He took another long drink. "But let's just say, I've seen it cause people's lives to fall apart. Sometimes it was vindictive and personal. Sometimes it was just because they were a pawn in a greater scheme. I think honestly, the latter is more heartbreaking to me. People become disposable."

Roger's words sent a chill up my spine, something I didn't feel very often. He eyed me worriedly. "Why are you asking about this? Do you think you've run into one?"

Instinctively, I thought of the mysterious figure in the sweat-shirt. Standing outside Pete's, trying to break into Melanie's, following me at the diner.

"I'm not sure," I said. "But if I did, it would explain some things that have been troubling me."

"My advice. Stay away from whoever you think it is. Nothing good will come from interacting with them."

"I'm not sure I have a choice."

"You always have a choice," Roger said, turning back to his beer for a long sip. "Now, if you don't mind, I'd like to talk about happier things."

The conversation had ended, but I couldn't shake an eerie sensation of being watched as I turned and scanned the pub's clientele again. Everyone was chatting, laughing, without a care in the world. It made it all the more unsettling, that someone could be lurking in an otherwise hospitable environment.

Deceiver.

If what Roger said was true, if a person like this did exist, and they were pulling the strings behind the kidnapping, the ransom, the disappearances… was I safe anywhere?

Oh god, I thought, glancing down at my phone in a panic. What about Drew? Where was he right now? Was he out wandering in public like a sitting duck?

I bolted upright onto my feet. Roger looked at me with alarm.

"I'm sorry," I said. "Thank you. I have to go."

The old man nodded. "Be safe, son," he said earnestly.

I threw a twenty on the counter and headed for the exit, then took the usual left toward Sentry. If there was anywhere I was safe, it was there. I pulled my coat collar up and sank into my scarf as I carefully glided between pedestrians. I felt like a terrified child, watching them for ill-intended movements, waiting for an obscured snake to strike. Whatever bravery I'd earned the day before, I struggled to hang on to it desperately.

***

It was only a few moments before I stepped into the lobby of the Sentry building, very empty on a weekend afternoon. I checked over my shoulder as I walked toward the far corner, my eyes catching the security guard's as she clocked the panic in my stride.

Once I was in the corner, I dialed Drew's number, my first time reaching out to him since our infiltration at Pexler the day before. He picked up immediately.

"I'm an ass," he said.

"Shut up."

"A huge ass."

"Listen to me," I said in a low voice. "Do *not* go outside, do *not* open the door for anyone."

"Whoa, okay, we just escalated into zombie apocalypse territory."

"We need to talk."

"Okay. Yes. Great."

"Where are you right now?"

"I'm in the car on the way to lunch."

I groaned. "You need to go home. I'll meet you at your place."

"Just come grab a bite with me," Drew said. "You need to eat."

"Okay. Fine. Pick somewhere that we haven't been before. Somewhere secluded."

"Well, that's romantic. Should I pack a picnic basket?"

Silence.

"Sorry," Drew muttered. "Sorry, sorry about… myself."

I hung up the phone and glanced around the lobby, when my eyes rested on a security camera hanging from the ceiling nearby. I looked curiously into its lens, gazing silently back at me, and a thought occurred. I needed to go meet Drew, but while I was here, I could investigate something first.

"Excuse me," I said, walking up to the security desk. "I'm from Sentra Data Security, Alex Hemsley, CTO and in charge of security." I held up my employee badge. "I'd like to see some surveillance footage from last week."

The security guard reached for my badge, studying it carefully. My heel jumped anxiously against the floor.

"Alright, Mr. Hemsley," she said. "Follow me."

In the security suite, another guard was sitting in front of the screens, his legs outstretched, eating yogurt. A football game played on his phone.

"Kurt, look alive," the lady said as we entered the room. The man sat up quickly and turned to the monitors.

"I need to see some footage from last week," I said.

"Sure," the man said. "What floor?"

"Actually, I need to look outside the building." The man gave me a questioning look, and I elaborated. "We had a break-in last week, I'm sure you remember. I just want to see the person arriving and leaving." I paused. "To see if they were alone."

"Ah, yes, I remember," said the man. "What day was this again?"

"Thursday, around seven fifty PM."

The man at the terminal looked at the screen to his right, where he opened a folder of timestamped video files. He tabbed down the list, going back in time.

"Thursday…."

"Yes."

The man leaned forward, punching the keyboard as he navigated further down the timestamps. Suddenly he stopped.

"What in the world," he muttered under his breath.

I felt myself stop breathing. "Is everything okay?"

"We're looking for seven fifty PM, right?"

"Yes."

He tapped his finger anxiously against the mouse. "It's… not here."

I blinked. "What do you mean it's not here?"

"The file's just… missing."

"Like it got taped over?"

"No," he said. "We keep video logs for six weeks. Each file is a fifteen-minute recording. We've got the file before and the file after. But this…." He leaned forward, squinting. "It's like it's been deleted."

Deja fucking vu.

"But you have the next segment, starting at eight o'clock?" I said. "Can I see that?"

"Yes, sir."

He clicked on the filename, and video of the building exterior filled one of the monitors.

"Jump ahead to eight oh-five, please."

The man scrubbed ahead, stopping just as I saw Melanie pushing open the lobby doors. She was alone, leaving at a casual pace, her head looking down at the phone in her hands. No one accompanied her, and no car came to pick her up. She proceeded down the sidewalk and out of frame.

"So we have her departure, but not her arrival," the man said, his voice a mixture of confusion and embarrassment. "I'm so sorry, sir. I'm not sure what happened."

However, I was becoming less unsure.

"How many people have access to this footage?"

"Only two of us."

I stood in silence, considering.

"I'm sorry, sir," the man said. "I don't know what happened."

"It's okay. Thank you." I turned and left the security office.

SUSPICIONS.

"Hold up. Wait a second." Drew lifted his fork in the air and pointed it at me. "So you're telling me, there's another type of person out there running around with special powers like you, except they're the opposite?"

"Yes," I said, speaking quietly.

We were on the Upper West Side, eating outside at a cafe in the early afternoon. The clouds were parting slightly, allowing the smallest glimpse of sunlight to spatter the concrete patio. Only a few others sat at the tables around us.

"And you think that's why Melanie faked her death and snuck in after hours? That someone pushed fake memories into her, to have her try to download our data?"

"I know. It sounds crazy."

"You're right. It does."

"But nothing else makes sense." I prodded at the scrambled eggs on my plate, my stomach too uneasy to muster the enthusiasm. "It explains Pete's behavior too," I added.

Drew cocked an eyebrow. "This guy you know absolutely nothing about?"

"I saw how he left the morning after. He was acting too calm for someone who was just involved in a kidnapping and murder. It's because he didn't remember."

"Sounds like his actions didn't bother him." He set down his fork, wiping leftover yolk from his lips. "I think they just call that being a criminal."

I sighed, putting my head in my hand. "You're not listening to me."

"I'm sorry, I'm sorry," he said quickly. "I hear you." He rested his hand gently on my shoulder. "Have you seen anyone suspicious? Anyone following us around that could be a threat?"

"Yes." I paused. "Maybe. I can't be one hundred percent sure. Someone in a red sweatshirt keeps popping up in memories. They trailed me to dinner last night." I looked up at Drew. "That means you, me, we need to be careful. Keep an eye out for anyone suspicious wherever we are."

I could see Drew's body tighten at these words, as the gentle chatter of the patrons around us felt suddenly very present and close. I cast an eye toward a nearby table, where three young women were carrying on, laughing as though everything with the world was right.

Drew leaned forward and lowered his voice. "So, what do we do now? How does this help us find Analise?"

I had no answer for that.

Drew sighed, plunging his hand in his coat pocket and pulling out his phone. He gave it a morose look. "One of the reasons I was trying so desperately to get a hold of you was because I got a new message." He pulled up a text thread and handed the phone to me. It was the same thread with Gideon and the kidnappers. "We have a deadline now," Drew whispered.

My heart pounded in my ears as I read the message on the screen before me.

Good afternoon. You will send us the data by tomorrow night at midnight via the following web address.

An upload link to a third-party transfer service, with an unknown recipient. The message continued.

If we do not receive your data, you do not receive Analise.

No cops.

It was official, we only had a set amount of time left. No more games. I could feel the color drain from my face as I handed the phone back to Drew.

"What about the guy at Pexler?" he said. "The one who got fired the day before the incident. What did you say his name was?"

"Carter Young."

"You should pull him."

"I left him a message asking him to meet up. Haven't heard back."

"What's his number? Let me call him. I can be persuasive."

My breath hovered uneasily in my chest. I glanced away with a fleeting bout of shame. "There's a new problem, though."

Drew tilted his head. "What?"

I held up my gloved hand. "If there's a pusher out there pulling all the strings, and I pull them, nothing stops them from pushing me right back. They could feed me fake memories to try to influence my behavior."

Drew's eyes widened. "Shit."

"But we can't sit here doing nothing. I need to meet with Carter as soon as possible. However, there's one condition."

"What's that?"

"You are going to be there with me, and you're going to record the whole conversation on your phone."

Drew raised an eyebrow. "And why will I be doing that?"

I leaned forward on the table. "Because, if there is a pusher out there, we can't trust our own memories. There's only one solid truth we can lean on." I pointed to my camera phone. "Surveillance."

I readied for a smart retort. But instead, Drew considered what I was saying and nodded. "Okay. Understood."

Satisfied, I pushed the last remaining chunks of egg around my plate.

"How are you doing otherwise?" Drew asked.

I looked up, surprised by his earnestness. "Functioning, I guess. But I'm wearing down. I was out cold last night, slept all night for the first time in days. Like ten hours. You?"

"Same. But man, I keep having dreams about men with guns coming after me." Drew gave a tired glance toward his coffee mug, then lifted it and took a long sip.

Just then, I was distracted by something I saw over his shoulder.

A woman leaned out from a far table, her obvious gaze shrouded by sunglasses and a raised hood, wearing a familiar burgundy sweatshirt over her small, slim frame.

Quickly I averted my eyes.

"She's here," I whispered.

Drew stared at me. "What?"

"The stalker I saw at the diner last night. And at Melanie's and Pete's. She could be the pusher."

I dared a glance up again, and when our eyes met, she jumped up from the table and began to run.

"Alex?!" Drew said.

But I had already shot to my feet, and I tore across the patio after the stranger. Heads turned as I hopped over a chair and darted around the corner of the restaurant.

"Hey!" I shouted. "Stop!"

I wondered if anyone on the sidewalk might notice the pursuit and attempt to stop the young woman. But that wasn't likely with a man twice her size trailing after her. Some people moved as I hurtled down the sidewalk, others kept their heads down over their phones, scowling when I bumped into them.

"Stop!"

It wasn't as crowded as the night before, so I was able to keep her in my sight for two blocks until she arrived at the corner of Central Park West just as the pedestrian signal hit zero. She went for it, speeding across the crosswalk as the light turned yellow, her feet slamming into the grit on the other side as she halted before a group of children.

The traffic had resumed by the time I arrived at the intersection. She turned and looked at me, and I saw her full face, her sunglasses having fallen off earlier in the run. She looked to be in her early thirties, with pointed features. Her hood had fallen down to reveal a pixie cut of dark purple hair. She clocked my obstacle, taking a few deep breaths, then turned and continued into Central Park.

I watched as the perpendicular cross signal began counting down from twenty-five. *Come on.* She would be long lost in the Saturday afternoon crowd by the time I got to the entrance.

Twenty.

I breathed heavily as I watched her purple hair disappear into the mass of people.

Fifteen.

Going… going… gone.

Ten.

I didn't overthink it.

Five.

I removed the gloves.

Zero.

Spigot.

I ran as fast as I could, darting across the street and through the entrance to Central Park. My direction was simply straight for the first hundred feet, then I began to approach a fork in the path.

I held out my hands.

And I focused.

My right hand hit someone's wrist first, three fingers brushing against a watch. They had seen the purple-haired woman approaching the fork, but not the direction she had taken.

My left hand bumped against a set of knuckles. They had seen the purple-haired woman, steering out of her way as she dodged through the crowd. They'd watched her continue down the path. She'd gone left.

As I veered left, I hit another person's arm. She'd sprinted straight, progressing farther down the path.

Another hand. She had left the path and crossed over the grass.

I ran as fast as I could, never stopping, my hands darting out and making contact wherever I could. The memories of strangers numbly washed over me like gallons of water, but I kept moving, kept sorting through the timelines. My brain was firing on all cylinders.

I moved down Terrace Drive and past Cherry Hill Fountain, and for a brief moment I saw the woman darting into the trees.

Almost there.

I tapped a final hand to see which way she had gone as the path rounded near the water. She'd gone left, down a vacant flagstone walkway, her pace slowing. She was heading down to the bank.

I stopped at the top of the path, catching my breath, then walked as quickly and as quietly as I could down the stone fragments. The sounds of ducks and distant laughter were only just beginning to hit me, as I listened for any motion ahead, fighting the sound of my beating heart in my ears. I plunged my hand into my pocket and pulled out my phone, opening the camera app and hitting record.

As I rounded the final corner of trees, I could hear her breathing. She was as out of breath as I was. I readied for her to run, either away or directly at me. But when she came into view, she was standing there waiting for me. Surprisingly, she was also holding her phone.

"Alex Hemsley?" she called, staring at me through the phone screen. "That's your name, right?"

I stopped about fifteen feet away from her. "Who are you?"

"You knew Melanie Abrerra," she continued. Her tone wasn't threatening. In fact, it seemed accusatory, like a journalist interviewing a perp.

"How did you know Melanie?" I asked, the interaction becoming more puzzling by the second.

The woman reached into her sweatshirt pocket, pulling out an inhaler. Quickly she held it to her mouth and pumped a dose. Her breathing began to slow.

"Why were you chasing me?" she asked.

"Why were you following me?"

We watched each other warily from behind our phones, looking up and back down at our screens.

"I saw you last night at Melanie's," she said. "What were you doing there?"

"I was looking for her. What were you doing there?"

"Looking for her. Looking for anything."

Something was beginning to dawn on me. I relaxed my shoulders, easing my posture to appear calmer.

"You're looking for the pusher, too," I said.

Her brow furrowed. "I don't know what that means."

I kept the camera recording, but I held my hands out so she could see I meant no harm. "My name *is* Alex. I *did* know Melanie. She disappeared and I've been trying to find out what happened."

The woman listened and nodded. "You work for Sentry? Your brother is the CEO?"

"That's right."

"He was sitting with you at the restaurant."

"Yes."

Why did all this matter?

Then it hit me.

"You work for another data storage firm," I said.

I could see in her eyes that this was the truth.

Like Melanie, she'd been pushed. A pawn to infiltrate.

"Which one?" I asked.

The woman lowered her phone. "Ackheim."

Holy shit.

In my head, I could see the email sitting in Melanie's inbox with the data from Ackheim, the sender address so taunting at the time.

"And your name?" I asked.

She hesitated, then said,

"Abigail. Abigail Friend."

FRIEND.

I CALLED DREW AND told him to meet us at a nearby gazebo, small and private. The day was cooling and in the distance, dark blue clouds were beginning to move in. A cool, moist breeze swept across my face as Drew stepped up onto the wooden structure, then stopped, taking a wary look at Abigail at the table where we both sat.

"It's okay," I said. "She's looking for answers, like us."

Drew pulled his phone out of his pocket, pointing the lens at us. "No offense."

Abigail slid her phone toward Drew. "If you wouldn't mind doing mine as well."

Drew looked confused at first, holding up her phone too, one in each hand, both recording the interaction.

"My name is Abigail Friend," she began, reciting like it was a deposition. "I was a security engineer at Ackheim until my termination this past week. I was terminated for transferring un-encrypted information from our databases to an external source, which is not permitted by our company's security policy. The security policy *I* wrote.

"I cannot honestly say why I sent the data. As I go over the reason in my mind, it makes no sense. There are several things leading up to that day that don't make sense. And to top it all off—I emailed our confidential information to an employee at a rival company."

To Melanie, I thought.

"Okay. So, why were you following us?" I asked.

Abigail frowned at the table. "I will admit my memory is fuzzy. I am looking for any kind of clue as to why I would have done this. You work at the company who I sent the data to, you were looking for the person I sent it to. So I followed you, because I need an answer. I...." Tears had formed in her eyes as she spoke, and she wiped one away with her wrist. "I'm so sorry. This sounds delusional."

I felt sorry for her. I leaned in further on the table, speaking gently. "Can I tell you something that also sounds delusional?"

She looked at me with appreciation, that I was listening instead of laughing. "Yes," she whispered.

"I have a special ability. I can see people's memories."

She didn't flinch, didn't laugh. Instead, she saw the sincerity in my eyes and nodded calmly. "I've heard of people like you. What is it they call you again?"

"Pullers," I said. "And I'm looking for someone with another kind of ability. Someone who can push memories onto people."

Abigail thought quietly for a moment. The tree leaves rustled around us as a gust of cool wind blew past, quieting the birds.

She spoke quietly. "I think I should show you something then."

Drew perked up, his head whipping wildly back and forth between us. "Absolutely not."

We both looked at him. "You have the cameras," she said. "We'll know if one of us isn't being honest."

Drew opened his mouth to speak again.

"It's fine," I said.

Then I turned back to Abigail, sitting directly across from me at the table. Slowly, I extended my hands.

"Show me."

She reached her hands towards mine, then hesitated. She was evaluating the risk one last time. But this was her only shot at getting a clear answer. Slowly, she set her fingers into my palms.

★★★

I watched each memory in real time with her, still sitting at the gazebo as she drove, the sensory connection tethered by our hands resting on the table. In her memories, I saw her sitting at an office desk, the room dark with the shades drawn just how she liked it.

Abigail spoke from the present. "This was several weeks ago. Just a regular afternoon, when I learned some big news."

Her boss walked in, stiff and quiet. He stood by her desk, flummoxed with emotion, as he began to speak. "Ackheim has been bought by Sentry. Over the next few weeks, we'll be transferring our assets over to their system. With hope, you'll be able to keep your job working for them."

I frowned. "Sentry never tried to buy Ackheim."

"Tell me," Abigail said to me, "do you notice anything strange about this memory?"

I stared at the man in the suit, his curt behavior unusual for someone who was normally a boisterous spirit. But I supposed bad news made everyone act differently.

"Not really," I said. "Did you notice anything strange?"

"Only when I look back now. It just seems… off. My boss' reaction. The walls of the room seem closer. Even the lighting doesn't seem quite right."

As she said it, I could sense the flimsiness of the setting around us. There in picture, but not fully right.

"I'll show you another," Abigail said.

We glided over small details, emails about the coming merger, announcements of executives stepping down. We arrived at another office, this one much brighter, Abigail seated across from a woman in a pink blouse who was studying a set of papers on the desk before her.

"You were the head security engineer at Ackheim," the woman said, "for… six years?"

"Yes," the Abigail at the desk said.

"Certainly you possess the skills necessary to merge into our own security department." A shuffle of papers. "Numerous certifications. Soaring letters of recommendation. For salary, we can discuss, but I'm confident we can come to an agreement on a benefits package comparable to what you received at Ackheim."

"Great."

The two women rose to their feet.

"So nice to meet you, Ms. Friend," the recruiter said, extending her hand. "I think there's definitely a spot for you here at Sentry."

I raised an eyebrow. "What? I've never even seen this woman before. Or this office."

Abigail spoke from the present. "Does anything look out of place to you?"

"Godawful sixties wood paneling."

"Yes, it's dreadful. What else?"

Again, the room didn't feel quite right. It gave the odd sense of a stalking animal hiding among the woodwork, disguised as something innocent, masking a lurking predator underneath. But those were complicated feelings to have about something as simple as a room.

"This fluorescent lighting." I held my hand over my eyes. "Not a very welcoming environment for an interview." The tubes seemed to radiate beyond their casing.

"Yes, it doesn't seem right. Let me show you one more."

The room at Sentry dissipated, and Abigail now sat with the remainder of her team at an Ackheim conference table. Her boss spoke, again in a jarred and choked-up manner unlike his normal demeanor. Their jovial leader had crumpled before them as the final day of Ackheim came to a close.

"It's been my deepest pleasure to work with all of you. You are my family. You are my kin." He rested his fist against the lapel of his tweed suit as eyes around the table grew misty. "Let's go celebrate our time together. Drinks on me at Everett's Tavern."

The team grabbed their coats and flipped the light switches for the last time, stacking into the elevator down to the lobby. Outside in the cool winter dark, they pulled their coats tighter and chattered amongst themselves. Abigail was just walking up to the side of one of her team members, when she heard her boss' voice behind her. "Abigail."

She stopped and turned to him. He spoke in a low voice. "Did you remember to initiate the transfer?"

Abigail was confused. "What?"

He tapped her phone. "They sent the instructions this morning. I assume you saw them."

Abigail navigated to her inbox and found a set of instructions that had arrived earlier in the day. She'd set it aside for after lunch and then forgotten to execute the transfer, something very unlike Abigail.

"They need this tonight," her boss said. "We're shutting down the servers in the morning. Can you go back inside and take care of this transfer real quick?"

"Absolutely," she said. "I'm so sorry."

But she was struck by the casualness of the transfer protocol laid out in the email.

Compile all assets into a single CSV file and email to:
Melanie Abrerra.

"Fuck," I whispered.

"Wait," Abigail began, frowning at her phone. "I don't think I—"

But her boss spoke again, sadly, as he gave her wrist a gentle squeeze. "Please, Abigail."

She looked up into his eyes. He was in pain. She understood, he just wanted it all to be over.

"Sure thing. I'll see you in a little bit at Everett's."

She turned around, her arm sliding out from his hand, and walked back into the building, her silhouette dark against the lobby lights. But as I watched the Abigail in the memory disappear into an elevator, something caught my eye.

The lobby lights glowed eerily through the windows and doors in the evening fog. Yet something about them had shifted. I rewound to just before Abigail had left the gentle grip of her boss' hand, before she'd turned and walked away.

"Do you see something?" Abigail whispered.

I studied the backdrop around us. There was a sort of shimmering detail dancing in the lobby lights, almost otherworldly. I had never seen it before, but it mesmerized me.

"Yes," I replied.

I looked closely at the apparition. It wasn't fixed to a location. I glanced around for some kind of source, but there wasn't one.

"What is it?" she asked.

"Some kind of visual imprint."

"Like a glitch?"

The light danced before my eyes. "An artifact," I whispered.

I reached out to touch it. There was nothing to grasp, it was not tactile. But as I looked closer, I saw it was sitting overtop something. Like a plastic sheet of film covering a glassy surface. It was so obvious now, how fake and flimsy the memory was. I could almost just peel it away. Somewhere behind it, far away, I could hear muffled speech.

"This memory is not real," Abigail said.

I looked at her. "This never happened?"

She gave a sad chuckle. "No. As you said, Sentry never acquired Ackheim. I never interviewed for a job with them, and this interaction with my—former—supervisor never transpired."

Around me, the setting changed to a dimly lit office, her boss standing in the corner, disappointed and speechless, while two employees in suits interrogated her.

"This one is real," Abigail said in the present. "And it had very real consequences of unemployment. Shame. Betrayal. I tried to explain to them that I had been instructed to send the information, but I could not find the email I'd been sent, and my boss...." She sighed. "He had no idea what I was talking about."

I looked for the sign of an artifact, the tell of shimmering light, but there was none. This memory was solid, set in stone. Every last unfortunate detail.

"I was so distraught," Abigail said. "This place I had worked at for so long, the respect of my peers, all of it—was suddenly gone. For days I've sat and stewed over everything. Sifting through all the bad information. And the memories I showed you in particular... there's something *not right* about them, at their core. It's hard to explain."

"Like cheap flimsy copies," I said. "Taped over the originals."

The office evaporated before my eyes as we returned to Central Park, still sitting under the gazebo, the gentle sound of lapping water nearby. Abigail withdrew her hands and sat taller, crossing her arms, a newfound light in her eyes. "If what you say is true, about the existence of a 'pusher,' then this could explain everything that happened to me."

"I'm confused," Drew said, still standing with the two phones in his hands. "If the pusher wanted Ackheim's data, why did they have you email it to Melanie?"

"Well, if Melanie was pushed too," I said, "then I bet they have access to Melanie's email account. The fact that I even saw that email was probably an accident."

"Does it not make more sense that Melanie is the pusher?" Abigail said. "That she had me send her the Ackheim data and then ran off?"

A cold breeze shook the leaves around us again as I sat with that thought. I wanted to say it wasn't possible. But nothing was impossible at this point.

Drew broke the silence with another question. "Does the name Carter Young mean anything to you?"

"No," she said. "Should it?"

"Or Pete Brown?" I asked. But I knew before she shook her head that she had never known that name.

Shuffling through the memories, I brought up another subject. "You're staying with your sister right now?"

"Yes. I went there that same night to housesit. But she doesn't want me to be alone right now, so I'm still staying there."

"That's good," I said. "I don't want to scare you, but you should know there's been a pattern of unexplained departures surrounding all this. Beyond just Melanie."

"Wiping memories," Drew chimed in. "Full-on *Total Recall.*"

The color drained from Abigail's face.

I shot Drew a disapproving look, then turned back to Abigail. "Go back to your sister's," I said. "If I were you I'd get the hell out of here. At least until this boils over."

Abigail nodded, her lips pulled taut. "I think you're right."

I took out my phone. "I'm going to text you my number. If you remember anything, see anyone, just call."

"Alright. My number is—"

I pointed up to my head. "I know."

"Oh," she said. "Right."

"That never stops being weird," Drew murmured.

The phone in Drew's left hand buzzed as I sent the text. Abigail extended her hand. "You can give that back now." She looked at me and smiled. "I trust you. Thank you for your help."

I nodded. "And yours. I hope we'll see each other again soon."

With the encroaching dark clouds, the noise of the park around us had silenced. The rippling lake water nearby lulled gently with the warnings of the birds. Another breeze crept by, bringing the scent of rain. Across the table, Abigail flashed me a final look of gratitude. But she had already been ahead of the game before I'd come along. Truth be told, she had many of the hallmarks of a puller. She was intuitive and observant. She was withdrawn but compassionate. I hoped, prayed, that she would be okay.

Drops of rain began to spatter the ground around us. Abigail rose from the table and gave a final nod to Drew. "Take care, both of you." She lifted her hood over her head, then she walked up the path and beyond the trees, into the storm.

POUR.

"We really should have offered her a ride," I said in the car over the roar of incoming rain.

"No thanks," Drew said in the passenger seat. "Too close quarters."

Outside, night had fallen along with the rain, blurring the city lights as we navigated the soggy streets. People huddled under their hoods and black umbrellas. Horns blared as drivers struggled to get their bearings through water cascading over their windshields. We pulled up to the end of a line of traffic, barely crawling.

"Fuck, man," Drew muttered. "Times like this, I wish I took the train more. What an absolute shitshow."

A clap of thunder rolled through the city. I was already feeling paranoid. Under my sleeves, I could swear I had goosebumps.

"Look, maybe you should stay at my place tonight," I said. "Or vice versa. Safety in numbers."

"So you can wake up in the middle of the night and remember you're supposed to choke me out?" Drew scoffed.

"That's not going to happen," I said. But I wasn't confident about anything anymore.

As we waited for the traffic to move, I scanned through some of Abigail's memories again, the night she was pushed. How she'd continued into the Ackheim building and up to her office. She'd prepared the file and typed in the email address of her new future coworker, Melanie Abrerra. My throat caught as she hit the send button.

And then she'd exited the building through the back, a shortcut to get to the tavern quicker. I wondered if she would have been intercepted had she returned through the front lobby doors.

And of course, Abigail's confusion when she'd arrived at Everett's to find none of her colleagues. She texted one of them. *Did you guys already leave?* A few minutes later she got a reply: *What are you talking about?*

Abigail was crestfallen to have missed the event, but it had been an emotional day and she was ready to call it. She'd shifted her backpack on her shoulders, packed with overnight items, and continued on to her sister's.

I slammed on the brakes as a car cut in front of me from a side street. A wave of water slapped the tires of the oversized SUV while I cursed under my breath.

"Honk at that motherfucker!" Drew spat.

"What good will that do?"

Drew sighed, looking back out the window at people running on the sidewalk. "What makes you think we should be so scared of this mysterious pusher anyway? They seem to be targeting lower-level employees, staying under the radar. They already got Melanie."

"Yes, they got Melanie, and they tried to access a top-level client, and they failed." I looked at him. "And who's got the password for those clients?"

Drew gulped. "You and me."

"That's right, you and me, pal. Which means we've got targets on our backs."

Drew thought to himself in silence. Outside, the speed of traffic picked back up, and we closed in on the troublesome intersection ahead. "Alright," he said, "give me your best guess."

"Honestly?" I said. "Gideon."

"Mr. Pexler himself?"

"The man's a sociopath," I said, spitting the words angrily. "Plus he's got the bunker, the gloves…."

"The gloves? Nah, nah, he's a germophobe. He's known for it." Drew shook his head. "But I don't buy it. I think it's some dumb ploy he made up to be more interesting."

"Think about it," I said. "He pushes all these pawns to infiltrate his rivals, but he can't get what he wants from Sentry. He decides to fake a ransom, so he hires some goons to do his dirty work."

"And… what, kills his sister?"

I threw my hands in the air. "You heard him, he couldn't have given two fucks about her life." I steadied myself, lowering my voice. "I saw for myself. He was such a self-obsessed prat growing up, he barely ever spoke to Jessie."

"I don't know, Alex. Gideon's a psycho, but I don't think he's a murderer. Plus, why would we receive a flash drive of Pexler data if he's behind all the breaches?"

I stared at the water crashing over the windshield, the world outside as blurred and unclear as the end of this mystery.

"No, I don't buy that scenario," Drew said, shifting in his seat. "Allow me to present door number two."

I sighed, loosening my grip on the steering wheel, placing aside my rage.

"Door number two," said Drew. "Some person we've never met wants to get our data and Pexler's, but they fail, right? They push Melanie, but she can't access the top-level data, and the flash drive they sent from Pexler gets intercepted and returned to Jessie."

"Right."

"So this pusher does some research, looks at social media, and sees us all hanging out. Just four fucking sitting ducks. And they arrange this insane kidnapping so Gideon and I will hand the goods over." He paused. "But here's the kicker. They wouldn't even need to pay these goons money. Just…"

"Plant a motive in their minds."

A wave of nausea flushed over me.

Drew checked his phone. "We really need to talk to this Carter guy. I say we go to his—"

Suddenly, the growl of engine and a screech of tires cut through the air. Out of nowhere, a bright yellow sportscar slid through the intersection on a red light, its wheels sliding as the brakes failed to stop its immense speed against the flooded pavement. It slammed into the SUV in front of us with an intense crack of metal and glass.

"HOLY SHIT!" we cried.

The two cars sailed into the building on the corner, barely clearing the pedestrians and coming to rest on the sidewalk. Bright orange flames began to flicker from the crumpled heap of metal.

I unbuckled myself and flung open the door, my feet hitting the water, pounding against the current as I sprinted across the intersection. From the corner of my eye, I could see a couple others joining me. We all hesitated once we arrived at the radius of the growing fire's heat, shifting on our feet as we analyzed the wreckage, identifying any opening where we could help the drivers and passengers.

My face burned, hot and wet, but I could see movement in the SUV smashed between the sportscar and the building. It was the driver, struggling to pull himself free from his seat belt just beyond the obliterated windshield. I braced myself and leapt onto the hood, the metal softening under me from the heat of the flames. I stretched out my arm, hand still ungloved, and grasped his.

I might've been pulled away into his memories had I not been through so much in the past forty-eight hours. But my mind steeled itself against the current, and I stayed in the present, focusing on extracting the man from danger. My other hand yanked at the seat belt, giving him room to wrestle his body free. His shoulders emerged from the car, and then he pulled his legs free, one of them crumpling beneath him as we staggered backward across the hood of his car and onto the sidewalk.

"Are you all right, man?" I said between gasps of air.

The man said nothing, completely dumbstruck, overwhelmed with pain and shock. Of course he wasn't all right. But he was alive.

The fireball roared louder as I watched two other good Samaritans extract the unconscious body of the sportscar driver onto the sidewalk nearby. The flames shot higher in the air, licking the sky, fueled by gas and metal, enclosing the twisted heap.

And then a cold sweat came over me.

I looked at the man next to me, my hand still resting on his arm.

He hadn't been alone.

I didn't think about the heat, or what I was about to do. I just jumped to my feet and ran. I didn't think about the yells of the people around me as I dove back onto the hood, the flames licking my limbs, as I plunged into the SUV through the sinking windshield frame. I couldn't think. I just knew. Knew when I reached into the backseat that there was someone else there who needed help.

There, somehow preserved in a small cavern of leather and metal frame, was a small child in a car seat, his cries only just now piercing through the sounds of the fire. His small blue eyes looked up at me, full of terror, reflecting the flames around us.

I pulled him up through the belt of the car seat and pivoted next to the steering wheel, facing the diminishing windshield, the only exit collapsing before us. I wrapped him in my arms against my chest, and I rolled, my arms grazing the shards of glass as I tumbled out onto the car hood, now a crumpling pile of hot metal. The roar of the fire was deafening, the heat nearly boiling my brain. But then my body hit the cool, solid reassurance of concrete, and several pairs of hands pulled me and the child away from the wreckage.

"Oh my god!" screamed the man. "Oh my god, Oliver!" He plucked the boy from my arms and wrapped him in his own, kissing his head, shushing him gently. The man turned to me with tear-filled eyes. "Thank you," he muttered over and over. "Thank you, thank you, thank you...."

I could still feel heat on my face, and when I looked down, my beard was on fire. I smashed it into my scarf, the ashy smell rising directly into my face. I lay for a moment on the ground, heaving, the fresh air scouring my smoke-soaked lungs as the sound of approaching sirens bounced off the buildings around us.

★★★

"Hold still, hero. Breathe again." The paramedic placed the cold stethoscope beneath my shirt. All over me, my skin was cold. My jacket had been butchered, my burnt scarf discarded, and the right half of my beard singed away. I hadn't been this exposed in a long time. It felt good.

"You really should go to the hospital for a full analysis," the paramedic said, adjusting her gloves. "You had some decent smoke inhalation."

"Okay," I lied. I wasn't about to trap myself in a public building with scalpels with a pusher on the loose.

The commotion around the intersection had increased, despite the yellow tape sectioning off the sidewalk and traffic officers directing cars away from the area. Emergency responders marched around the scene, their radios buzzing. Firefighters inspected the wreckage to ensure the fire had been fully put out.

Beyond the tape, a couple news vans had pulled up to cash in on the chaos. I turned to look, and stared directly into a camera nearby, pointed at the ambulance. I quickly turned away. "Fuck," I muttered.

The paramedic frowned at the camera crew. "Hey!" she shouted, waving her hands. "Not at the victims!"

Next to us, another ambulance was being loaded up. An EMT carried the small child into the vehicle, his tiny arm in a sling. His father followed behind him, dazed and groggy on a stretcher, his pant leg torn, his body not exactly in a natural shape.

"Are they going to be okay?" I asked.

"Yes. But I can't speak for the asshole who was racing his sportscar up the block."

She continued to dab at the cut on my shoulder, her fingers working under latex gloves. I'd only been touched up by a doctor once before. The feel of thinly veiled fingers on my bare skin was intriguing. Almost pure touch, with no consequences. *This is what it's like for everyone else.*

The adrenaline was still burning off, a sharp pain creeping into my head. "Can I have some painkillers?" I asked.

"Yes, I'll go grab some."

As the paramedic stepped away, my phone buzzed in my pants pocket. I was honestly surprised it had made it through the incident in one piece. I pulled it out and looked at the screen. Drew was calling. I answered and held the phone to my ear.

"Oh, good, you're alive," he said.

"Yes, I'm all right."

"I parked your car. I'm sitting here about half a block back, next to a mass of people trying to get a look. Are you going to be able to leave?"

"Yes, very shortly."

"Okay. Fair warning, it's like a crowd at Coachella over here."

"I have no idea what that is."

"Okay, great. Try not to get touched."

I hung up the phone and looked at the soaked wad of cut up fabric that had been my coat, as the paramedic returned with two aspirin. Around us, rain continued to pour, drumming against the roof of the ambulance.

"Do you have a poncho?" I asked.

***

DRESSED IN THE finEST layer of plastic sheath, like a human condom, I stepped away from the ambulance into the rain, water pelting me and sliding away. The lights of the city shone bright in the nighttime around us, the sound of activity never ceasing.

"Sir!"

"Excuse me, sir!"

I turned away from the newscasters as they tried to call to me. I didn't want anyone broadcasting my face on TV right now.

Two officers stood at the police tape, calming people down, telling them to step back. Various people held their phones, livestreaming the whole ordeal. An officer nodded at me as I approached and held up the tape for me to cross under.

Into the soggy, crowded mass I entered, shielded by my rain-resistant veil. The sleeves were long enough to cover my hands, and I reached up to pull the hood almost entirely closed. I glanced warily at the people around me, each step a relief as I passed people who stayed focused on the police activity and kept their hands on their phones. I headed in the direction of Drew and the car.

But then someone stepped in front of me, halting my stride.

A man in his twenties, bearded, tall, in a puffy jacket. He spoke urgently.

"You're running out of time."

My heart jumped. *This is him*, I thought for a split second.

But then I saw the look on his face change. Urgency melted away to confusion. He looked at me questioningly. He had seemed so sure when he addressed me. Now he looked like he had no clue what he was doing.

I whipped my head around wildly, surveying the crowd. My heart raced.

The pusher. They're here.

I took a step forward, passing the confused man, and another person approached from my left.

"You need to hurry," a woman said with pleading eyes. Then her face relaxed, her head tilted in question.

I stepped past her and kept looking. *Where are you, you mother-fucker.* But there were so many people pressed against each other, their hoods raised, umbrellas bobbing.

Only one other person was looking at me, a young boy I approached, about ten years old. He lifted his eyes to mine and spoke.

"They won't wait much longer."

The boy looked away and stepped beyond me, disappearing between the legs of adults standing packed together, hip to hip. If I was meant to follow him, it was impossible.

I waited for another, but no one else came. Standing in the pouring rain, I looked desperately at the people around me, but there was no way of identifying anyone.

The pusher had slipped through my grasp.

SMOKE.

I was on autopilot, exhausted by the time I got home and showered the smoke off, simply going through the motions. Standing in front of the bathroom mirror, I stared at the burned patch of hair on my jawline. Sluggishly, I pulled out the trimmers and began to chisel away my facial cloak, short golden curls littering the counter, until what was left was a very polished and respectable thin goatee. My eyes scanned my reflection as though I was a stranger. But I wasn't a stranger at all. I just hadn't seen that man for some time.

My muscles ached, my eyes barely stayed open. I stumbled to my bed and landed on my back, staring up at the ceiling. There was much left to do. But I had no energy, and I could feel that sleep was seconds away. Memories floated before my eyes like specters, interconnecting around me to cushion my landing, their voices floating past my ears like wisps of wind.

I let myself sink away, falling backward, deeper and deeper, past subconsciousness and into sleep.

★★★

I was in a crowded space, the people around me dressed formal, their words indiscernible, pinging and melting together like the lines of a watercolor inside the dimly lit venue. I drifted forward, heading for a doorway draped with curtains, leading to a side room bathed in shadows and velvet.

As I stepped to the threshold, I couldn't believe my eyes.

There was Jessie, standing alone at a table, her back to me. Her brown hair draped over her shoulders, which rose gently as she breathed into her living body. Only a few others mingled in the room, scattered among tables along the walls.

I approached slowly, as if I risked scaring the apparition away. With each step, more of her face came into view, and the sounds of the people around us faded until I arrived at her side. When my heel came to rest, her body shifted as if startled, and she looked up, her brown eyes gazing straight into mine. And in that moment, I could see the glimpse of her warm smile, stretching forever.

But then her eyes moved, continuing around the room. Because, I remembered, I wasn't really there. She surveyed the others around us, wearing the same nametag lanyards as she did, a green braided cord lying over an elegant business suit. We were at some kind of corporate convention, the kind I received invitations to but never attended. Had I done, would I have met her here? Would we have had more time?

Deciding not to bother engaging in small talk with the boring array of strangers present, Jessie picked up her martini glass and exited through another chamber, parting the sea of cocktail hour enthusiasts on their company's dime. She emerged into a large, carpeted lobby, its grand ceiling spanning opposing staircases from several stories above, opening up to the heavens. And as she stopped to take it in, she looked up and saw a familiar face.

Gideon Pexler, lurking like a gargoyle alone in the mezzanine, stared down at her, his jaw set tight. Neither of them smiled, only watched the other, studying carefully. Jessie would not have expected to see him at such a populated event, yet here he was, outside of his bunker. A chill ran down her spine, and so it did in mine, and she set her martini glass on a nearby table and walked out of the lobby into the cold, foggy Manhattan night.

At the curb she waited for her car, her breath billowing before her mouth. The wisps of warm air danced against the lights of the city, twinkling like stars on an eerily silent night. Had the city ever been this quiet? A warmth tingled in my palm. I looked down to see a little boy clinging to my hand. Little Oliver from the car crash smiled back up at his dad.

No, that wasn't right.

The child disappeared, and when I looked up, Jessie was gone from the curb. Drew stepped up next to me, smoking a cigarette. He repeated something he'd told me months earlier. "God, imagine being eaten up by this city. No anchor, just taken where the current goes. That's what terrifies me most. Not having control."

I'd lowered my head and said nothing about the perpetual battle being fought in my mind. Instead, the car rolled up, and a man stepped around from the driver's side to open the back door.

My heart stopped when I looked into the eyes of Pete Brown.

"Right this way, sir," he said politely.

The ground opened up beneath me and I fell, fell through the void. Somewhere I landed in a darkened forest at dusk, looking out behind a tree at a small figure walking away, its silhouette rippling in the mirage of the summer heat.

And then I heard the sound of a floorboard creak behind me, somehow indoors, and when I turned I was standing in a den. The low light of a lamp cast shadows off the man standing before me holding a knife.

"Please, no," the strange voice from my throat wavered. But at the same time the calculus was running in my head to reach for the lamp before the knife could swing, to disarm the intruder. I couldn't be weak. I had to defend myself. I leaned for the lamp as the knife traveled quick, too quick, toward my abdomen. And just as the sharp pain hit, the room flashed white.

I was sitting on the floor of a claustrophobic space lined with concrete bricks. The scent of sterility stung my nose, the intensity of the white paint on the walls blinded me. I shrieked, leaping to the metal door and pounding it relentlessly with my fists, screaming, "Let me out! You can't keep me in here! Let me out!"

No, no. You're doing it again.

I lowered my arms and stepped back from the door, closing my eyes and slowing my breathing. This wasn't my memory. This wasn't me.

The cell faded gently away, as I settled back into my skin.

Just sleep, I told myself.

It was like I was floating in the pool again, or maybe the deprivation tank. Total darkness. Just the sound of lapping water. Like a koi pond, dark and mysterious, gliding protectively between myself and the rest of my mind.

★★★

IN THE MORNING I stood by the river, the city cold and gray, a fog rolling lazily over the Hudson. My muscles ached. I was nearing physical and mental exhaustion, but I couldn't keep sleeping once the light had woken me up. The occasional jogger passed by, dressed warm for the morning cold, but I didn't pull my scarf tight this time, didn't close my jacket or wear gloves on my hands. I wanted to feel the cold. I wanted every bitter sensation this world had to bite me and propel me forward.

I didn't care that I was out alone where someone might touch me, might erase my mind or push me to do their bidding. Somewhere over the past forty-eight hours, that fear had melted away. What scared me more was how little time we had left.

For perhaps the fifth time, I pulled my phone from my pocket and glanced down at the text message Drew had forwarded me this morning.

Midnight tonight. Clock's ticking.

A reminder from the kidnappers. The previous photo of Analise's terrified face stared back at me from further up the thread.

Find her.

A twinge caught the back of my throat. *I'm trying, Jessie.*

I opened my call log and tapped the number for Carter Young again. Holding the phone against my ear, I listened to it ring as I watched the water pass before me like sand dwindling from an hourglass. Again, I was greeted by his voicemail. I hung up the phone.

A small sailboat began to pass slowly before me, and my eyes locked on the lone man steering it up the river. He was older, grizzled and graying but steady in his motions, packed warm in his winter coat. He tended carefully to a nearby rope, adjusting his sail as he glided against the current pushing out to sea, staying his course. His movements were sure and calm. And for a moment, the ease of his self-direction brought a strange peace over me.

My eyes shifted to the buildings across the water, to the shadows of the ones around us. How perverse it was that in this serene moment, this man and I were surrounded by a bustling black hole of human activity, a claustrophobia that used to drive me mad.

Used to.

Today I felt different, standing on that bank. I did not feel trapped. I did not feel panicked and immobile. Instead, I felt the strangest sense of space, my lungs filling with the vast air around me. Nothing pressing in on me. Just me, in my body, and that itself could not be encroached.

I had been in this city for almost a year, and I had spent most of it cowering inside, afraid to step out and be a part of its teeming brilliance. It had been such a threatening presence to me for so long, it was almost heartbreaking how beautiful it seemed today for the very first time.

I felt a vibration in my pocket, snapping me back to reality. I extracted my phone and saw that a text had arrived from an unknown number.

Then I remembered. It was the number for Carter Young.

Let's meet. Bryant Park 2pm.

Come alone.

MEETING.

"So, remind me again. This guy is like Melanie, but for Pexler?"

"Yes," I said, sitting next to Drew on the bench. "He got caught downloading data, presumably onto the flash drive I received. Jessie fired him the day before the kidnapping."

We watched people come and go as the sun bathed the park in winter sunlight. With the holiday season coming up, the park had transformed its grassy space into an ice skating rink, and vendors were drawing heavy crowds of shoppers in with their seasonal offerings. The sweet smell of kettle corn drifted through the air, but I wasn't hungry, I couldn't eat. I was too focused on the task ahead. Today was the last day.

"Okay," Drew said. "So how do we know this guy isn't the pusher? Like it's some kind of trick?"

"We don't," I said. "We still need to be careful."

Drew waved his phone in his hand, the camera open to record. "Oh, I will be."

I'd texted Carter our approximate location in the park. We sat back from the path, a safe distance from people strolling among the shops. We would be able to tell if anyone was approaching us. So far, we had yet to see Carter.

Drew checked his watch. "He's not exactly prompt." He fidgeted nervously, a coffee cup balanced between his fingers. He'd been quiet for most of the time we'd been there. "How are you feeling?" he asked. "After last night?"

"Some aches," I said, twisting my neck. "Headache's mostly gone. I slept better than I've slept in years."

"I'll admit I was wide awake all night."

Time ticked slowly by. Drew's leg bounced anxiously beside me, so I rose and walked to the footpath for a better look at the crowd near the rink. Plenty of young people dressed warm, but none of them looked familiar, and none of them were Carter. I checked my watch. It was nearly three.

"Where the fuck is he?" Drew said, irritated, as I returned next to him on the bench.

"I don't know," I said. "Something isn't right."

"Damn right it isn't," he muttered hoarsely.

I turned to look at him. "Hey. You okay?"

"Fuck," he whispered, taking another careful look around us before angling toward me. He rubbed his face with his hands. "No, man. I'm not okay."

I studied him, reading the fear in his face. He continued, speaking quietly.

"I just…. Ever since yesterday, I've been a little spooked. I thought this was all some sci-fi fantasy bullshit, but then it all got very real, very fast. I watched you and Abigail hold hands yesterday like some kind of ritual, and I listened to her talk about being used as a puppet and how her life fell apart. I watched you fucking run into a fireball and thought you might not come back out."

My heart softened at his concern.

"And then the pusher sends fucking parrots up to you to deliver messages like it's some kind of horror movie. And…." He hesitated. "And there's something else. Remember when I told you they hadn't heard from the Ackheim CEO after the breach earlier this week? Well, they found him last night. In a bathtub of his own blood, like he killed himself."

I could see the fear in his eyes as he looked at me.

"I'm scared, okay," he said. "I'm scared. I'll fucking admit it."

Carefully, I reached out and set my hand on his shoulder. He took a deep breath, steadying himself.

"And this text this morning," he said. "This is the last day. And Alex… we aren't any closer to finding Analise."

I didn't know what to say. He was right.

"So what do you want to do?" I asked.

He stared at his hands. "I don't know."

He did know. He just didn't want to say it.

Drew looked out again at the people casually walking by, going about their lives as usual.

"We're in over our heads," he said. "At least I am. And I think it's time we seriously consider what our end game is going to be."

"Like going to the cops?"

"Maybe that." He looked back at me, hesitant. "Maybe just handing over the data like they asked. Give them what they want so they leave us alone."

I was surprised to hear that defeat was an option. That told me, more than anything, that he was afraid. He was ready to fold.

Drew checked his watch. "It's almost three. If I put out a call now, I can hold an emergency meeting with the board before the end of the day. If we're really about to send these assholes our data tonight, then I need to start showing up and getting ready to do some damage control."

"Even if we decide to go to the cops?"

He shrugged. "Either way, we're fucked. A story breaks that we're a target of a kidnapping in exchange for company data, it's not going to look good. I need to get ahead of it now." He chuckled to himself. "Believe it or not, the company actually needs me right now. And that doesn't happen very often."

"Okay. I understand. You should go."

"What'll you do?"

I looked back out at the people walking by. "I'll stay. I'll wait for him."

"The fuck you are."

"I'm staying," I said again, firmly. Drew's eyes pleaded with me, but I couldn't run anymore. "This is all I can do. It's what I have to do." My throat tightened. "For Jessie."

The start of a rebuttal croaked from Drew's throat, but he threw it away with a heavy sigh. "Okay. Okay fine. Just text me, man. Send me something every once in a while, let me know you're okay. And hey." He pointed to his phone. "Don't forget to use the camera."

"You got it."

Drew set his hand on my shoulder, and for a fleeting moment, I felt a shared feeling of brotherhood. Genuine love, not masked intent. We gave each other a small nod. Then he rose. Checking nervously over both shoulders, he walked off, keeping his distance from the crowd, until he disappeared beyond the park boundary.

★★★

THE SUN SLOWLY LOWERED in the sky, mirroring the diminishing prospect of meeting with Carter Young. Groups came and went, tourists in bright colors, locals holding their skates, people simply browsing as they sauntered by on their cell phones, speaking to an invisible other. Occasionally, someone somewhere would blast music from their phone, causing people nearby to turn and frown, disrupting the idyllic park afternoon.

Another hour passed, but still no one showed.

That's it, I thought. *He's not coming.*

I rose from the bench and began to walk toward 40th to catch a taxi. Maybe I would go to Sentry, lock myself in my office, and force myself to comb through everything one last time. There had to be a missing clue somewhere.

And... if not?

Then I would prepare the transfer. And hope the kidnappers kept their word. My stomach turned with apprehension.

Suddenly, my phone pinged with another text. I expected it to be Drew. But instead, there was an update from Carter.

Be there in 10. Sorry.

I breathed a sigh of relief, eagerly pushing my previous thoughts from my mind. But then my heart began to pound. I needed to be ready to protect myself.

I looked around for a good meeting spot. I didn't want to sit next to him on a bench. I spotted a group of green tables ahead, mostly vacant, sitting off to the side of the path. I took a seat and armed my camera, watching for the man I had seen in Jessie's memories.

Sure enough, ten minutes later, I spotted the tall, sharply dressed man in his thirties, wearing a long tan overcoat, walking calmly and confidently. I didn't wave. We made eye contact, and he appeared to know who I was. His long strides carried him directly to my table.

"Alex Hemsley," he said, his voice deep.

I nodded. "Carter Young."

He nodded back. "We meet at last."

CARTER.

CARTER TOOK A SEAT in the chair opposite me. Discretely, I pressed the button on my phone perched on my leg to begin recording. A second of silence passed as we studied each other, unsmiling. He was private, hard to read.

"You must have some questions for me," he said. He spoke slowly and controlled, keeping eye contact.

I could pull this man. That would answer all my questions. But I couldn't risk it if he might be the pusher.

"What do you want to tell me?" I countered.

The corner of his lip rose just the slightest. He shifted his weight in his chair, crossing his legs, waiting patiently for me to lead. It reminded me of my interrogations at the precinct. This man knew how to play ball.

What I knew for sure, was what I had seen in Jessie's memories. "Tell me about the leak," I said. "The data you stole from Pexler."

"How do you know about that?"

I shrugged. "Through Jessie."

Carter scoffed. "That cunt."

"*Excuse* me?"

"Sorry, sorry." He waved his hand as though erasing the comment. "That was rude. I guess you could say I harbor some hurt feelings from working with the company."

I nodded slowly, hiding the disdain I was starting to feel for this man.

He continued. "I was up for a promotion three months ago for the position of CTO, but at the last minute, Gideon decided to give it to his sister. A *nepotism* hire." He looked at me, waiting for some kind of reaction, a sign that I agreed with him. I stared quietly back.

"Well, it was a bad fit from the beginning. There was no real management. People came and went as they pleased, our security team got too relaxed, there was no real oversight and accountability. Then...." His voice tightened. "She had the nerve to tell me that the code I was writing was incorrect, riddled with mistakes, when in reality it was her work that was inferior."

This man had a severe superiority complex, but I listened calmly.

"So you were mad at the company," I said. "You were overlooked and wrongfully criticized. Who wouldn't want to retaliate?"

Carter nodded. "Exactly. Call me human."

I looked at the man, his relaxed posture, his hands resting on the table. I crossed my arms, pondering my next step.

"And how far did your retaliation go exactly?" I said.

Carter shrugged. "I downloaded everything, like they said." He cracked a smile. "And I still have it."

This puzzled me. "You still have it?"

"For the right buyer."

I blinked. "You didn't send it to anyone?"

"Not yet, I haven't."

This wasn't right. I had received a flash drive with the Pexler info in the mail last Monday. There was an incongruity. Or he was lying.

"I assume that's why you wanted to meet today," Carter said. "That's why I met with Arthur Charlan, the CTO at Ackheim yesterday. They've given me an offer for a position as well. Apparently they just lost their lead security engineer."

At last, I frowned. I wasn't going to play along with this charade. It was becoming quite clear, his interests lay in selling data he supposedly didn't even have. Whoever we were up against wanted to obtain the Pexler data, not sell it.

"Let me ask you one more thing," I said.

"Shoot."

I set my arms on the table and leaned in, studying his face. "Do you have any idea the whereabouts of Jessie or Analise Pexler over the past few days?"

He shrugged, uninterested. "Why the hell would I know?"

For a moment, we sat there looking at each other. Me, considering. Him waiting for me to make the next move. The laughter of the pedestrians nearby wove in and out as daylight was slipping away.

"Alright, Mr. Young," I said. "Name your price."

"Name a number. I'll tell you if Ackheim was higher."

"Sixty."

He blew air between his lips.

"Fine, one-twenty."

"Warmer."

"One-fifty. And a quarterly payment of fifteen thousand over the next two years, for your discretion."

Carter beamed. "We're speaking the same language now."

I flashed a smile back. "Think it over. You have my number. I look forward to hearing from you, assuming you don't run off with any other suitors."

I held my hand across the table, and Carter eagerly grasped it.

"It's been a pleasure chatting with you, Mr. Hemsley."

His voice echoed in my head as I let myself fall backwards, floating into the darkness of his memories.

★★★

CARTER WATCHED WITH JEALOUSY as Jessie walked into her office that very first day. He watched as she reached forward and lifted a note off the desk. No doubt something sweet from her big brother. He scoffed as his eyes lingered, his brow crumpled with envy.

The shadows tilted and time progressed, fast-forwarding. I listened to the snippets of conversations bubbling around me, weaving in and out of discussions with coworkers in the suite.

"Can you believe he hired his sister?" Carter asked.

"I don't know, she seems nice," someone said.

"And she doesn't micromanage," said another.

"I come in late all the time." The person shrugged. "Never a word."

In fact, it seemed that Jessie often preferred to work with her door closed. I could relate. Some days she simply worked from home, and would allow others to do the same. The atmosphere in her department at Pexler was relaxed. People liked feeling they were trusted. But that didn't work well for Carter, who preferred the tight oversight of older men akin to a military squad, and had long bathed in mutual admiration of his former supervisors over the years.

One day, about a month ago, he was summoned into Jessie's office and asked to take a seat.

"Your work is sloppy," she began, her tone curt.

"I'm sorry?"

"There are mistakes in this configuration for the firewall. Anyone can breach it. You need to step it up."

Carter blinked, baffled. "The code is perfectly fine."

She scowled at him. Her behavior startled me.

"I've been cleaning up your messes since day one. You think your poor performance goes unnoticed?"

A fire raged inside Carter. Choice words floated before his lips. Instead he kept his mouth shut tight, his teeth grinding.

Jessie slammed her fist on the desk. "Do you fucking hear me, Young?"

I stared in disbelief from the corner. Carter shot to his feet and stormed out the door before he could say anything he could be fired for. A burning disappointment washed over me.

And then the lights flickered.

I squinted, scrutinizing the memory around me. The corners seemed hazy. The sounds of the office, now that I focused, seemed to warble.

Artifact.

Jessie stood frowning at her desk with her hands on her hips.

This was not real. This conversation, Jessie's harsh criticism and offensive behavior, far out of her character, had never occurred. It was entirely fabricated.

Someone had fed him this memory.

But what wasn't fabricated was the simmering resentment Carter now felt for his boss. He tossed and turned at night, seething with anger. He came in late and left early, barely working, his heart no longer in it. He stared at her office door in a way that made my skin crawl. In a way that made me think he might send harm after her.

There was a noise somewhere behind us. Carter and I both turned to look.

I couldn't believe it.

It was Gideon.

Standing at the entrance to the hall, dressed in a black t-shirt and glasses, his posture like an alien's, he gazed down the Engineering suite. All the workers in their offices went quiet. You could hear a pin drop.

Gideon stared at his sister's office, the door closed. No motion, no expression. Just stared.

And then a moment later, he simply turned and walked away.

Fucking creep, thought Carter.

A month of apathy passed. It was burning him alive, not being motivated to work for praise. And finally, one day as he was staring at his monitor, he thought, *To hell with it.*

I watched him as he opened the database and began downloading assets, pulling a vacant flash drive from his desk drawer. His leg bounced nervously as the files pooled on his local system, then queued to transfer to the thumb drive. When it was finished, he removed the drive from the computer and set it on his desk.

This is where he'll put it in the envelope, I thought.

But instead, Carter reached for his coat. He shouldered it on, then leaned forward to power off his computer. He picked up the drive and tucked it into a tiny breast pocket in the inner lining of his jacket.

I watched my surroundings carefully, observing the lamp in the corner barely lighting the shadowy room. The leaves of the fake plant sitting on Carter's desk. His motions as he picked up his messenger bag and rose from his chair. I watched carefully for the tell of an artifact.

But there wasn't one.

Okay, I thought. *Maybe he mailed it at home.*

I flipped ahead to the next memory of the flash drive. That night, back at his condo, Carter extracted the drive from his pocket and set it carefully in his safe, next to his revolver. I stared over his shoulder as he smiled at the little plastic drive, a sleeping bomb, and what it was going to do for him.

He never did mail the drive, after all.

To this day, it remained slumbering in his safe.

So how the hell had a flash drive of Pexler data ended up on my desk? Who had sent it to me? Apparently I wasn't going to find the answer here.

Over the next few days, Carter listened carefully for any sign that he'd been found out. He figured he probably wouldn't be, that Jessie and the rest of the team were too stupid to catch on. But sure enough, the following week he was called into her office. In fact, it was last Tuesday, the day after I'd given Jessie the mailed drive. Jessie sat at her desk, flanked by another VP and an HR rep.

He simply sat and smiled as they recited the reason for his termination. It was straightforward business, sign here please, gather your things. As he stood to leave, Jessie spoke from behind her desk, in a somber, regretful tone.

"Why did you do it?"

He held his head up high. "If you have to ask, you'll never know."

Jessie stared at him in disappointment, not feeling the weight of the words as he'd intended. But he didn't notice. He just reminded himself that he was smarter than her, and he gathered his things and walked proudly down the hallway, opening the door to leave the Engineering suite.

We're done here, I thought, preparing to return to the present.

But what I saw as Carter opened the door caught my eye.

There was a man I recognized.

No… it couldn't be.

Dumbfounded, I stumbled forward, trailing fast on Carter's heels as he turned into the hallway. There I could see everyone coming and going, workers walking with their coffees, pointing at papers and discussing meetings.

I couldn't believe my eyes.

There, dressed in a button-down shirt and wearing an employee badge, in all his receding hairline glory, was Pete Brown.

I stared at him, walking toward me, speaking to a colleague at his side. His gait, his gestures, his voice, all matching what I'd seen in the memories of his neighbor. In the security footage at his building.

It was him.

And he was a fucking Pexler employee. An accountant, to be exact.

I stared in disbelief, gawking as he and his coworker walked away, the hall slowly disappearing as Carter's consciousness moved elsewhere.

Carter Young may not have been behind the attack that night. But someone at Pexler definitely was.

STRINGS.

I CAME BACK TO the present, my muscles still maintaining a foreign smile as I looked into the face of Carter Young, our hands still clasped. I shifted in my chair, and my phone fell from my leg, bouncing against the metal table.

Carter looked down, frowning. "Were you recording me?"

His grip on my hand tightened. I wanted him to let go.

"What are you, some kind of fucking cop?" His voice was rising.

There was so much bouncing around in my head that was way more important than me being here. I needed him to let go. I needed him to leave.

"No, I'm not a cop. It's so I can relay the information to Drew, our CEO," I lied.

He scowled. "You legally have to tell someone you're recording them. That shit won't hold up in a court."

"Yep. You're right." *Please leave.*

Carter shook his head angrily, then finally released my hand. Turning to leave, he pulled his coat tighter, the drop in temperature noticeable as night had fallen. He marched away, his strides faster and angrier as he disappeared into the growing crowd.

But I couldn't care about any of that now. I picked up my phone and stopped the recording. Then I dialed Drew.

"Come on," I muttered as it rang.

His voicemail chattered in my ear. Maybe he was in his meeting. I ended the call and set the phone on the table.

No matter. There was work to be done. I needed to mine for information. I took a deep breath to center myself and steady the walls of my mind.

Focus.

The distant sound of laughter faded away.

I dove into Jessie's memories, looking for interactions between her and Pete. Scanning quickly, like I was flipping through a rolodex, I saw a few fleeting moments with his face. But she hadn't even known his name. He was a bean counter in another department. She hadn't ever worked with him directly.

I hesitated before moving on, remembering the fabricated altercation Carter had recorded with Jessie in her office. If I found that interaction in Jessie's memories, what would I see from her side?

I pictured the setting as Carter had seen it and scanned through Jessie's memories, looking for a backdrop that matched. I swam further and further back until, about a month prior, I found a memory that looked similar. Jessie sat at her desk, and Carter sank into a chair opposite her, having been summoned.

"I just wanted to give you some feedback on your performance," she began.

Carter's jaw twitched.

Jessie smiled. "You're doing an excellent job. Really, this work on the firewall is… genius."

Carter beamed, nodding at her. "Thank you."

"I might even have some questions for you. If you have a second."

I watched from the shadows as this new memory unfolded. As I suspected, the content was entirely new to me. It did not exist in Carter's memories, because it had been replaced with a different version. Jessie had not been so brusque as he remembered; in fact she had acted entirely in character. Carter scooted forward up to the desk and was speaking excitedly about authorizations and data packets, Jessie fully engaged and nodding with each point. Why would someone have wanted to alter this?

To breed contempt, I thought. Someone had wanted Carter to feel anger and hurt toward Jessie. That must have been the catalyst planted, to make him send the drive. Influence him to betray his company. It had almost worked.

I was about to leave the memory when something caught my eye, pulling my gaze away from the conversation. It was the room. The walls seemed unsteady, floating like ghosts. The corners were hazy. The lights were dull. And even in Jessie's voice, I could hear the slightest ringing.

This wasn't right either.

I stepped forward into the room, reaching my hand out toward the light shining overhead. As I turned my hand and curled my fingers, the light bent unnaturally, wrapping around my skin like thin plastic.

Fuck.

My heart skipped a beat.

Artifact.

Jessie had been pushed.

A million implications flooded my mind.

The most obvious, of course, was that whatever had actually transpired in this conversation was still a mystery. It was somewhere under here, the real memory, just beyond recovery. I stared at the dancing lights in Jessie's office, the unfocused corners, trying to pull the film back with my mind. *Please.*

But it did not budge. There was nothing there to recover. The memory was gone.

Someone had pushed Carter to believe his new boss had told him off, sewing a hatred that would consume him. But someone had also pushed Jessie to cover up the same conversation. *Why?*

I thought again of Gideon standing at the end of the hallway, his sunken eyes staring toward his sister's door. Carter had noted what a rare occurrence it was to receive a visit from their elusive boss.

Had he been there to manipulate one of them?

But beside all of that was the greater revelation that if this memory of Jessie's was false, at some point, she'd been in contact with the pusher.

Which meant any of her other memories could be false.

Already, I could see hints of artifacts revealing themselves on various memories. On long days inside her office, toiling away at her computer. On walks from the Pexler building to the subway, intercepting her return home.

My god, I thought. She'd been a pawn too.

But what had she been pushed to do in those hours she was offline? I had no way of knowing, because she herself hadn't known.

My mind jumped to the conference I had watched her attend in my dreams the night before. Standing there in the lobby with her, I'd watched her eyes meet with Gideon's, brother and sister regarding one another like bugs under a magnifying glass.

I followed her outside and watched her closely as she waited at the sidewalk for her car, her breath floating in the cold night air, moist droplets hung against the void night sky.

But they didn't disappear.

Wrong, it was all wrong. The pocket of breath hung there in a state of unnatural perpetuity. The sound of the city jolted around us. The lights on the buildings twinkled.

She'd stepped outside and then been pushed. Right after Gideon had seen her.

It was all adding up. It couldn't be a coincidence. A reclusive mastermind at the center of it all, pulling the strings of his puppets in his own company, destroying the reputations of his competitors.

My consciousness fluttered back to the present. Around me the constant buzz of people was setting me on edge. I needed to go somewhere, anywhere I could bury my head and focus. I turned on my heel and marched out of Bryant Park, heading north. I pulled out my phone and tried desperately to call Drew again, but was met with his voicemail once more. I left a message.

"Listen. It's Gideon. He's the pusher. And Pete, he was a fucking Pexler employee." I kept rambling. "Jessie was pushed, God knows what he had her do. Just… watch your six. And call me back."

Already the sky had turned a deep, dark blue. Patrons were filing into restaurants. A nearby vendor was hocking halal plates to a long line of people waiting patiently in their coats against a crisp winter wind that had filled the sun's void.

As I passed the open door of a bodega, a jacketed duo exited in front of me, halting my stride. It was as I gave a half-turn to the storefront that something caught my eye. A television hung behind the register, where a news anchor was gearing up a local news segment. The banner unfolded along the bottom of the screen with the headline in big black letters.

And suddenly, I couldn't breathe.

Tragic death of young CEO.

I stepped forward through the door, locked in a trance, the world around me gone except for the voice of the news anchor.

"Some heartbreaking news tonight in the tech world, the passing of *another* bright young mind. Police have identified a man who died earlier today in a traffic incident."

No.

"He was the CEO of an up-and-coming database security company, lauded by many as a pioneer in the field."

Please no.

Every cell stood frozen in my body.

And then a picture of a man appeared on-screen.

"Gideon Pexler, CEO and Founder of Pexler Technologies, was the victim of a fatal traffic accident early this morning."

I released an immense sigh of relief, crashing over me like ice on my skin. But still I stared at Gideon's face, just as shocked to see his severe gaze looking back at me.

B-roll played of an ambulance parked in the middle of a city street, bathing the shadowed morning with its red and blue light. In fact, it was the street just outside the Pexler building.

The newswoman continued. "A witness nearby said that they saw Pexler rushing toward the street when a taxicab was approaching, and sadly a collision occurred. A reminder to be vigilant when navigating our streets."

Now a small crowd of people were shown on-screen rubbernecking by the ambulance on their way to work. The last people whose attention Gideon would ever grab.

I couldn't believe it. Gideon Pexler, genius child prodigy, was dead. Hit by a taxi as he ran into the street.

"Unfortunately, this is the second death of a CEO of a Manhattan-based tech company in the past few days," the newscaster said from her desk. "A disturbing trend we hope won't continue."

I tilted my head in thought, the voice on the TV fading away.

Who were you running from, Gideon?

KEY.

I sat at the bar, spinning the shot glass in my fingers. I had ordered one and only one, just enough to loosen my mind, then promptly requested a glass of water. A change of pace for me.

Behind me, the crowd in Knoxley's was sparse. The dinner rush had gone, and only a couple tables remained with folks determined to put off the completion of the weekend for as long as possible.

I glanced soberly at the empty stool next to me. I had hoped the old man would be here, not for solace this time, but as another set of ears. Maybe, I thought, if I told him everything I'd learned, he could piece it together, see the forest for the trees. He was the only other person I knew in this world who could understand what I was dealing with.

I lowered my head and concentrated again on the memories I'd collected from Jessie when she was still alive. When she was blissfully unaware of any ill intent billowing around her. Grabbing her morning coffee and taking the elevator up to work. Greeting her team members as she walked down the hall. And then, a filmy grain plastering her office as she opened the door, like an old movie playing as she sat at her desk and wiggled her mouse.

What had she been told to do?

I heard the door open behind me, and when I turned, my eyes met my brother's. He looked around anxiously as he slid between the tables, holding his arms close to his chest.

"Okay, no more splitting up," he said as he climbed on the stool next to me. "I've seen horror movies. That was a dumb idea."

I sighed, feeling a sense of relief to have him sitting next to me.

The bartender popped up to the counter. "Can I get you anything, sir?"

"God, yes. Whiskey neat." Drew turned back to me when the bartender walked away, loosening the scarf around his neck.

"How'd the call go?" I asked.

"About as terrible as you'd expect. But everyone's on their toes. We've got PR statements ready. If word gets out, we'll be prepared." He softened his voice. "Did you see the news? About Gideon?"

I nodded, unable to muster any words of remotest sympathy.

Drew sighed. "It's fucked up. I didn't much care for the guy, but he didn't deserve to die."

I inspected the perfect curves of the shot glass in my fingers, the way they refracted the light passing through from the other side. The bartender returned with Drew's glass and began to bus tables as another party departed the pub.

"I still can't believe Gideon's not behind all this," I said.

"He would've died before we got the final text this morning," Drew said. "He couldn't have sent it."

"Then it has to be someone else with access at Pexler." I set the shot glass down and turned to Drew. "Jessie, Carter, Pete, that's three employees that were pushed."

"Carter was pushed?"

I sighed. "Yes. Someone planted an altercation with Jessie in his memories. Then he downloaded the data from Pexler."

"So he's the one who mailed you the flash drive?"

I paused. "No."

Drew blinked, shaking his head. "This shit is giving me a headache with every minute."

"And Jessie," I said. "I can see all the fake memories that were planted in her. Someone was using her. Just like all the others."

"Why didn't you see them before?"

I shrugged. "I didn't know how to find them until Abigail showed me. I didn't even know pushers and fake memories existed until yesterday."

"Could it mean something else though?" Drew said, thinking as he sipped more of his whiskey.

"What do you mean?"

"I mean, what if she was being wiped for a different reason?" His eyes lit up. "What if she saw something she wasn't supposed to see? Or some*one*?"

I nodded slowly, backtracking through the handful of artifacts I'd collected. Jessie at the computer. Jessie in the hallway. Jessie leaving the building.

"Maybe she did something that made someone very angry?" Drew said.

Something snagged my mind's eye. A slight movement in the shadows of a memory.

Drew took another sip, still hypothesizing. "I mean, hell, maybe her murder wasn't even an accident."

This sent an angry heat spiking through my veins. But I was following something, someone. I needed to figure it out what it was.

"I see something," I said.

Drew perked up. "What?"

I was stepping into an empty hallway, squinting in the dark. It was after hours, the night before the kidnapping. Jessie was working late, and everyone had gone home. She was just closing the door to the Engineering suite when she saw someone moving in the distance.

"Hello?" Jessie called.

The sound of a faint click.

Drew's voice intruded. "I'm just saying, it'd be real convenient to—"

I raised a finger to silence him. "Holy shit," I whispered.

Jessie walked to the door down the hall, the one she could've sworn she just heard close. A door with sheet plastic poking out from underneath. *What would someone be doing in here this late?* she thought.

I recognized the door. I'd seen it myself when we were at Pexler. It led to a suite that was being renovated. Construction workers had filed in and out during the day.

But who had Jessie just seen slipping inside?

She lifted the security badge from her pocket and pressed it against the door sensor. It beeped, the little LED lighting green. Cautiously, she extended her hand to the handle.

And then she froze.

The lights danced, the walls trembled.

And under the film of the artifact, I watched Jessie retract her arm and continue down the hallway, leaving the building.

I raised my hands so quickly, they made contact with a glass object. Back at the bar, the shot glass smashed onto the floor behind the counter.

"*Shit,*" I whispered, turning flustered to the bartender who looked up from wiping a table. "Sorry, sorry!"

I turned back to Drew, manic, my mouth working fast to keep up with my mind. "I've got it. I know where we need to go."

"What? Where?"

"Someone's using a hallway at Pexler that's been closed off," I said to Drew. "I think Jessie caught them sneaking into it the night before she died."

"Shit," Drew whispered. "And you think that could be...?"

"Where they're keeping Analise," I answered. "Maybe. If not, maybe we'll find another clue."

An energy began to buzz under my skin, between my brother and me. He fidgeted in his chair, setting down his rocks glass.

"So what do we do?" he said.

Find her.

"We go," I said. "We go and we save her." From my pocket, I pulled Jessie's spare security badge and dropped it on the counter.

Drew looked warily at the badge and took a deep breath, mulling it over in his head. "They could be there waiting for us."

"There's no reason for them to expect us."

"If it's what you think it is, you don't think there'll be some kind of surveillance?"

"Maybe. That just means we have to be fast."

Drew studied the badge longer, thinking more. I leaned forward and touched his sleeve.

"You can stay, but I'm going," I said. "I can't just sit here and let it all wash over me, I can't just hide. I have to do something, because I *can*. I have to do this."

"Like hell you're going alone." Drew sprang to his feet and reached for his coat. "I'm coming with you. But first, I need to go back upstairs to my office and grab something. A little insurance policy."

"What's that?"

He looked at me seriously. "A gun."

★★★

"You keep a *gun* in your office?"

My car raced up the thinning streets of Sunday night Midtown. It was nearing eleven o'clock.

"Yeah, man. All this competition, it makes me nervous someone might stop by for a visit and try to pull something."

I scoffed and shook my head.

Drew smirked. "Not such a bad idea now, is it?"

On my leg sat my phone. I had tried calling Abigail, thinking she might be interested in joining us to face the person who had wrecked her life. An extra set of eyes could prove helpful. But she hadn't answered, so I'd sent a text. *Hey, you ok? Call me.*

"We owe Carter Young a hundred fifty thousand, by the way," I said jokingly.

"Dude, I'll pay anyone a million dollars just for this night to be over."

The mood had changed from apprehensive to energetic. Adrenaline was warming up our veins as we charged up the street, diving headfirst into our last resort.

"We're close." Drew pointed out the window. "Take this open spot here."

I pulled the car over to the curb. Drew tucked his handgun into his waistband.

"Hey, be careful with that," I said.

"Frankly, this isn't exactly the weapon I'm worried about."

We looked out the windshield at the tower looming two blocks away. It stood cold and gray against the misty winter night. As we stepped outside, the cold wet air stung my face, no longer protected behind a thick beard.

I looked over to Drew. "Ready?"

"Ready."

We began our walk over to the building, my heart pounding in my ears. The sidewalk was almost completely empty, the occasional pedestrian walking by with their head tucked down into their jacket.

As we closed in on the last block, my phone dinged in my pocket. A response from Abigail.

In the text thread, I could see my message from earlier: *Hey, you ok? Call me.*

Underneath, she'd replied. My stomach gave one final turn.

Who is this?

PART III.

FIND.

THE GLASS PANELS ALONG the ground floor were dark and un-yielding as we approached the lobby doors, coated with a fine layer of the night's moisture. I held out the security badge to the sensor mounted on one of the door frames, and the latch to the door released.

Inside, the lobby was dim and shadowed, and a lone security guard sat before the glow of her monitors, her eyes heavy and tired. She looked up at us questioningly.

I flashed the badge along with a nod from across the room. *Just another employee.*

Her eyes went back lazily to the monitors.

We proceeded to the bank of elevators, pressing the call button and rolling back the doors of the nearest car. Quickly we stepped into the elevator and I swiped the badge, feeling like all the gates of the world were finally opening before me. I pressed the button for floor twelve and smiled as it illuminated.

Once the doors closed, Drew released his breath, leaning against the wall. I watched the numbers climb, the floor of the elevator like a rocket beneath my feet. I slipped off my gloves and tucked them into my pockets.

Ding.

Pexler, twelfth floor.

The doors opened, revealing a darkened lobby, the reception desk unattended. As we stepped out of the elevator, a motion sensor signaled for various low lights around the room to illuminate. Small, subtle lights backlit the letters spelling out the name PEXLER behind the desk with an eerie glow.

It was still. Nothing made a sound but the gentle hum of the HVAC. Drew and I barely drew breath, for fear of disrupting the quiet.

The hallways we had seen the other day were now behind closed doors, each with a badge reader above the doorknob. I turned left toward the hall to the Engineering suite. Carefully, Drew pulled the gun from out of his waistband, gripping it in both hands. I held the plastic badge to the reader, and it lit green, unlocking the door. I turned the handle and pulled.

Motion-sensitive lights marched down the hallway before us, but other than that, there was no sign of activity. We stepped forward into the carpeted hallway. Drew closed the door behind us.

Slowly, silently, we stepped past the doors on either side of the hallway, sleeping wooden giants holding back unknown assassins just on the other side. I clocked a camera in the corner of the hallway, reminding myself that we might not have much time.

We rounded the first corner, and there, on the left side of the hall, was the door, the one from Jessie's memories. I saw the tufts of plastic sticking out from underneath, the dark stains of footprints on the carpet outside. An overhead light shone down, illuminating the rivers of grain in the wood.

Drew looked at me, then back at the door, confirming this was our destination. He took a deep breath in, readying his stance, his grip tightening on the gun. "This is it," he whispered.

Game's over, motherfucker.

I braced myself for anything. Gunfire, knives, a grizzly old man lunging at my neck. I was ready.

Drew and I gave each other one final nod. Then I pressed the badge against the sensor.

The light flashed green. The lock released.

I pressed down on the handle and pulled the door back.

The floor of the hallway was covered with a run of plastic sheet. I cringed as my first step crumpled the material under my foot. The walls were half painted. The doorways of eight or so offices lined the walls. Some had doors, some didn't. Some had a wall busted out to expand the room, the studs behind the drywall peeking through. It was like we had entered some partially deconstructed world.

Carefully, we checked each room. I assessed the ones on the left, Drew the ones on the right. Two fluorescent panels housed the harsh light for the entire hallway. Everything else was dark. My eyes tried to adjust as quickly as possible, scanning between rooms.

Halfway down the hallway, the plastic sheet ended, and my footsteps quieted on plywood subfloor, avoiding crumbled chunks of drywall. Up ahead, a floor-length window gazed out over the darkening city of Manhattan.

With each passing doorway, my heart pounded harder. We cleared each shadowed alcove as we went, until at last we were down to the final pair of rooms. We checked the open one on the right, desolate in the darkness. The one on the left had a closed door.

On that door was a badge sensor.

Drew and I looked at each other.

Everything that had happened, that had puzzled us, that had threatened us, had led us here. This insane fantasy story that had been chasing us for days, we had finally chased back. My brother and I positioned ourselves, ready for whatever was about to come at us on the other side of that door.

In my mind, I thought once more of Jessie, smiling at me on the stairs outside the restaurant.

I reached forward and pressed the badge against the door.

The light flashed green. I pressed the handle down and pushed.

The room beyond was unfinished, the walls bare, the floor covered with large squares of unanchored carpet. Two lights in the ceiling illuminated the cold, harsh surfaces of the room. The smell of sweat and drywall drifted out.

And there, sitting on a folding chair in the center of the room…

Was Analise.

GOOD.

"Analise!"

Drew ran to her. I froze.

Analise was not tied to the chair or restrained in any way. Yet she did not move, and when she looked up at us, her eyes filled with fear. She flinched as Drew knelt beside her. "Oh my god, Analise, are you okay? Are you hurt?"

"Wait," I said to Drew. "Something's not right."

He stepped back and studied her. She leaned away, hiding her face in her hands. She had not spoken a word, only murmured terrified under her breath. Her body shook, from fear, maybe even hunger. He looked at the gun in his hand and handed it to me. I stood there with it hanging at my side.

There were only a few other items in the unfinished room with us. I noticed a sealed bucket in the corner, with a bag of cat litter sitting next to it. A blanket lay in a heap on the floor by the window. And along the front wall of the room was a basic folding table with another chair in front of it. On the table sat a laptop, open with its screen dark.

"What's wrong with her?" Drew asked.

I looked back at Analise, tucked the gun into my waistband, and slowly approached her. "It's okay," I whispered. "We're not gonna hurt you."

She lowered her hands, glancing nervously at me. The fear was not an act, it was real. Something had petrified her. Or someone.

"Hey. It's okay. We're here to help you." I kneeled down in front of her and held out my hand. "Let me help you."

Analise was listening, her hands slowly extending to mine. Gently, I let the warmth of my hands soak into her cold fingers as I peered into her memories.

Immediately, I noticed something was wrong.

I was standing in a void of white.

I'd never seen anything like it before. I shuffled through the timeline, more blank slates of white flashing before me.

"What do you see?" Drew asked.

"There's... nothing."

"What do you mean?"

"I mean there's nothing here. She has no memories."

I landed at last on the faintest trace of a memory, but I couldn't make out its contents. It was as if someone had scrubbed it with steel wool, hastily erasing it, leaving only a transparent residue behind.

I came back to the present, still kneeling before Analise. She looked desperately into my eyes, her hands now gripping mine. I felt an overwhelming sadness for her. She had no idea who she was, why she was here, how to even speak.

I patted her arm. "We're going to get you out of here."

I spoke over my shoulder to Drew. "We need to go." I was fighting back the fear as best I could.

"Hold on." Drew was now over by the table, looking at the laptop. "You need to see this."

I rose, returning the gun to my hand as I walked to his side. He'd turned on the computer and was staring at the contents of the screen. A list of files, dated and timestamped, filled the frame.

"Is this...?"

"Security footage," Drew said.

We were looking at the interface of a surveillance program. A familiar name was emblazoned at the top.

"I recognize this," I said. "This is the surveillance company our building uses."

Drew tapped down the list, generating a video preview for each file he highlighted. "Looks like these are from several locations that they monitor."

I looked at the labeling on the interface. "This company stores their surveillance in the cloud. But it looks like this a local collection, saved to this laptop."

"Wonder why?"

We watched the videos as Drew kept tabbing down the list. There were multiple angles of Pexler, people streaming in and out of the lobby on a busy day.

"Wait a minute," Drew said, watching a video at a new location. "Is that Ackheim?"

I leaned in toward the screen. Sure enough, I recognized the building. And that wasn't the only thing.

"Holy shit," I whispered.

A small woman with colored hair was exiting the lobby doors, dressed in her coat with her bag over her shoulder.

"That's Abigail!" Drew said.

Then suddenly, at the edge of the shot, she was stopped by a person wearing a jacket and a hood, just barely in frame, obscuring the movements happening between them. I knew what was going to happen next, but it still sent a rush of nausea as I watched her pixeled figure turn around and walk back into the lobby.

My stomach knotted. "That was the pusher."

We shared a look of dread.

I leaned back in and looked at the other locations associated with the filenames. Another caught my eye. "Click on this one."

The facade of a familiar brick building filled the screen. A balding man in a jacket was walking up from the sidewalk toward the front door, when the top of a hooded sweatshirt just barely bobbed into view at the edge of the frame. They must have called the man's name, as he turned and walked over to them, a look of surprise on his face, then stopped. His eyes glazed over, then he turned around and marched inside the building. Presumably to pack up his family and leave.

"Pete Brown," I whispered.

Behind him, the hooded figure in the sweatshirt pushed through the door and followed him inside.

"*Shit*," I murmured, shaking my head. A lump was starting to form in my throat. Of course, they'd needed to go upstairs to push the whole family to get them out of town agreeably.

"That's Thursday morning, eight AM," Drew read from the list.

I frowned. "But this footage was supposed to be missing."

Drew scanned the list of files. "Wait a minute. This one has our address in the filename. This is from our building, two Thursdays ago."

"The night of the break-in," I said.

A new video opened. The exterior of our ground lobby filled the shot. I could feel my pulse quicken as I watched our home territory being observed through enemy lens.

A car pulled up to the curb. The door opened, and my throat tightened.

"Melanie."

Melanie Abrerra stepped out of the car, turning to speak to someone else in the backseat. She gave a final nod, then shut the door. The car drove off as she approached the lobby.

"This is seven fifty that night," Drew said.

"She was arriving to try to log into the database. After we thought she was dead. There was someone else in the car. Who was she talking to?"

Drew scrubbed back in the video. "I bet we can see a plate. This would have been useful for us to find earlier."

But I was remembering my interaction with the security guards the day before.

"There was nothing to find," I said. "The security team told me this exact video was deleted from the logs."

We shared another look.

Someone knew exactly what they were doing.

"We need to go," I said. I turned to go get Analise.

"Wait!"

I stopped at the urgency of his tone.

"There's one from today."

I turned around. "Where?"

"At Sentry. From this afternoon."

"What?" I rushed back to the table.

We watched as the video began to play, the same camera capturing the outside of the lobby. I studied the faces of people coming and going, not recognizing anyone. Then about fifteen seconds in, I finally saw a familiar shape in the low-resolution cluster of pixels.

My brother, Drew, was exiting the lobby.

I could hear him hold his breath beside me.

In the video, he walked toward the edge of the screen, checking his phone, when he looked up suddenly, his face filled with shock. It was as if he had recognized someone. He stopped right on the edge of the screen, but before he could speak, the slightest shadow fell across his face.

Someone was touching him.

Their body was not in frame, but I could barely make out the shape of their hand, touching his cheek. It lingered for only a second, then it was gone. Drew immediately turned, heading back to the lobby.

"No," he groaned beside me. "No, no, no. Where am I going? What am I doing?"

His figure disappeared inside the building.

I looked at him, standing next to me. His hands shook as he began to panic.

"Drew. What did you do this afternoon?"

"I had my call with the board," he rambled, "then I prepped some documents. I downloaded the top-tier files and deleted them from the server, like you asked, and I—"

"What?" I snapped. "Stop, stop, stop. What did you say I asked you to do?"

His eyes widened, the pitch of his voice soaring higher. "You called me and asked me to!"

Without thinking, my hand shot out and clasped his wrist. He continued to speak as I watched his recollection of the events from his afternoon. "You called me!" he pleaded again.

I could see him sitting at his desk, answering a call.

He continued in the present, his voice shaking. "You said I should remove the files from the server for safety. And put them on a drive and keep it with me. So no one else could try to hack it."

I watched the conversation play out in his memory. The lights over his desk sizzled, the room swirling, full of artifacts.

I turned and looked at him next to me, my hand still on his arm. Slowly, I shook my head.

"Fuck," he said, his energy manic. "Fuck! No, no, no." He pulled his arm away and covered his face with his hands, pacing in a circle.

"Drew?"

He stopped.

Gravely, I asked, "Where's that drive?"

Our eyes met.

He'd put it in his pocket.

It was still there.

"We have to go," I said. "*Now.*"

Drew ran to Analise, shaking as he guided her to her feet. My heart was racing as I turned toward the door, then I had a thought. Surveillance had been the key, the one solid truth. The laptop here was full of evidence. Maybe the police could stitch together an identity from the crumbs left behind. I spun on my foot and went to collect it, setting the gun down on the table as my hand gripped the screen.

But what I saw stopped me in my tracks.

The video with Drew had ended, and the next file had begun to play. I recognized the setting immediately. I'd been there before.

The familiar vast concrete steps of a restaurant filled the screen. Lights strung overhead, the faintest hint of snow. Two people stood in the middle of a landing.

Me and Jessie.

The police had told us there hadn't been any surveillance. But here it was. Had they lied? *No*, I thought, *this must have been deleted as well.*

My eyes stayed glued to the screen as Jessie bid me goodnight and walked down to the sidewalk, Analise following just behind her. Then suddenly, a big black SUV pulled up to the curb.

But something was different.

A man got out of the driver's seat. A man I recognized immediately as Pete Brown. But he did not wear a ski mask. He did not carry a gun. He did not shout. Instead, he simply opened the back door, and Analise stepped into the car, thanking him with a smile.

What the fuck.

He then closed her door and returned to his seat, and the car drove away, leaving without event.

It felt like cold water was pouring over me.

Jessie remained standing at the sidewalk, very much alive. She turned and walked back up the steps, motioning to someone. I watched as Drew entered the frame, coming to a stop beside me. The three of us stood on that landing, talking amongst ourselves.

None of this was right.

My mind was racing back to that night.

And suddenly I saw it. I saw it everywhere. Artifacts. It was like the entire memory was on fire, the truth burning all around me.

My memory was a fake.

In the video, the three of us faced the street, Jessie standing between me and Drew. Another car pulled up to the curb. It was our ride.

No. It can't be.

I could hear a voice echoing in my ears. *Do you think what we're doing is good?*

Jessie raised both her arms, setting her hands on our shoulders, her fingers draped over the bare skin on the back of our necks.

I could feel her touch. I could remember it clearly, the fake memory dissolving, floating like ashes among the snow.

Her head turned. Jessie looked directly into the security camera. She smiled.

And somewhere from across the room, a voice said,

"Hello, Alex."

ARTIFACT.

I couldn't believe my eyes.

There she was, standing in the doorway, living and breathing, with a gun in her hands.

"Jessie," I whispered.

Her brown eyes focused on me above a knowing smile, but without her usual warmness.

"You're the pusher."

Her grin widened just a little more. "Well done, Alex." She stepped further into the room. "I knew it would take a sharp puller to follow my trail of breadcrumbs, but you came through with flying colors."

Somewhere in my dumbfoundedness, a wave of dread spread over me. *She knew about my ability.* All this time I thought I'd been covertly closing in, but suddenly I felt like a dumb animal led blindly to slaughter.

"What's the matter?" Jessie said, looking at Drew across the room. "You look like you've seen a ghost."

"But you're dead!" Drew sputtered. "We watched you die!"

"Yes, you did," Jessie said, her gaze fixing on him with amusement. "Well, you *thought* you did."

I looked at Drew's pistol sitting on the table next to me.

"Don't get any ideas," Jessie said, pivoting her handgun in my direction. "Move away." She gestured with the barrel of the gun. I quickly stepped away.

Stunned beyond belief, I studied Jessie's face, that same face that had seemed so endearing before, now completely unfamiliar. Without her glasses, she seemed raw. She was Jessie and she wasn't. My face reddened and my heart stung as the feeling of betrayal sank deeper and deeper.

"How?" I said, still in disbelief. "*Why?*"

Jessie looked at me, and I could see a glimmer of sympathy behind her eyes as she sighed. "I know you must have a lot of questions. You've made it quite far. You're much more apt than any other puller I've ever met."

I was confused by the compliments. By everything. "I don't understand. You faked your death?" From behind Drew's shoulder, Analise emitted a small whimper as she began to cry. I gestured to her. "You hurt your sister?"

Jessie's smile fell. "She's *not* my sister."

Drew turned to look at the woman standing behind him. I watched as Jessie regarded her with disdain.

"And Gideon," I said, my mind clicking up to speed. "He wasn't your brother."

"I would have killed myself long ago if I'd been related to those two worthless sacks of shit."

"Hey!" Drew scowled, his hand gently touching Analise's arm.

"You're not a Pexler at all," I said.

The corners of Jessie's lips rose again in a knowing smile.

I shook my head. "Is your name even Jessie?"

In my mind, the collected memories of her youth wavered with artifacts. The two girls playing together. The absentee father. The standoff to spare her sister from his blow. They all dissolved, leaving me with no trace of who this woman really was.

Jessie took a deep breath before she began. "The Pexlers possessed something I needed. And they had the influence to connect me to others who also possessed things I needed."

"So you inserted yourself into their lives," I said. "And into their company."

She shrugged. "Not really that hard for someone like me. I found Analise and she became my doting sister. My interview for the job ended after the first handshake. The beautiful thing about the Pexler family is, they're very private. No one at the company had any idea about their CEO's family. So when an overshadowed sister emerged, with the supposed recommendation of their leader, what was there to question?"

A flash of a memory in my head: Carter watching Gideon appear at the end of the hallway, gazing warily toward Jessie's office door.

"But Gideon knew," I said. "You couldn't get to him."

"Quite a recluse, that one, always stowed away in his bunker. Amazing how the company just churned away without him while he shut himself away to play with his toys. I tried for months to crack that barrier."

In my head I could see it again, Jessie's memory of marching into the atrium on the top floor, stopping under the camera. *Gideon, we need to talk!* But it had been futile.

Until today.

"So it was you," I said, my throat catching. "You killed Gideon?"

"As much as I'd like to take credit for his demise, sadly, that was not me." She shrugged. "I just wanted to play with him a bit. But the moment he saw me waiting for him outside the building, he ran the other direction, and well, straight into a taxi. Pretty brutal to watch if I'm honest."

Drew shook his head. "Fucking monster," he whispered.

She whipped her head toward him along with the gun, startling him.

"You want to talk about monsters?" she snapped, stepping closer to him. She pointed the gun at Analise. "Do you know what this bitch has done? What her brother has done?"

Drew backed away, huddled over, his arm extended back to keep Analise behind him.

"Why don't you ask her?" Jessie said, then she snickered. "Oh, I guess you can't."

"Stay the hell away from us!" Drew shouted, his voice cracking.

Jessie stared at Analise with a predatory gaze. "Don't you remember, darling?"

Analise shook her head fearfully.

"Then let me enlighten you. She ran her Lexus over a child on Fifth Avenue. He died in the hospital after five hours of agony. Her alcohol level was twice the legal limit, and it wasn't the first time she'd been caught driving drunk. She should have gone to jail, case open and shut. But big brother made sure she got the best lawyers, he even arranged a deal with the DA, to make sure she didn't face any real consequences." Jessie glowered at Analise down the barrel of her handgun. "A child killer, bound to kill another, walking free thanks to the privilege of wealth."

Something came over Analise's eyes as her face began to tighten. It was realization. It was memory. It was shame, pouring from her eyes as she sniffled. "Oh god," she cried. "Oh *god!*"

Drew stared at her in disbelief. "Hey," he whispered, touching her arm, but she stepped away from him and collapsed on the floor next to the folding chair, sobbing hysterically.

Jessie looked Drew soberly in the eye. "I'd say she remembers." She stepped toward Analise, in shambles on the floor, and extended her hand. The hairs on my neck stood up as I watched her make contact near Analise's ear, an almost sisterly touch. And suddenly, the crying stopped. It was as if the distressing memory had melted away. The young woman on the floor looked up with wet eyes.

"There, there," Jessie said. "You're a good girl now. Isn't that right?"

Analise nodded. "Yes, sis."

My eyes widened as I clocked the third manifestation of Analise in this room tonight. First she'd been an empty shell. Then she'd remembered an echo of her former self, haunted by the memory of her actions. Now, she was back to the Analise we'd known before, the one we'd dined with. Playing the role of Jessie's sister. A puppet.

My eyes flashed to the open doorway that Jessie had stepped away from, a clear escape. But across the room, Drew was now cornered against the opposite wall. I could make a break for it, but I couldn't leave him behind. And we couldn't leave Analise.

I looked at the woman holding the gun, now a complete stranger. I needed to learn more about her. And I couldn't pull her, not without risking being pushed. I'd have to do this the hard way.

"The fake kidnapping," I said. "How did you pull it off?"

She turned and stepped back toward me, smiling. I could tell she was pleased to answer. "That truly was my magnum opus. The hardest push I've ever done. It's one thing to stage something so elaborate, but to have a puller involved…." She shook her head. "It was a huge risk. I didn't want you to doubt me. And I knew you would be able to see any discrepancies in your brother's memories. So once we sent Analise on her way, the three of us rode over to your place."

I could almost see it, the faintest trace of it lingering in my mind's eye. The three of us sitting on my couch, Jessie in the middle holding our wrists, as she bowed her head and concentrated carefully on the story she was weaving.

"We sat there the rest of the night, until I was sure I had all the details filled in. Then I escorted Drew back home while you slept, and I went on my way."

Drew piped up. "But we went to the police station. We gave statements!"

"Oh, Andrew, of course you didn't." Jessie cocked an eyebrow. "Weren't you wondering why they never called to follow up?"

"And the gunmen?" I said. "And Pete?"

Jessie shrugged. "Pete was the only one who was there, as our humble driver. I wanted you to recognize him from a memory at Pexler. And you did."

"It was all so real, though," I said, thinking again of the tattered memory of the kidnapping.

"I'll take that as a compliment. You see, I've interacted with pullers before. You're a very hard group of people to deceive." She grinned widely. "It's taken me a lot of practice, but I've learned it's a lot more convincing if a push is based somewhat on the truth."

My mind spun on her last words. It had been so obvious to see Abigail's pushed memories because they had been planted in an instant with very little effort. But so much care had been taken in overwriting my own recollection of the night of the kidnapping. The ripples had been harder to see, until I knew for a fact none of it was true.

I registered the silence around us as I'd become lost in my thoughts. I needed to keep her talking.

"So you're doing all this to steal data from our companies," I said. "Why?"

"Let me ask you something. Do you know what exactly your brother's company does?"

I nodded. "We protect clients' confidential information to keep people safe."

"Sure," she said dismissively, "but exactly *who* are you protecting?"

I shrugged. "Regular people."

She sighed. "I'm going to need you to be more specific."

I paused. "Legal witnesses... government spies...."

"Go on."

I thought of the top-level client Melanie had tried to access, a police department.

"Informants."

"*Criminals*," Jessie snarled, "who were given freedom and protection in exchange for a few words of information. People who have hurt others and are now hiding behind a shield. Is that about right?" She turned to Drew. "You've capitalized on protecting people who don't deserve to be protected."

Drew said nothing, glowering back at her.

"What are you going to do with their information?" I asked.

"I have a connection with an interested party, a group of like-minded people," Jessie said. "They're willing to pay a high price to right some wrongs. You see, that upload link I sent goes straight to them, and they'll publish the names and locations for any vigilante that's interested. And then they pay me. And I leave Manhattan."

"This is just for money?" I spat. "Endangering these people's lives?"

"Of course it's not." She looked me in the eye. "Alex, I've seen all kinds of people throughout my life. And I know you have too. All shades of good and bad. You and me, we both have an ability to make the world a better place. So that's what I'm doing. I'm eliminating the protection given to these people who are not good. That's what this is about."

I mulled over her words. "And you think you have the right to do that? To just wipe them from the earth without trial?"

"Absolutely," she said firmly.

I shook my head. "You're right, I *have* seen all kinds of bad in this world. But you can't play God with people's lives. It's not your call."

Jessie frowned at me. "Why not? If I don't use my ability to make the world a better place, how am I any better than the people on your lists?"

I wasn't sure how to answer.

She took a step forward, staring intently into my eyes. "And you, sitting back, wallowing in self-pity, letting these people live their lives. How are you any better?"

"That's enough," Drew growled.

"How are you making the world a better place, if you destroy innocent people's lives in the process?" I asked. "Like Melanie's?"

Jessie sighed. "Ah. Yes, that one was unfortunate. I do what I can not to disrupt innocent lives. But there was nothing I could do. So I sent her and her husband to start an exciting new stage of their lives. In North Carolina, I think. Rest assured, nobody was harmed, and nobody's life was 'destroyed.'"

"You uprooted them, made them leave their friends behind." I thought of Priyanka. "They just disappeared without a trace. The damage was still done. People are not pawns."

Jessie smirked. "People are whoever I need them to be in order to achieve a greater good. I am still human. I am not the strongest, or the fastest. I am also, inconveniently, very recognizable by law enforcement."

I could hear Roger's voice in my head. *Most of them do end up in jail.*

Jessie continued. "Because of this, I have to be very careful to cover my tracks. Sending other people to complete tasks." She gestured to the laptop on the table. "Removing any surveillance footage that could possibly lead the police to me."

I eyed the computer, a treasure trove of evidence. If I could make it out of here with that laptop tucked under my arm, I could turn it over to the police. But as the thought was materializing in my head, it was as if Jessie could see it as well, and she walked over to the table. She pointed the gun over the keyboard, over the hard drive, and pulled the trigger.

The gunshot echoed in the room as the bullet thudded through metal and plastic, into the wood floor. Analise yelped and Drew jumped, screaming, "Shit!"

"I was saving those videos just for you to see," Jessie said. "No need for them anymore."

I stayed grounded, my eyes shifting to Drew's gun still lying on the table.

"So you sent Melanie to do your bidding," I said, still working to keep her talking.

"Yes. I had Analise arrange for you two to come out to dinner that night, so you would be away from the building."

That was the night we'd first met, at the rooftop lounge with Drew's friends. He'd been so eager to infiltrate the enemy. Turns out, the opposite had happened.

Jessie continued. "You could say Melanie thought of me as a lifelong friend. At least, after I tailed her and her husband on their way to work. I tried to convince her the company had come under poor management, and she needed to bring me the data to keep its subjects safe. I thought we were on the same page, but then she pulled out her phone. I could tell she was conflicted. She dialed someone to ask for a second opinion."

Priyanka, I thought.

"I had to stop her there, and unfortunately, I had to be quick. I erased any memory of her friends at work. To her, it became a completely hostile workplace. After that, she was more than eager to fulfill my request, believing she was simply carrying out a security protocol." Jessie sighed. "Unfortunately, I am unable to put back memories I do not know. Her memory of her workplace and her coworkers had been permanently altered. I knew she could not go back."

"So you sent her away."

"Yes. With her husband, so they could be together." She raised her eyebrows. "See? Not so bad."

I ground my teeth. "She was a good person."

"And she still is. Just somewhere else."

Drew spoke, his voice high in pitch. "But you didn't get the data."

"Yes, Andrew, you're right," Jessie said, sitting on the edge of the table, her gun trained on him casually from her knee. "Melanie either did not know, or neglected to mention, she did not have access to the clients I requested. I was quite disappointed to meet up with her after our dinner empty-handed."

"What about Abigail?" I said. "What did you do with her?"

Jessie shook her head. "She was a surprise, indeed. You were never supposed to meet her. I had no idea she was so in tune with her psyche. Practically a puller, that one. She was my in-and-out at Ackheim. That data has already been sent to my contact. But she was clearly bothered by the conflicting memory. I had intended to tidy her up once she came back out the building that night, but somehow she slipped away from me. For a little bit anyway."

My heart sank. "Where is she?"

"She is with her sister in another state. New Jersey, I think. She's applying for new jobs. The thoughts that troubled her are long gone."

Drew sputtered from against the wall. "You may have gotten the Ackheim data. But you won't get the rest of what you're looking for. Pexler, Sentry. We never sent it. And now we never will. Not unless you let us go, with Analise."

For one silent moment, Jessie and Drew stared at one another, their shared gaze intensifying with each passing second. Then Jessie doubled over with a burst of laughter, her gun bobbing up and down as it pointed at Drew. I edged closer to the gun on the table.

"Oh, Andrew." Jessie sat back up and gave a shrug. "I downloaded the Pexler data the day I came here."

Drew gulped in silence.

"I didn't lie about my skill to get this job. I am actually pretty adept at database structures, security protocols… you name it, I've breached it."

In my head, I could see it. The false memory from Carter, her dressing him down for his incompetence. The false memory from Jessie, her building him up for his excellence. And the truth, submerged somewhere underneath.

"You were caught," I said. "Weren't you?"

Jessie turned to me, smiling once again.

Behind the memory, I could hear the muffled shouting. A man and a woman, arguing within the closed office.

"Carter Young," I said.

"Self-entitled bastard. He marched right in to tell me he would be letting Gideon know I was moving data. Of course, I stopped that in its tracks. It's amazing what a little workplace discontent will drive someone to do." She shrugged, the gun tipping sideways. "I didn't even tell him to steal the data! He just did it himself. Tell me, did he offer to sell it to you?"

My lips tightened. Jessie released another laugh.

"Once people realize the source of the information leak is Pexler, the company will immediately look to him. Amazing how that all just fell into place."

She left her perch on the desk, drifting back toward the center of the room.

"And he proved useful again today, when I needed him to keep you distracted."

My heart skipped a beat. The meeting in the park with Carter. I had been busy interrogating him, while Jessie was at Sentry pushing Drew to gather the data.

"You sent Carter," I said.

"Yes."

"No, no," Drew said, looking back and forth between us. "We asked him to meet us."

Jessie sighed. "Who do you think convinced him to do that?"

Drew's face sank again, his skin white and covered in sweat. "But then... how the hell did you know I'd left Alex at the park? How did you know I was at Sentry without him?"

Jessie regarded him with a bored gaze. "Phone monitoring app."

"What?" we both said.

"Do keep up." She pulled her phone out of her pocket. "When we were sitting in Alex's apartment the night of the kidnapping, I installed a monitoring app on both your phones. All your activity, including your recordings and locations, I've been tracking."

The blood drained from our faces. This whole time, we thought surveillance had been our cornerstone for safety. But it was the opposite. All our efforts to protect ourselves had betrayed us. Jessie had been watching all our discussions, all our movements.

"I know," she said, putting her phone back in her pocket. "Kinda blows, huh?"

"Wait," I said, still puzzled. "So you had the Pexler data from day one. And Carter still has his copy. So... who sent me the flash drive?"

A wide grin stretched across Jessie's face.

"It was still you?" Truly baffled, I said, "Why?"

She shrugged. "It brought you here, didn't it? You came to retrieve the drive after I died, and you saw this hallway, and you found my extra badge. Puzzle pieces you would need to end up here tonight." Her voice softened as she studied my face. "I'll admit, I also wanted to see what kind of person you were. If I could trust you. I gave you an opportunity to cross me, to damage my position, and yet you brought it back to me, no strings attached."

In all her sternness and confidence, in her assured actions and carefully planned moves, I did not expect the shield to come down ever so slightly as she looked at me.

"You really did good," she said. "You found all the little clues I left for you. The license plate in Drew's memory. Learning more about Pete and finding him in Carter's memories. And the little hints I left in my own, about this hallway."

I was growing frustrated the more she congratulated me. "But I don't understand. Why do *all of this*? The fake kidnapping, the fake push, the fucking puppets." I waved my hand at my brother.

"You could have pushed Drew days ago to get the data, clean and simple. Why do all this?"

Jessie and I stared at each other for a moment. The distant sound of late-night Manhattan faded away, the breathing of our bystanders silenced.

"I wanted to test you."

"*Test* me?"

"I wanted to force you into action. See how far you could go with your ability."

My jaw would not close. I released an exasperated breath. "What does this have to do with *me*?"

"We have more in common than you think." Jessie began to pace. "Tell me, does the name Thomas Portmeau mean anything to you?"

I shrugged, shaking my head. "I've heard it before. But I don't know who that is."

Her fierce eyes burrowed into mine. "Come on. Think harder."

I sighed, lowering my gaze as I submerged into the depths of my mind, illuminating darkened corners I hadn't searched before. He wasn't in Drew's memories, he wasn't in Carter's or Abigail's.

And then I saw it. A report lying on a table, the detectives discussing quietly as a man was led into an interrogation room. One year ago.

His name existed in my own lived time. He'd been tied to the case with the rat. Portmeau had let him use his house, an old shack in the woods, no questions asked. But then he'd turned and offered testimony against the rat, sparing himself any jail time.

I lifted my eyes questioningly to Jessie's. She could see the dots connecting in my head.

"A mutual friend of ours," she said, her smile falling.

And then something else floated before my eyes. A memory emerged, half forgotten. A man in a long coat, walking at a distance, following two young girls on their way to school. That glance back at the man, with no wavering or shimmering, had been real.

Jessie continued, running her thumb along the barrel of the gun. "I believe you are familiar with his friend, Lester Drake."

The rat. How had she known I'd been involved in his case?

"Are you looking for him?" I said.

"Oh," she said, her eyes darting up. "Didn't you hear? He's no longer a concern to this world."

I blinked.

She shrugged. "Heard he walked right off a building."

It was as if frigid ice had been dumped over my body, immobilizing me in fearful disbelief. Then an immense surge of heat, my face turning red, as the thought of him sitting at that table, cackling with laughter, ran through my mind like a flash of fire.

No, it couldn't be. The man was like a cockroach that couldn't be killed.

"I understand he hurt you," Jessie said. "Just like he hurt many, many others. What he did was unforgiveable. And he no longer has to rot this world with his existence." She cocked her head. "Tell me, Alex. Does this news make you happy?"

I didn't know what I felt. I was so rocked by this reveal, my mind thrashing like a sea upon rocks in a storm. Drake had been like the devil himself, a plague that wouldn't relent, and yet supposedly he was now gone.

"And now you're after Portmeau," I said.

"He played a vital part in Drake's early days," she said. "Scouting children, providing his home as a location for him to bring his abductees."

I studied her stance, her grip on the gun becoming tighter. She was near the opposite corner of the room. In fact, it was dawning on me that she'd maintained a distance from me this whole time. When she drifted toward her hostages, it was always toward Drew and Analise, but never toward me. She'd likely brought the gun because she'd seen Drew with his. But she kept her real weapon, her touch, far away from me.

She's not going to touch me.

She didn't want me to pull her. She didn't want me to see something she knew.

I felt the presence of the gun on the table next to me once more.

"You and I, we're of the same fleece," Jessie said to me gingerly. "And you were touched by this man's treachery. I just wanted to give you the chance to play a role in the downfall of the coward who enabled him."

I kept her gaze, feeling the connection once more, this moment of knowing between us.

Then the energy in the room shifted, and Jessie's eyes fell back on Drew. "I believe we've reached the end of our little show-and-tell." She nodded toward him. "The drive in your pocket, please."

"I don't have it," Drew sputtered.

Jessie cocked her head again. "Come on, Drew. I'm the one who told you to put it there. We both know you have it."

Drew shot me a nervous glance. I kept my eyes on Jessie, though fully aware I was only a few feet from the gun on the table. What I would do with it while Jessie held her own gun, I had no clue. But we needed to buy just a little more time.

"Just tell me one more thing," I said.

Jessie sighed and looked at me.

I thought wistfully of the woman who had made me laugh at the rooftop lounge, who had shared a beer with me and discussed the elusive purpose of our lives. Here she was, and yet still she felt dead, cold in my arms.

"Was any of it real?" I asked. "Was any of it… you?"

I could see the briefest flash of regret on her face. "I'm afraid I can't answer that yet," she said. "Not until I have your trust. Not until you give me the flash drive, and I know we're on the same side."

"You said a push is convincing if it's based on the truth," I said. "So some of it *is* you. There is some good inside you."

"It doesn't matter who I am, Alex. Or who you are. All that matters is what we choose to do with our powers. I know you used to help people, but you got hurt, and you stopped. I'm doing the same. I'm trying to help people too. Just in the way that I can."

"*Bullshit,*" Drew hissed.

"I wouldn't lie to you, Andrew," Jessie said, tightening her grip on the gun. "We're in this together now. We have a bond from this thing we've gone through. All of us." She looked over at me again. "You understand what I'm trying to do here, and I hope you would agree with it. And I hope, for that reason"—she turned back to Drew—"you will hand over that drive in your pocket."

Drew was breathing heavily, sweat beading on his face.

"Come on, Andrew," Jessie coaxed. "Do some good for a change. Don't protect these people."

"You're so full of shit," Drew whispered shakily, stepping back against the wall as Jessie loomed closer with the gun. Then she stopped, lowering the weapon and flashing a smile.

"You know I don't have to use this," she said. "I can just *make* you give me that drive."

The hairs on the back of my neck stood up. I scowled, my nostrils flaring. "Don't you fucking touch him."

"Language!" She regarded the terror on Drew's face with a playful laugh. "Fine. It doesn't have to be you. We can use a bystander."

Without warning, Jessie's hand shot out to her right, grasping Analise's shoulder where she was watching quietly on the ground. Suddenly she began to whimper and cry, her breaths turning to broken wails, pain emanating from her shuddering body.

"Stop that!" Drew screamed, dancing in place. "Don't touch her!"

"The drive!" Jessie yelled over Analise's cries.

"Okay, okay, just *stop!*"

Jessie released her grip on Analise, and the young woman slumped over onto her hands, her breaths tearing into the silent urgency fallen over the room.

I was standing right next to the table, the gun only two feet away from me. I could reach it easily and point it toward Jessie, but she was standing so close to the other two, it was too much of a risk. My mind raced, trying to think of something, anything I could do.

"Now," Jessie barked, extending her empty hand toward Drew. "Or I'll make the memories even more painful."

Drew nodded frantically and inched his hand into his pocket. Jessie's eyes lit up as his fingers withdrew, clutching the flash drive clumsily.

"Bring it here," she said, her voice softening as though she was about to receive a fragile charge.

I glanced once more at the gun sitting nearby. Across the room, Drew sighed, looking down at the end of his company sitting squarely in his palm, any last fighting words fading from his mind.

Then, next to Jessie, there was a sudden, swift motion.

Analise, with a face wet from tears and full of rage, rose to her feet and lunged at the gun in Jessie's right hand, dangling before her. She latched on, throwing Jessie's weight and nearly toppling her over, catching her off guard before she could act.

It was all I needed.

In one quick move, I took the gun from the table, and I pivoted to the two women across the room. Analise, her hands clawing at the gun gripped in Jessie's hand, was beginning to lose her ferocity. Her eyes widened as her sister's touch sank in, and just as a look of confusion and bewilderment spread across her face, I pulled the trigger.

Analise and Drew screamed, and Jessie ducked, as an explosion of drywall rained over them. Drew stepped away, his hands over his head. Jessie looked over her shoulder, clocking the gun in my hands.

"Don't fucking move!" I yelled.

But then Analise rose to her feet, the gun in her hands pointed at me, her eyes smoldering down the sight of the barrel.

Fuck.

I ducked beneath the table, but as I looked up to see where the bullet would land, Jessie placed her hand once more on Analise's arm. The younger sister did not fire. Instead, they both turned and ran for the door.

"Stop!" I yelled, scrambling to bring the gun around toward them. But I knew that nothing would stop their flight. They disappeared through the doorway, footsteps pounding from ply-wood to plastic down the hall.

I pulled myself out from under the table, looking over at Drew to make sure he was okay. Leaning against the wall, panting, my brother gave me a nod. He held up the flash drive and stuck it back in his pocket.

Then he spoke, his voice cracking between breaths. "Analise. We can't let that psycho have her."

From down the hall, I could hear the door being flung open, bouncing off the wall.

"I'll get her," I said, turning toward the door.

"I'll go too."

"No, stay here. Call the police." If I was certain about one thing, it was that Jessie did not want me dead. She'd stopped Analise from pulling the trigger. And she didn't want to come anywhere near me. It was as if I had invisible armor on me.

And armed with that feeble, shaky confidence, I tore out the door and ran down the hall after them.

STOP.

MY FEET POUNDED DOWN the crinkling sheet plastic and into the carpeted hallway. I heard a click from my right, and as I rounded the corner, I could see the door to the Pexler reception area swinging shut. I clasped tightly to the gun as I barreled forward, unsure what the hell I was going to do once I reached that door.

She had to be stopped, Jessie. I didn't need to lethally wound her, just disable her so someone could put her away, away from other people. Analise might not come quietly either.

I slowed my last few steps at the door and carefully nosed it open with my shoulder, my eyes darting for any kind of threat. But no one was waiting for me in the reception area. Instead, I could hear the final mechanisms of the elevator door closing.

She really is going to make a run for it, I thought, sprinting to the elevator bank. I jammed my finger repeatedly against the call button for another elevator, catching my breath as I watched the numbers over the departing car count down to the lobby.

Then I heard a slight noise to my left. I turned my head and clocked a heavy metal door just barely ajar, its silver latch peeking beyond the frame. Next to it was a sign that read *Stairs*.

I looked back at the numbers over the elevators. The first car had fully descended to the lobby, and mine was fast approaching. It would have been obvious for Jessie to lead me to the lobby. And that's what made it wrong. I pivoted to the left and ran to the stairwell door.

The corridor was concrete and echoey. I slowed myself, masking my steps as I gently shut the door behind me. Below, I could hear the faint sound of movement, an occasional whisper. I stayed next to the wall as I descended the stairs to avoid casting any shadows in the scant fluorescent light.

"Here," someone whispered, not too far below. Then the small electronic beep of a door sensor. I moved faster to get a sense of how many floors below me they were.

But the stairwell door shut before I could locate them, the slap bouncing off the walls around me in a disorienting way. They were maybe one, two, three floors below me?

Then I remembered. In Jessie's memories, I saw that the technical leads had access to the eighth floor, where the servers resided in a vast temperature-controlled room. I darted ahead, still trying to muffle my footsteps, until I reached the door marked with a large eight. I pulled Jessie's security card from my pocket, gripped the gun tight once more, and pressed the badge against the sensor. The lock flashed green and beeped.

I was met by complete darkness on the interior of level eight. If there were motion-activated lights, they weren't programmed to operate this late. I slowed my breathing and listened as I stepped into the hall. If I was quiet enough, they would have no idea I'd followed them. But I didn't hear anything, no movement or voices, as the sizzling silence pressed against my eardrums. They could be standing next to me, I thought, and I wouldn't even know. But if I couldn't see, they couldn't either. *She can push people, not see in the dark.* I stepped swiftly away from the door, against the opposite wall, unworried about a collision. Jessie wasn't going to hide somewhere where I could accidentally touch her.

To the right, the hallway opened up to a large room with windows running ceiling to floor. The dulcet lights of a sleeping Manhattan cast a muted glow against the walls, my shadow moving with me out of the corner of my eye. I approached slowly, rolling my feet carefully against the carpet as I listened for any trace of movement.

Suddenly, a door slammed somewhere in the distance, its reverberations bouncing into the hallway. I proceeded forward, listening for the sound of footsteps. As I reached the end of the hallway, I heard the gentle creak of a floorboard, suspending my heartbeat in alarm. But I looked down and discovered it had been triggered by my own heel. Gingerly, I removed my foot from the board and pressed on.

Bathed in the light from the city, the large room was some kind of common area with a sparse scattering of chairs. A long reception desk ran the length of the wall opposite the windows. I inched along the desk, scanning the chairs, and the one lone door on the far side of the room, made of thick metal. There was some kind of faint noise behind it, inarticulate, hard to place. It grew louder the closer I crept. Then I realized what I was hearing was the wash of echoing dialogue in the chasm of the server room ahead of me, and accompanying that realization, the thud of approaching footsteps. I ducked around the reception desk and crouched on the ground, listening as the heavy security door screeched open.

One set of footsteps walked slowly into the room, just a few feet on the other side of the desk from me. Quiet and careful. As they passed, I inched toward the edge of the desk, stealing a glance.

Jessie.

She surveyed the room, her hands held out from her sides, ready to deploy. Her brown ponytail swung as she scanned behind a small gathering of chairs, then headed toward the far end of the reception desk.

I retracted my head, steadying my heart rate, calming my breaths. I didn't move a muscle as I sat waiting with the gun, her footsteps moving farther away. As far as I could tell, she was alone. Without her minion at hand, this would be the easiest way to immobilize her.

I heard the sound of the creaking floorboard, the siren call at the entrance to the room, as Jessie proceeded into the dark hallway. Now was the time.

Slowly I rose, my eyes glued to the corner where she'd just disappeared. I moved without making a sound, the gun waiting between my hands, shining eerily like a ghost in the city light. Once I rounded the corner, I'd see her in the dull illumination from the window, her tall slender shadow moving along the wall. I brought the gun higher as I readied to pivot into position.

And in that moment, there was a click behind me.

Then a bang.

Drywall exploded behind me as I ducked, dashing toward the cluster of chairs. I raised the gun and aimed vaguely for the legs of the blonde woman shooting at me from the other side of the room, standing next to the server room door. Another shot burrowed into the floor next to me.

"Ana!" Jessie cried from the hallway.

Footsteps ran past me. I looked up and Analise had dashed into the hallway toward her sister's voice. Then I heard the ping of the elevator car arriving.

I shot to my feet, turning to the darkness of the hallway, praying that any fired shots would keep missing.

"Stop!" I shouted.

I squinted as I ran into the shadows, but by the time I could make out their shapes, they were rushing into the dim light of the elevator.

The distance between us was closing. Thirty feet, twenty, ten. But I wasn't going to make it. I skidded to a stop in front of closed doors.

This time they were in the car, there was no doubt, as I watched the numbers above the door descend. They were headed to the lobby, there was nowhere else to go. I turned to the stairwell and took off as fast as I could.

Down the concrete steps I went, the slaps of my footsteps and the force of my breathing washing over me, numbing my senses. I cut the corners, hopping down steps, moving faster than I'd moved in years. It seemed like an eternity, but barely a moment later I was arriving at the lobby door. Adrenaline pounding through my veins, I burst through the door, eyes darting for the runaway target.

The security guard.

I turned toward the front desk, but I didn't see anyone there. Just the flash of a closing glass door at the front of the lobby, and a wave of blonde hair disappearing into the night.

I ran toward the door, when I clocked the security guard hiding under her desk, crouched and whimpering. Here I was, standing with a gun. Analise had a gun. But the weapon on the guard's hip quivered with her as she made eye contact with me then looked fearfully away.

She's been pushed, I thought.

But I hadn't stopped running, and suddenly I was out in the cold night air, looking frantically in the direction that the women had run. Somewhere to the right. *Don't stop now.*

I raced to the corner of the intersection and examined my options. To the south, a stranger walked hunched over in a jacket a block away. To the west, a taxi was pulling up to deliver its occupants to their hotel.

And then to the north, someone began to shout.

"Help!" It was a man's voice. "Please, someone help me!"

I crossed the street to the man pacing next to a bus stop. Middle-aged in a puffer jacket, he was in a state, looking wildly around him, gasping and crying.

"What is it?" I said.

"They took my car," he sputtered frantically. "I stopped at the light here and they took my car."

I reached out and touched his face, ignoring his look of shock. I could see his dilemma playing out before me: two women, blonde and brunette, forcing him from his car with a gun before hopping in and speeding away.

But it wasn't true.

The lights on the dashboard danced. The streetlight simmered in its haze on the windshield.

"Please!" the man gasped again as I withdrew my hand. "They went that way!"

But he was just a decoy. Ignoring him, I turned and surveyed the area around me again.

And then something farther up the street caught my eye. A pair of subway gates straddled the road, and at the stairwell opposite, a woman in a fluorescent vest was slowly climbing the stairs. As she reached the top, I could see that she was a security guard.

I watched as the woman sighed, exhaustion heavying her eyes. Purposefully, she reached down and unclipped her belt, decorated with tactical gear, and dropped it to her side in a heap on the ground. Then, as if bored, she walked lazily away into the night.

It was uncanny. And that was exactly what gave it away.

I left the man in his fabricated distress and sprinted for the subway stairwell.

As I approached the top of the stairs, I slowed and squinted into the darkness, watching for any signs of movement as I descended quietly into the cave. At the base of the stairs, the turnstile bank sat abandoned, the handicapped door left hanging ajar. I passed through to the final set of stairs leading down to the platform, stepping along the dirty concrete, the air warmed and still. Carefully, I glanced around the corner.

There they were.

Jessie and Analise pacing at the far end of the platform, unaware, believing they had the entire station to themselves.

I analyzed the situation quickly. Analise stood closest to me, the gun hanging at her side. She watched her captor carefully, waiting for an order. Jessie walked in a circle with her arms crossed, studying the floor, not anxious but impatient.

If I could disarm Analise, that would take care of the matter of the gun. And if I immobilized her, she'd have nowhere to go. Once removed from Jessie's influence, she could hopefully be restored to some state of her former self, God willing there was enough therapy. But if she was immobile, Jessie would likely leave her behind to make a safe getaway up the stairs on the opposite side of the platform. She could come after us again for the data, wreaking havoc on more people's lives.

On the other hand, if I could land a shot on Jessie, I would be exposed for Analise, who very well could decide I was worth killing if I maimed her sister. But then maybe she'd stay if she had no one to tell her where to go.

My ears perked at the sound of the handicap gate opening around the corner behind me. I hid the gun in my coat as I turned and waited for the source of the approaching footsteps.

"Goddammit," I hissed when I saw them.

"You're an idiot if you think you can do this alone," Drew said, rushing quietly to my side. He nodded toward the stairs. "They in there?"

I nodded back.

"We need to get the gun," he said.

"We need to get the pusher."

"Well, I guess we know our respective targets." Drew stretched his neck, leaning forward to steal a glance at the platform.

Suddenly, there was a vibration beneath our feet, and the walkway began to rumble.

There was a train coming.

We watched as Jessie and Analise hurried to the edge of the platform, watching down the tunnel intently. But the train was not slowing, its power only rocking the station even harder as it blew past the platform, a late-night express train that wouldn't stop here on its way to Brooklyn.

"Now!" I whispered.

With the women distracted, their heads turned and watching dismayed at the departing train, we scurried down the steps, the massive sound cloaking our footsteps. But just as we hit the bottom step and I raised my gun toward Jessie at the other end of the platform, the final car clacking by, Analise whipped her head toward us.

I stepped quickly behind a pillar, blocking me from her gunfire but with Jessie still in sight. The pusher had clocked the incoming attack and turned to flee to the opposite steps, but I fired just feet in front of her, the bullet whizzing past her kneecaps as she skidded to a stop. She looked over at the source of the gunshot and let her eyes land on mine. Somehow, there was no fear, only the look of pleasant surprise as she slid behind a nearby column.

I could hear another shot squeezed off from elsewhere on the platform, the curved tile of the train tunnel cracking to my left. The sound of struggling pulled my attention to other side of the platform, where Drew had gotten his hands around Analise's on the gun.

"Please stop!" Drew shouted desperately. "I don't want to hurt you!"

Analise fought hard, stomping her feet against Drew's ankles. Seconds later, with a final swing of their arms, Analise stumbled backward, and the gun flew from their hands, clacking against the cement floor ten feet away and sliding even farther. For a short moment, I felt a sense of relief, that we were finally about to hold the cards.

Then Jessie stepped from behind her pillar, receiving the gun just as it stopped at her feet.

"*Shit.*"

Quickly she pivoted back to her cover, and I could see the tip of the barrel extending toward the struggle happening at the opposite end of the platform.

"Drew!" I yelled.

But he had been watching, and quickly detangled from Analise, running behind another pillar as a bullet from Jessie's gun just missed his head.

I glowered at her, my blood boiling over the kill shot.

"So nice of you to join us, Andrew," Jessie called. "I do enjoy courier delivery."

"Oh, *fuck off!*" Drew wailed.

"I'll strike a deal with you two," she said. "Give me the drive, and I'll leave you Analise."

The younger woman turned and shot Jessie a bewildered look. *What?* she mouthed.

"I've got another deal for you," I called. "Leave Analise, and we'll let you go." A lie.

"That deal won't work for me. Come on, Alex. Don't you want to do some good? To save innocent lives? After this journey you've made?"

We stood there for several seconds, breathing heavily behind our structures of cover, Analise the only one standing out in the open, resentment growing on her face. I turned and looked over toward Drew, who glanced at me with questioning eyes. *What now?*

Then the sound of footsteps pricked our ears. We both turned to see Analise striding toward Jessie, a whisper emitting from behind the pillar. *Come here.* The butt of the gun protruded, an invitation to take control.

"No," I said, watching from across the platform. "Analise, stop!" I raised my gun, but she proceeded, stopping directly in front of Jessie, who extended a hand to her shoulder. And then, Analise screamed, her voice filled with excruciating pain.

I jumped from behind my pillar, and to my horror, Drew did as well, sprinting across the platform. I rushed forward, Jessie's whole body just coming into view as she was raising her gun toward Drew.

"No!" I screamed.

Drew yelped as the bullet grazed his shoulder, stumbling dangerously close to the platform's edge. I raised my gun toward Jessie's head, but suddenly Analise was running toward me, closing the twenty feet between us with impressive speed, and she tackled my midriff, sending me backward off my feet. The gun flew from my hand. Analise clawed at me, ripping the skin on my neck, but I was able to cast her aside and roll onto my knees, then scramble to my feet.

The clamor was only strengthened by the sound of another approaching train. With everyone's senses flooded, I sprinted toward Drew, and together we spun behind a wide pillar near the base of the stairs, another bullet just missing his stumbling body.

"Are you okay?" I shouted over the piercing sound of grinding metal.

Drew nodded, looking exhausted. But he wasn't giving up yet. "You have to pull her."

I shook my head and opened my mouth to speak, but he held up a hand. "It's the only way," he said. "There's something she doesn't want you to know. Maybe it's a way to stop her."

Our words were concealed by the sound of the passing vehicle, another express train that wouldn't stop. But its final car was clacking closer. I thought longingly of Drew's gun sitting at the far end of the platform, out of reach.

"I'll distract her, then you go," he said. "If she doesn't see you coming, maybe you'll be okay."

Sitting there out of breath, cradling his arm, his wits still about him, I had never seen my brother this brave before. I flashed him a final look of appreciation, followed by a short nod.

"Wait," he said. He pulled the flash drive from his pocket and slipped it into my own. "Just in case."

The train was gone, its distant lights receding from the tunnel tiles, its ghostly whisper lingering in the air. In one quick movement, Drew pivoted around the column and began to sprint across the platform.

"Analise!" he yelled. "Come with me!"

I leaned out just enough to catch a glance of Jessie raising her gun toward Drew. He scrambled behind the next pillar, panting and continuing to yell. "She's controlling you! Don't listen to her!"

Jessie's back was to me as she tracked Drew's movement from pillar to pillar, Analise cautiously spacing herself from him as he edged closer. Carefully I stepped forward, my shoe just barely scraping the grit beneath. Jessie spun around, our eyes locking down the barrel of her gun.

But then Drew leapt from his final perch, and his hands grasped Analise's arm. "Let's go!" he yelled. "We have to leave!"

Jessie turned back to the struggle. "Hey! Release her!"

Drew leaned on his left foot and dragged Analise with all his strength, spinning her around and right into Jessie's shoulder. Jessie pushed back hard, shoving her sister away, Analise bouncing like a ragdoll between the two. In that brief moment that Jessie was recovering her weight, Drew lunged toward the gun in her hand.

That was the moment.

I could feel time slowing as I swept forward in two large, long strides. Jessie was swinging her arm up, her eyes locked on Drew, countering the incoming attack. She had no idea I was behind her, closing in, extending my hand toward the base of her neck. It could only be a tap, I told myself. If I lingered any longer, she could take control of me.

I kept myself moving, running past her like a cutthroat game of tag, as my fingers began to lace through the fine dark strands of hair above her shirt collar, the fuzz of vellus canopy over warm skin. This time, I did not think to worry about what darkness I might find.

At last, the tips of my fingers brushed her skin. Time stood still, and the clamor of the subway station disappeared in an instant.

JESSIE.

"Sissy. Help me."

I was standing in a quiet, dimly lit room. In front of me, two young girls worked with a plastic doll.

"See the Velcro there?" the older sister said, pointing to the back of the doll's shirt. "That's how you remove it."

I'd seen this before. It was uncanny how familiar this scene was, and yet it wasn't. There was something different. I wasn't standing in the pristine, brightly lit room of an affluent family's mansion. No, this was not that at all. The room was worn down, dark and brown, the wallpaper falling away in spots to reveal the wood underneath. The floor was barren and covered in dust, except where the girls played on a thin, chewed-away rug. Clutter was strewn around the room, on crooked tables with crumbs and ashtrays, past-due bills peeking like dried leaves from beneath smeared paper plates. There were no parents to be found though. Just the two girls, in the house by themselves, temporarily forgetting their bleak surroundings.

The younger girl smiled, a small tongue poking out between her lips as she looked up at the display her sister was constructing from cheap wooden blocks. "Whatcha building?"

"It's the Louvre," the older girl said. "It's a museum in France. Where the Mona Lisa is."

"It's a triangle," the little one said curiously.

"Yes. It's the strongest shape there is."

Among the dilapidated furniture, Jessie's brilliance struck me differently in this worn-down house. These were not children of means. They were the opposite of the Pexlers.

But who was this younger girl? The little blonde sister. Her appearance was the same as in the fabricated memory from before. Yet it couldn't possibly be Analise.

There was more to find out. The sun shifted in the room and the girls melted away. A tired woman, in her late twenties but appearing two decades older, leaned back in the stained couch, one foot propped on a chair, staring blankly at the far window as she smoked a cigarette.

"Mom," the brown-haired girl cooed as she strode into the room. She could tell her mother was tired after a long day of work. "When are we having dinner?"

"I don't know, sweetie," the woman said delicately, unable to look her daughter in the eye. "Maybe see what you can find in the cabinet."

But then the woman's eyes rose to the sound of a car pulling up outside. The little girl became excited, a smile breaking across her face. Her mother, however, was displeased, and she brought herself to her feet and walked out the front screen door, the wooden panel clacking against the threshold.

Her mother was angry, as the two adults began speaking in hushed tones. "Why don't you give us more money? Why don't you bring more food?" But the argument did not last long, as the woman did not have the energy to press much further. She came back through the door, sighing as she walked down the hallway to resign to her room, and a middle-aged man stepped into the house.

"Daddy!" The little girl smiled. She rushed forward to hug the man, the side of her face brushing against his shirt, breathing in his familiar smell. The man, with a weathered face and short red beard, rubbed his hand on the girl's small shoulder. When she stepped back, he placed a brown fast-food bag in her hands.

They ate together in the kitchen, the rays from the setting sun shining through the suspended dust particles in the air. The man asked about school, and the girl talked about her favorite subjects. He was a much better conversation partner than her mother, but she knew she shouldn't think that. The way she held his full attention made her feel not so small and helpless.

"Guess my favorite color," she said, leaning forward on her elbows on the table.

"Hmm, ok," the man said, scrunching up his eyes as if thinking hard. "Mud brown."

"Ew, no!"

"Okay, I'll try again." He tapped his finger playfully against her nose. "Red."

"Yes!" The girl was beaming, wriggling in her chair. "Guess my favorite subject."

The man pressed his finger against her nose again, part of the game. "Math."

"Yes."

She loved her father, the little girl. And she was always sad when he had to leave. His visits were so short, and growing more sporadic. Two weeks, sometimes an entire month would pass before he would come by. He was a temporary happiness, and then a reminder that happiness can never last.

He was not the father of the girl's little sister. That man was younger, and similarly an inconsistent character in their story. He'd all but vanished after his daughter's birth, but would come around a couple times a year asking for money, a place to sleep. He would stay a few days, their mother happy at first, then in tears as they screamed at each other as he departed. It was all noise on the older girl's ears. The man would beg attention from his daughter, but never from her, and she preferred it that way. He was nothing compared to her father.

⋆⋆⋆

THE BROWN-HAIRED GIRL LOVED going to school. It meant leaving her crumbling home and immersing herself in the world beyond. Textbooks held vivid pictures. Word problems involving money added up as they should. And there was always lunch.

Walking home from school one day, the girl saw a shadow sweeping over her from the sky above. She looked up in wonder, her mouth agape as a red-tailed hawk swooped down toward the grassy lot beside her and plucked up a mouse. She recounted the story excitedly that night as she lay with her little sister in the bed that they shared, her hand squeezing the other's.

"She came down so fast, she was almost a blur. And her talons were so big and sharp." Jessie folded her free arm behind her head, staring up at the ceiling. "I wish you could've seen it. It was so cool."

"But I did see it," the younger girl said.

"Don't lie."

"But I'm not."

The older sister withdrew her hand and propped herself up on her elbow, frowning. "Well then, what color was the mouse?"

The little girl thought for a moment. "Gray."

"Lucky guess."

"The bird held it in the right foot, and it flew toward the corner store. But it was hard to see because of the sun."

Jessie stared at her sister. The little girl had stayed at the preschool until their mother could bring her home after work, well after Jessie had gotten back. It wasn't possible for her to have been out walking along that road, to have seen the hawk. But the details had all been correct.

"I'm not lying!" the little girl pleaded.

There had been unusual moments like this before, little surprises, misunderstandings, things that didn't make complete sense.

But this was the first time Jessie realized just what the source of this uncanniness might be.

★★★

As the girls grew older, Jessie used her power to show her sister special moments from her day as they lay in bed before sleep. A butterfly on the playground. A class video on sharks. A beautiful sunset on the river. For several years, it was something just the two of them shared.

"Show me something," the little girl would say, her eyelids heavy.

And Jessie would touch her arm gently, feeding her the image of a happy Labrador puppy she'd encountered on a walk that day. "See the puppy?" the older girl would say, so the sister would know that was a shared memory. The little girl would smile and nod, drifting off to sleep.

Another time, the younger girl's father came by, freshly intoxicated and out for blood. Yelling had echoed down the hallway as he quarreled with their mother. He had tried to take the little girl with him. She lay in bed with red, wet eyes and bruises around her wrist.

"Show me something, sis."

The brown-haired girl stared blankly at the floor, sitting shell-shocked and empty. What did she have to show her sister that could cheer her up? Nothing extraordinary had happened that day. It had been another day of dust, loneliness, and hunger. Her heart stung as she watched another tear slide down her sister's cheek, onto the hole-filled rag she clutched like a teddy bear.

It was then that Jessie thought to try something. She imagined a brilliant sky, a field of flowers, a family of rabbits, the warmth of the sun. It was just the two of them, crouching in the green, poking animals and lying in the grass. The older sister made a crown of dandelions and set it on the younger's head. In her mind, she placed it as the perfect evening, a replacement for the domestic chaos they had endured. Jessie squeezed her eyes shut and willed it to be as real as possible. Then she set her fingers on her sister's cheek, brushing her straw-colored hair behind her tiny ear. And suddenly, the child heaved a sigh of relief, sinking into the mattress, a new calm breaking over her.

Jessie didn't say anything, didn't dare reveal that the daydream wasn't real. As her sister drifted off to peaceful slumber, she raised her hand before her face and stared. There was more to this, it seemed, than she had originally thought.

★★★

AT fiRST THEY WERE small experiments. When she was standing in line at school, she'd reach forward and lightly tap the wrist of the classmate standing in front of her, transmitting a silent question. They'd turn around and say, "No, I don't have another dollar on me." Or, "Yes, it's pizza for lunch today." Sometimes it didn't work quite right, and she'd see a confused look flash across their face, as though they'd just had a bizarre fleeting thought.

She'd try asking questions to her mother through touch, never opening her mouth, but her mother turning as though she'd just voiced an inquiry. "Sure, we can have sandwiches for dinner. Go check the bread."

She was also growing old enough to understand why it was so hard for her mother to keep a job, to bring home food, to raise her head and interact when she was slumped over on the couch. One night Jessie walked into the living room and saw the foil on the cushion next to her mother, the familiar groggy, shaded eyes. She stood in front of her mom, watching her sadly.

Please, stop.

Then she pressed her hand against her wrist, her mother barely registering the interaction.

For the next two weeks, the foil disappeared, and their mother was lighter, happier, more determined. For she'd told herself it was time to stop, for her daughters. But a fleeting thought does not simply change a destructive addiction. At eleven years old, Jessie learned this firsthand. Some people couldn't be helped. She'd remember that well into adulthood.

★★★

THE GIRLS WERE GETTING bigger, hungrier. They stayed at the school as long as they possibly could, taking their long walks home in the setting sun when the temperatures were milder. And finally, one night, their stomachs growling and knowing full well there was nothing to be eaten at home, they stopped at a sandwich vendor. They had no change. But Jessie reached forward to touch the hand of the man at the register, and he returned with two warm, fresh sandwiches. Her sister's eyes lit up.

They were ravenous, devouring the meal on the way home, walking under the stretched shadows of tall trees like fugitives in the night. Jessie wasn't sure what should concern her more, that she'd essentially robbed someone, or that she didn't feel any guilt about it. What were they to do, starve? She and her sister had been failed by every adult around them. There was no one looking out for them. But with this strength, she could provide for the two of them. Herself, and more importantly, her sister. Her charge.

It was nice, not feeling powerless. When she got in trouble at school, she could make the teacher simply forget. When she was out of lunch money, she could still secure a meal. And when another kid made fun of her, she could plant an embarrassing memory to get them to shut up.

"Why are you so weird?" a boy blurted one day on the play-ground, surrounded by his friends, his face pink with laughter. "You're always touching everyone. Do you like touching people? Do you get touched at home?"

He thought he was funny, but he wasn't. Jessie reached forward to touch his arm, but he backed away, cackling. The anger flared within her, and as she stepped forward again, the boy leaned on one foot and rammed his shoulder into hers, knocking her to the ground. The kids around them laughed. But her hand had grazed his, and she looked up to see the boy begin to sputter, his face turning beet red.

"I—" He looked around worriedly. "I need to—"

Jessie smiled a knowing smile, looking him in the eyes. "Can't keep the piss in?"

The kids around them shut up and instantly turned to the boy. There was no telltale stain on the boy's shorts, but because he truly believed he had just peed himself, because he was acting so ashamed, the kids began to laugh. The boy turned and ran away.

★★★

NOT LONG AFTER, ON a simmering autumn weekend when her mother and sister were away, Jessie came home to find her father's car in the driveway. It had been months since she'd last seen him, his visits becoming even more sparse. But he was there to welcome her with a broad hug, to offer the warm comfort of his company, and a stack of takeout food on the table.

"You're getting so big," her father said, fishing the last lo mein noodle from his carton. "You act so grown up these days."

"Thanks, Dad. You're acting so grown up yourself."

He prodded her shoulder with a chopstick, causing her to giggle. His weightlessness, his smile, it all made the chaos of the world around her melt away. Which is why it hurt, like always, when he began to say goodbye.

"Why can't you stay?" she asked, finally brave enough after all these years.

The man sighed. "Sweetie, you have your mother. We're not together. I can't stay."

"But this is good. This right here. Why don't you want this all the time?"

Why don't you want me?

A look of guilt fell over his face. But it didn't change his answer. If anything he appeared to be steeling himself, gathering his things hastily and turning for the door.

"I'll see you next month, sweetie."

She was losing him again. She balled her fists, the fury growing inside her as he moved swiftly to make his exit, leaving her behind to resume her empty life of squalor.

The thought came to her quickly.

She didn't have to let him leave.

The girl stepped forward as her father was standing at the sink, and she pressed her hands under his shirt against his back.

There was a crash as a plate fell into the basin. The man gasped, his head whipping around, looking out the window and then toward the door. He began to hyperventilate, panicking as he dropped to the floor, shaking as though gripped by fear. He waited, not daring to move toward the door, lest he meet what he thought was waiting for him outside.

He sat there for a moment, heaving and wheezing. Then his breathing began to slow, his body started to relax. A look of realization washed over his face. Solemnly, his eyes lifted to look at his little girl. Jessie held his gaze at first, but the longer his eyes bore into hers, the more uncomfortable she became, like he could see directly into her soul, into the nothing she really was.

The man finally looked away. He sat in thought, staring vacantly at the wooden cabinets around him. Then, in one solid, swift motion, he rose to his feet and walked to the door, leaving the spilled food and cracked plates behind him.

"Dad?" Jessie said quietly.

He pushed open the door and stepped outside, the panel clattering shut.

"Dad!" She raced after him, leaning out the door. "Dad, stop!"

But he did not change course. He stared silently ahead as he strode to his car and opened the door.

"*Dad!*" she screamed, tears forming in her eyes.

He looked up, one last time at her. A look of remorse, of regret. It hit her hard like a punch in the gut. Then, he lowered himself into the car, shutting the door and starting the engine.

Jessie walked out onto the grass, watching his car as it disappeared down the street. She continued to call after him, tears spilling down her cheeks. I watched her from the other side of the yard among the trees, feeling the pain that she felt. I was sorry for her. I wished I could help her.

She continued to stand there as the last light of sun passed behind the horizon, watching the end of the street, noting its emptiness with each passing second.

She would never see her father again. She would never rely on, or trust anyone, again. She only had herself, and her sister.

★★★

YEARS LATER, A SIXTEEN-YEAR-OLD Jessie was standing in line at the corner market, staring at a black-and-white flyer with the portrait of a young girl wearing a Winnie the Pooh sweatshirt.

"It's real sad," her sister said next to her. "They haven't seen Shauna for two weeks now."

Jessie regarded the word MISSING in big block letters below the girl's picture. "I'm sure she just ran away. Wasn't she always getting in fights with her mom?"

The old lady at the register dragged their snacks across the scanner. "Two eighty-five," she lowed. Jessie dropped the change carefully into her hand. She didn't use her ability much these days, only when it was necessary. She was reminded of the look on her father's face with each use, and the shame was too much to bear.

"Come on. I'm gonna be late for practice," the younger girl said.

Jessie collected the bag from the counter. "I don't know why you still go to gymnastics," she said dejectedly, her eyes moving over the mismatched clothing on her sister. "It's not like Mom can actually buy you a team uniform."

"So what, we just stay home? You can't hide forever." Her sister led them through the market door, stepping into the sunlight. She stopped and sighed, breathing in the autumn air. "Sometimes you have to let the sun in, sis."

The girls continued on their walk to the school. A gust pushed brown, dried leaves down the concrete, causing Jessie to pull her jacket tighter. They were walking into a nice middle-class neighborhood, surrounded by green manicured lawns. Hardly anyone was out today, until they had gone a couple blocks, then Jessie looked up. She felt strangely wary of a man in a pale trench coat approaching them, rather unkempt with shaggy hair, about fifty feet away.

"Let's cross over here," Jessie said, turning at the next crosswalk.

She could feel the man's eyes on them as they diverted their path, passing each other from across the road.

Don't be scared, she told herself.

They walked another block, and when she turned to check for him, he was now on their side of the street, trailing them. The older sister reached for the hand of the youngest.

"Don't worry," she said. "He can't do anything."

The girls picked up their pace, exiting the residential neighborhood and crossing a busy road, the school in sight at the top of the hill. Jessie took one more look, and the shadow was gone.

They didn't stay as late as usual. Still irked by the interaction earlier, Jessie insisted they start their walk home before the sun was setting. The amber rays were just fading from the bricks of their house when they arrived back. Their faces fell at the sight of a familiar rusty pickup in the driveway.

"Where's my money, Shar?" a voice grumbled from the front room as they snuck into the kitchen.

"*Your* money? How about your late support check for your daughter?"

The sound of an impact, flesh on flesh, and a grunt.

"Fuck you say to me?" His voice was filled with rage and alcohol.

Jessie grabbed her sister's hand. "Come on, let's go back to our room."

But the little girl, having grown braver and fiercer with age, shook her head, and marched toward the front.

The little girl's father continued his drunken ramble. "I oughtta take her right now for payment."

The mother began to cry. "Don't you dare!"

"Dad! Stop it!" the little girl commanded as she strode into the room.

"Speak of the devil," he murmured, then stepped toward her. Jessie watched in horror from the shadows of the kitchen. "You're coming with me. Teach your mama a lesson."

"No, Dad. You need to leave."

The man released a cackle of laughter, swaying in his boots. He was easily six feet tall, the smell of whiskey drifting all the way to Jessie's nostrils.

And like a snake, his hand shot out, the sound like a crack of thunder as it struck his daughter's face. She released a small scream, turning and rubbing her reddened cheek, trying to recover the bravery from seconds before. Behind her, Jessie glowered at the man, a familiar rage building up inside her.

"You belong to *me*," the man said, glaring down at her. "You do what *I* say. Say, '*Yes, Daddy.*'"

Tears formed in the little girl's eyes as she remained turned away, unwilling to look at his face.

"Say, '*Yes, Daddy!*'" the man snarled.

Their mother cried hysterically from across the room. His hand rose again.

Before Jessie even realized it, she was bounding toward him.

"Leave her *alone!*" Her outstretched hand grasped his raised forearm.

The man, so filled with drunken rage before, immediately folded into himself, releasing a loud shriek and backing into the wall. His eyes were filled with terror as he whimpered pitifully, flinching with each step Jessie took toward him, practically crouched in a ball on the floor.

She spoke slowly, each word filled with a heavy malice. "If you *ever* come here again, if you ever threaten either of them…." Her eyes burned down into his. "I'll fucking kill you."

The man nodded fearfully, and he truly believed it, she could see it in his eyes. For now he believed he had no strength, had always been a weak and whimpering child, and that he had seen her kill others, torture his family, stalk him as he slept. My mind burned thinking of the thoughts she had shared with him.

"Now get," Jessie whispered, "the fuck, OUT."

The man clambered to his feet and shot out the door, running faster than his beer belly had ever let him. She could hear the sound of the pickup ignition failing repeatedly, each attempt in quick succession like a plea, until finally the engine turned over and the truck peeled out of the driveway.

Jessie knelt beside her younger sister, sitting on the floor with her hands over her face.

"Are you okay, sis?" Jessie took her sister's hands in her own.

The little girl looked up at her with tear-filled eyes. Then she threw herself onto her sister, wrapping her arms tightly around her shoulders. Her protector.

The scene was an echo of what I'd seen in Jessie's fabricated memories, ending in the same sisterly embrace. As I looked down at them, the words floated through my head. *It's a lot more convincing if a push is based somewhat on the truth.*

***

At first, I thought I had seen all I would need to see from Jessie's childhood. I had just witnessed the same tipping point from the first version of her memories. She'd barrel forward as the protector, the avenger, just like before.

And yet that didn't feel quite right. The memory didn't hold the same weight as before. In fact, it seemed almost commonplace, just another confrontation with a malevolent spirit.

No, there was something else, I could feel it lurking behind me. I turned and looked at the scene forming amidst the darkness. It was a couple months later, and the girls were walking home from the library under a gray winter sky, dressed in secondhand coats. I stood off in the grass, watching them walk by. My eyes lingered on the younger girl, her blonde hair draped over her scarf, face pink with cold. She hunched her shoulders forward, shivering. "Mom said she has a job interview this week."

"That so? For what?"

"Receptionist at a dentist's office."

"Mm. She'll need to go to that everyday though."

"She's doing better," the younger sister said hopefully. Jessie wished she could believe in hope. On her mind were college applications, early admissions requests tucked away in her desk at home. Once she turned eighteen, she was planning to take her sister with her, away from this place.

The bleak afternoon light shone down through the bare trees around them, their branches reaching up like wiry hands into the watery sky. On the cracked street beside them, an old white van rattled by. They were just rounding the outskirts of the nicer part of town, on a route they didn't normally take, walking along a forest as they neared the mobile and prefab homes of their neighborhood. Jessie turned to look at a dirt driveway curving down the hill, arriving at an old station wagon and a small wooden shack in the trees. She stopped.

"Everything okay?" Her sister looked back.

Jessie stared, questioning her eyes, the blood in her ears beginning to rush. "Wait here," she said without looking away.

"I'll come with you."

"No," she said sternly. "Wait here."

Jessie stepped down the dirt road, watching for movement in the cabin or among the trees. Her little sister watched warily from the top of the hill. I left the sidewalk and followed Jessie, her feet crunching on lingering brown leaves and dying grass as she neared the station wagon. Her head cocked as the item in the back window became clearer. Finally, her fingers touched the glass of the rear windshield, her reflection dancing over the soiled clothing lying over a stack of boxes.

A Winnie the Pooh sweatshirt.

No, surely it was just a coincidence. But something in her gut fought otherwise, and she turned to look at the lonely shack at the edge of the woods.

Don't be afraid, she reminded herself. There was nothing she couldn't handle. She stepped toward the front porch, quietly ascending the stairs, trying to minimize the creaks between her steps. She lifted a hand to screen the light from her eyes, peering through the windows. She couldn't see anyone inside.

Something stirred in the reflection of the window.

Jessie whipped around and realized there was someone sitting in the station wagon. Steeling her resolve once more, she walked back toward the car.

"Excuse me?" she called gingerly. "Do you live here?"

The person was sitting in the driver's seat, visible through the open window on the passenger side closest to Jessie. A balding middle-aged man turned and looked out at her from behind his circular spectacles. He looked as though he was crying.

"Excuse me," Jessie said again, keeping her voice calm. "Is this your home?"

The man said nothing, only looked at her. His face was wrinkled with concern, dark circles beneath his eyes. Jessie registered it as panic. But I saw shame.

"You shouldn't be here," the man said, his voice shaking.

"What?"

"It's not safe."

The hairs on the back of Jessie's neck were standing. At her side, the fingers of her right hand twitched. Something wasn't right. She could touch this man and make him tell her what was going on.

But while she was standing there considering it, the strange man started up the car. With jagged, awkward motions, he turned the wheel and began to drive along the dirt road that snaked away into the trees. She watched carefully as the car disappeared among the gray, rotting trunks, the sleeve of the sweatshirt fluttering against the glass of the back window.

And then, silence. Jessie glanced at the woods around her, expecting someone or something to move. She gave one more look to the shack. Then she turned and hurried back up the hill.

Jessie expected to see her sister at the top, still waiting by the road, but she wasn't there. There was no one walking on the sidewalks, no cars driving on the old, cracked pavement roads.

"Mia?" Jessie called. Perhaps she had gone on ahead. Maybe Jessie had taken too long. She rounded the next corner, looking down the long stretch of road toward their home, and again saw no one on it.

It wouldn't have bothered her normally, but the strange interaction with the man had set her on edge. The blood began to rush in Jessie's ears again. *She just went home*, she told herself. Or had she gone back to the library? Why hadn't she called down to her that she was leaving? *It's nothing, it's nothing.*

Still, she shouted again, "Mia!" Her voice rang off the warped wood siding of the homes around her. "Mia! *Mia!*"

The man's words slithered through her mind again.

Something's wrong.

Jessie began to run toward their house, pleading with each step that she would see Mia's blonde hair come into view.

"*Mia!*" she continued to scream. She accelerated with each passing block, eventually sprinting that final quarter mile, nearly ripping the front door from its hinges.

"Mia?" Jessie shouted into the house, her eyes passing over her mother slumped over on the couch. She ran down the hallway to their bedroom, but her sister was not there. She came back to the living room and reached for her mother, grabbing her wrist. In an instant, her mother saw the memory of Jessie leaving Mia on the hill, walking down to the shack, and her disappearance upon return. *Mia's gone. We need to find her.* Her mother immediately sprang up, blinking furiously out of her daze.

The two of them ran out into the street, looking up and down the block, then loaded into the car, driving the route back to the library. When they did not see her, they drove to the police station, and once again, Jessie touched the hand of the nearest cop, relaying her urgent message. The Winnie the Pooh sweatshirt. The missing sister.

Within minutes, Jessie, her mother, and two cop cars pulled up to the shack at the bottom of the wooded hill. It sat just as before, empty and foreboding, its driveway unoccupied. The cops knocked down the door, their guns raised, but there was no one inside. Jessie walked in, her eyes wide and her mind racing, staring at the empty floors, at the bottle of bleach sitting next to the kitchen basin. Two cops went into the basement and began to shout. It was not Mia, they told Jessie, but she needed to leave.

The police put out an Amber Alert for the young girl, and Jessie and her mother were whisked back to the station. The officers brought Jessie into a private room to give a statement to two detectives.

"State your name for the record."

She gave her real name. Then she placed her hands on the table, palms up.

"Touch them," she said. "You'll see everything exactly as I did." The investigators looked at each other questioningly, then placed their fingers into her palms.

After that, there was nothing to do but wait. Her mother paced anxiously, occasionally visiting the pay phone to ramble to a concerned relative, more active and alert than she'd been in years. But Jessie sat at the end of the hallway staring at the floor, despondent. I sat across from her, watching her somberly as time marched ahead.

Six hours. Twelve hours. In the early morning, they called Jessie back to the table.

"Is this the man you saw?" A detective laid a picture of a balding, bespectacled man in front of her.

"Yes."

"His name is Thomas Portmeau. He's the owner of the shack and the station wagon. We intercepted him last night trying to leave the state."

"Did he have Mia?" Jessie asked desperately.

"I'm afraid not," the other detective replied.

"However," the first detective continued, "we've learned that there was another man using Mr. Portmeau's house. People in the neighborhood reported seeing him come and go the past few months in a white van. We're searching for him now. He's a registered sex offender. They identified him by this picture."

The detective set a new picture on the table. "This is the man we are looking for." Jessie and I leaned forward to see a grizzled man with a chubby face and shaggy hair.

Immediately, we both recognized him.

And the rest unfolded before me like an atomic bomb.

I could hear his wretched cackling in my ears. A rat of a man. The devil incarnate.

"His name is Lester Drake."

The rest of their conversation faded as I backed away, shaking, from the table. I could still feel his hands around my neck, the sounds of terrified children spiking in my ears, their fear coursing through my blood. I barely held on to Jessie's memory, almost collapsing. I leaned against the wall, slowly lowering to the ground as I heaved air into my lungs.

God, no, no, no.

The sounds around me changed, and when I looked up, I was sitting on the floor of Jessie's room the following night. She lay quietly in the bed, tears leaking down her face as she rubbed the sheet next to her where her sister would sleep.

Show me something, sis.

She would give anything to touch her own wrist and be transported away from this nightmare. She felt so powerless, worthless, with no one around to manipulate, no way to act to protect her sister.

"I'm so sorry," I whispered into the ether.

Her smiling little sister. I thought I'd recognized her as Analise. But in fact, it was another face I recognized. One buried deep, deep in a bed of memories I'd banished long ago. Memories that had broken me. I knew exactly what happened to Mia.

And I knew that Jessie would never see her again.

★★★

Two days later, Jessie packed a few things in a backpack and left. She had accepted the fact that she would likely never see her sister again. But instead of feeling powerless, something fierce was beginning to smolder inside her.

The police told her someone had spotted Drake and his white van the next state over. Jessie didn't think twice; she got on the bus and began to tail him. There, she pushed someone to gift her a car. When she ran out of money, she ate for free. After nearly freezing to death sleeping in her car, she started pushing hotel staff to let her into vacant rooms. It didn't matter anymore what was right and what was wrong for her to do. What was wrong was that this man existed, and he was walking free among the earth.

She wandered from city to city for months, looking for this shadow. Jessie wouldn't return for her final year and a half of high school, but it was no loss. She had been a sharp girl, top of her class, and there was little that books and academia could do for her now. Now, it was all up to her mind. How quickly she could build a story inside her head, as she reached forward to touch someone.

Of course, she encountered other shadows along the way. She stopped a man who had just robbed a couple at gunpoint, sending him back to return their things and turn himself in to the police. A woman who hit her child at the playground called herself in to child protective services. And a man who reached out one night on a dark street, placing his hand on Jessie's slender arm, recoiled with a scream, cowering on the sidewalk as she turned around to stare at him.

"You thought *you* were the one with the power?" she hissed, seething. A fire burned in her eyes, and slowly, one corner of her mouth began to rise.

The rat was elusive. Drake moved so frequently, leaving a trail of missing children in his wake. Jessie would move, opting to touch base with the local police and gather new information, until one day someone recognized her from a surveillance camera at a reported break-in at a hotel. They put cuffs on her, but she acted quickly and released herself from the situation. As long as she lived like this, she wouldn't be able to cooperate with police. She'd have to get better at covering her tracks.

One year after Mia's disappearance, Jessie came home to check on her mother, only to discover she'd been placed in the hospital after a suicide attempt. She watched her mother solemnly from the bedside as she slept, her eyes drifting over the thick bandages covering her wrists, her hands bound to the sides of the bed. Dark circles under her eyes, a lifetime of heartbreak etched in the wrinkles on her face. Jessie extended a hand and placed it on her mother's, her thumb rubbing along her knuckles. And slowly, she replaced her mother's memories. No longer would her heart ache over her lost daughters. Instead, she was a healthy, happy woman. No children, but a full life of adventures and traveling. Her mother had always wanted to see the ocean, so Jessie made it so. Her mother released a long exhale and sank deeper into the mattress, her nerves soothing and mind cooling. She gave her a different name, then Jessie called the nurse and pushed her to remove the bindings on her wrists. Then, after the nurse left, she gave her mother one last look, rose from her chair, and left.

***

For years she continued to move, following a distant target while dealing with the ones so clearly strutting around before her eyes. Her time as a helpless child had taught her the world was full of bad: deadbeat dads, negligent mothers, violent lovers, kidnappers, murderers. She could do nothing about the ones that had existed in her own life, but she had the power to remove the ones she saw now.

The easiest was to make them disappear. A violent shadow in a child's life would move away, suddenly and without explanation. People who stole began to fear retaliation from imaginary forces. But it was the worst offenders who were the most unstable. It was very rare that Jessie was forced to take someone's life. Instead, all Jessie had to do was show them the pain their actions caused, then stand back and let them make their choice. Sometimes, they chose to remove themselves. And if that failed, all Jessie had to do was wipe their memories and render their lives unlivable. It was coping, it was a new purpose. It was retribution for everything that had shaped her. For years, she did this.

Until one day, she heard the rat had been caught.

She sent herself into the police station two days after, reading over the records and transcripts. He'd been tight-lipped in his interrogations, unrevealing of the location of his victims. But then, a change of heart. He had spoken to a man named Alex Hemsley, not even an officer, some kind of volunteer. She studied his sheet closely, reading about the interaction, and how it had ended in his hospitalization in a psych ward.

Somehow, this man had cracked the rat. She knew, there was more to him than it seemed.

In the stack of pages of missing children, Jessie's eyes laid on her sister's face once more, smiling back in a photograph. And in the bottom corner of the page was a new note. Her final resting location.

It had been over a decade since she'd set out for revenge. At some point, it had become more of an ideal than a tangible goal. With each dark soul she had extinguished, it had been a symbolic cut into the dark ghostly flesh of this specter.

But then Jessie's eyes fell on the holding facility where the rat had been sent to await arraignment.

***

THE PRISONER SITTING ON the bus leaving Rikers was confused. Only moments before, he'd been told he was moving to a smaller prison and promptly escorted from the building. Once on the bus, a bag had been put over his head, where he now sat flanked by two armed guards, and rode quietly two miles down the road. There, he spoke no words as the guards marched him out of the bus and into a police cruiser.

The bag over the prisoner's head pivoted slowly as he listened to his surroundings. One driver, one passenger, saying nothing, only shifting occasionally in their seats. He could hear them driving into traffic, the car moving slowly and the sound of honking surrounding them. Then he felt the car shift, his back leaning into the seat, as they drove up a long, winding ramp.

The prisoner was led out of the car and set into a chair. He could hear the gun the person carried clamoring next to his ear. Then, they reached down and unlocked his handcuffs. Stunned, the prisoner brought his palms onto his thighs, wiping off the sweat. Then he heard the sound of gritty footsteps walking away, the car door shutting, the engine starting and the car driving away.

Still in the bag, the prisoner sat dead still, listening to the environment around him. The roar of city traffic, the breeze rolling across his hands. Finally, he reached up and removed the bag from his head.

The eyes of the rat locked onto Jessie's, sitting in a chair just before him, their knees almost touching, together on the rooftop level of a parking garage. His face broke into a smile, seeing that the only force he'd been left with was a young, unarmed woman. Indeed, he cackled delightfully, sensing his freedom was only seconds away. The woman did not flinch, did not move, only continued to stare. So he reached forward to grab her neck. But her hand shot forward, intercepting him at his wrist.

Suddenly, the grizzled smile dropped, and the man lost all expression, the light fading from his eyes. His arm was limp in her hand, barely able to hold himself up as he was leaning forward. I watched from nearby on the rooftop, unable to take my eyes away as she drained him of all life. Jessie cocked her head, smiling at the rat. *You look good as a husk.* In front of her, the rat was despondent, barely breathing, an empty shell of a man with no memories, only the faintest urge to keep breathing. It made my skin crawl.

Then Jessie tilted her head the other way, leaning close to the face of the man who used to be Drake. Still clutching his arm, she breathed into his face, the face that had watched her sister die. She fed him new memories, like an IV line through her fingers, absorbing into his skin. His face began to move again, into one of agony. He whimpered, crying, sucking air into his mouth in gasps, his chest caving under the immense grief pouring into him.

I know, Jessie thought. *They're all gone.*

She released his wrist, and he rose to his feet, burying his face into his hands, sputtering as he took shaky breaths. He looked up at the afternoon sky, at the tall buildings around him, lost in space and also within himself. Jessie leaned back in her chair, smiling as she observed him wandering about on the rooftop, crying to himself and shaking his head, obliterated by the new memories he possessed. I watched in a mixed state of awe and dread, overwhelmed by the strength of her power, the ferocity of her mind.

And it was only when the rat kept walking toward the low concrete wall of the rooftop that I realized the full potential of her power was still materializing. For so engrossed in darkness and pain was this man, that he stepped up on the concrete wall and gazed down at the city sidewalk some ten floors below, staring intently at a physical end to his pain. I could not move, could not breathe, as I watched him, suspended in motion, Jessie still sitting back and watching silently from her chair. Slowly, he brought his foot forward, and slowly, he let his weight take him. And the rat, the devil himself, vanished behind the concrete ledge, plummeting toward the ground.

He was gone.

My eyes landed on Jessie. Her eyes watered as she smiled triumphantly, having removed in her mind the deepest stain on this planet. But in my fascination and admiration, my stomach churned. It was a dark, warped sense of victory. It was righteous, it was vicious, it was powerful.

It was terrifying.

★★★

THE REST OF IT, I knew. It was just as Jessie had told us. I could see all of it, each interaction, rolling one after the other.

Jessie eating with Analise Pexler, listening as the vapid young woman bragged about her brother paying off the DA in her court case. Jessie's fingers itching, her eyes transfixed, as she watched the unrestrained confession of a killer with no remorse.

Jessie leaving a tech conference, stopping in the lobby to lock eyes with Gideon in the mezzanine above. I'd thought she had been wary of him, but I could see so clearly now, it was the other way around. He was squaring her with a look of suspicion. She stepped outside to leave his sight, waited a moment, then turned and walked toward a side entrance, climbing the stairs, looking for a way to get to him, unsuccessful.

Jessie cornering another dark mark on her list, the CEO of Ackheim, alone in his home. He had no knowledge of how to access his company's database, which was a disappointment. But there was more to her visit. For she knew a deep, dark secret of his, found buried in deleted texts. She watched, her hand on his, as his face flashed from anger to confusion to horror. All she had to do was make him forget who he was, and then remind him of what he'd done. She was long gone by the time he acted on it, by the time she heard he'd taken his own life.

And Melanie. Sweet Melanie. She was so helpful, so kind. Jessie had nabbed her and her husband as they were leaving the subway station for work. A simple conversation over brunch gave Jessie all the details about the data at Sentry and how it could be accessed. Jessie had already arranged for the higher-ups to be busy at a dinner that night with herself and Analise. All Melanie had to do was go in and download the data. Jessie's hand settled on Melanie's wrist, feeding her a new story. Management could no longer be trusted, and Melanie needed to download and scrub the collection of sensitive clients. There was one particular police department it was important she retrieve.

It shouldn't have been a surprise that the moment Jessie asked her to betray her company, Melanie was conflicted. She stared at her phone in her lap, then decided to dial a friend, a colleague from work who could help ease her mind and her doubts about Sentry. Jessie's hand flew to her wrist so fast, and Melanie's innocent smile melted instantly into a blank stare, dissolving away with any knowledge of her coworkers. Jessie led Miguel away from the table and pushed a memory full of grief, a memory that he'd found his wife dead that morning. He needed to call Sentry to report her death, so they wouldn't try to reach out to her or report her missing, and afterward she removed the false memory. Jessie took care to deliver Melanie personally to Sentry that night to ensure the push had worked, before being whisked away to dinner.

And of course, there was this young man, Alex Hemsley. She watched him from afar for weeks before their introduction, studying his coat and scarf, his gloves, his awkwardness, his distance from other people. He had to be one of them. He had to be like her.

She had to be careful. She had to execute everything perfectly. She would adapt the driver from that night at the restaurant into her own story with the kidnapping, to make it seem even more real. He'd drive the same car. And then she'd make him and his family leave, to avoid any possible police interaction, should a report ever actually reach the cops. There were plenty of options roaming just outside her door at Pexler.

And the holding location for her captive, a room at the end of the destroyed hallway that no one would bother to check. She'd put in a work order the week before to install a secured door. The night before the kidnapping, she watched as Analise slipped into the hallway to stock it with supplies for her stay. Not long after, Analise would be waiting there, her memory emptied, her only instructions to never leave the room nor make a noise.

She watched. She stalked. She pulled all the strings, smiling to herself as all the pieces fell into place. And then one morning, one missing piece walked out of the Pexler building, unaware that she was waiting outside. The look on Gideon's face when he turned and looked at her, standing only feet behind him. I hadn't seen that kind of fear on someone's face in a long time. It was just as she'd said: he bolted, took off. She ran after him, but once she saw him heading into the headlights of a taxi, she ducked away out of sight. His death disappointed her, to be honest. She hadn't wanted him dead. She'd wanted him sorry.

And finally, I stood behind Jessie as she watched hungrily from her laptop in the half-renovated hallway. Drew and I were about to walk right into her trap, and we were too dumb to know it. For Jessie, there was no apprehension, only excitement.

Because there was nothing, I realized. There was nothing I could do to stop her. She was too strong. Decades of memories had proven to me that nothing could break her. What I saw as an ability, she saw as power. And nothing could ever make her feel powerless again.

But as I watched her sitting there, listening to the conversation I had with Drew in the bar shortly before arriving, something astonishing happened. She turned her head and looked at me. Right at me, not through me.

Hello, Alex.

She knew one day, whether it was this day or another, I would be standing here, watching her in the memories she would share with me when I was ready. When she had my trust and my loyalty. She welcomed it. She was ready to meet her equal.

She'd show me how she'd killed the rat. She pictured us watching together, smiling. And then she'd ask the question that was lingering in her mind. Maybe, just maybe, her days of being alone were over.

And slowly, I let the memory fade, swimming past my ankles like a stream. I was coming back to the surface, the sounds of the city wash in the subway tunnel echoing in my ears.

In the present, time had progressed forward ever so slightly. For when I was fully back on the train station, my eyes focusing on the matter at hand, my heart stopped.

Drew stood perfectly still in front of Jessie. Her hand was on his shoulder, her fingers resting on the bare skin of his neck.

OFFER.

Jessie and I watched each other carefully, studying the other's emotions. She seemed discomposed, unused to being caught off guard, any trace of her confident smile long gone. Meanwhile I was sorting through all kinds of reactions, but mainly fear at finding my brother locked in her grasp.

"The drive," she finally said. "I need you to give me that drive."

Drew looked at me with defeat, apologizing through his eyes. He dared not move an inch under Jessie's touch, some fifteen feet away from me.

Analise stooped nearby to pick the gun up off the ground, and then waited. All eyes were on me, and my eyes were on Jessie. I knew her now, all of who she was. She bristled behind Drew, unkeen to have shared herself against her will, but it was no matter now.

"The drive," she said again.

"Drake," I whispered. "You killed him."

"I *burned* him right off the face of the earth," she seethed. "You see now why I have to do this. Why I can't just stand by and let people like Drake walk freely. They leave a path of destruction everywhere they go, snuffing out innocent lives, tearing them away from their families."

I stared at her, in awe, in fear. Both of us now seeing each other eye to eye.

"Now, hand over the drive."

"Don't do it," Drew sputtered to me, trying hard to muster courage.

I said nothing, the conflict hanging in my throat, seizing my resolve in a chokehold.

Suddenly her grip on Drew's shoulder tightened, and she pivoted him toward the edge of the platform, their shadows spilling over the tracks. "Tell me," she called over her shoulder. "Is it worth your brother's life?"

"Stop!" I pleaded.

"Or maybe," Jessie continued, "death isn't the answer. Maybe it's something worse." She turned Drew back around to face me. "If you don't give me that drive, I'll wipe your brother's memories."

Drew's face went white, her fingertips sinking into his shoulder.

"He'll be a husk, an empty shell of the brother you love. And I know," she whispered, "from one sibling to another, you don't want that."

She was exactly right. There was nothing to decide. I had seen enough, felt enough. There was nothing I could do but give her what she wanted, to save my brother.

I reached into my pocket and withdrew the drive. I could see Drew's face fall, his eyes looking desperately into mine. But it didn't matter to me anymore what would happen to the people whose names were on this drive, at least not as much as I cared about getting my brother to safety. I held the drive out in the palm of my hand.

Jessie nodded to Analise, who walked to my side. I curled my fingers over the drive. "Release him first," I said.

Jessie nodded again. The bullshit was over. She released her hand from Drew's shoulder as Analise plucked the drive from my palm. My brother stumbled over to me and I grasped his hand quickly, confirming Jessie had not tampered with his memories.

Across from us, Analise closed the distance to Jessie, holding both the drive and the gun. Like a homing missile, a devoted soldier completing the last step in her mission. Jessie held out her hand, and Analise slid the drive into her fingers. Jessie's eyes sparkled as she regarded the drive, the data she would sell, and the whereabouts of one Thomas Portmeau.

She broke the trance and tucked the drive safely away into her pocket. Her voice softened. "You probably know this by now, Alex. But gathering data has not been my sole focus these past few months." She looked back up at me, into my eyes. "You and me, we're not so different."

I felt Drew shift uneasily next to me, but I held her gaze. It was just the two of us in this conversation, pusher and puller. The rest of the world seemed to fade away.

"You know," Jessie continued, "I've met a handful of pullers in my time. Always so weak, so easy to break. But you, I could see you were different. You were so damaged when I found you, but I knew that if I pushed you, I could mold you into something extraordinary."

I said nothing, did not move, only listened.

"You've seen what I can do, and now I know what you can do. Imagine if we combined our powers. A pusher and a puller. Working together for a common purpose. Can you imagine what we could do?"

Her words laced into my brain like a string of temptation. I folded the thoughts over and over, my eyes unblinking, listening with a hunger.

"Every terrible thing you've seen in other people, we can prevent. We can do so much good working together. It's what you wanted, right? When you worked at the precinct? To help other people. To do good. You can do it again, only it doesn't have to hurt. I can handle the bad ones. I can even make every bad memory you've collected go away."

I inhaled a deep, shaky breath.

"We can do this," she whispered. "You and me. We can do this together."

Nobody moved a muscle. Her imploring words connected with me, touching deep in my tired soul.

And in eager, careful words, she spoke her final offer.

"Alex, will you join me?"

I stood there, locked into her eyes. I could feel the energy beneath them, the rage that filled her. It filled me too, from a different source. From all the memories I had seen, all the violence, heartbreak, senseless loss to fill centuries. We were the same, she was right about that. We were both trapped in a world that could not help us, lonely in our isolated lives, looking for something more. Together, we could find it.

But as tantalizing as it was to welcome her, to finally have a partner who understood me, there was something holding me back.

In my mind, I saw the torture she inflicted, the trickery she played in people's minds like they were toys. I felt the deception in how she had approached all of this, as a test, an amusing mind game. I knew she felt a respect for me, but it was not enough to guarantee that this wouldn't happen again. That I wouldn't constantly live in fear of her power over me, that she might alter my mind to tilt me into alignment with what she needed. Every morning I would wake, not knowing if my memories were my own. Not knowing if I had helped kill someone the day before.

Her power was amazing. And terrifying.

And I could not trust her.

It was for these reasons that I looked regretfully into her eyes, knowing the betrayal this would impart, and slowly shook my head.

No.

On the platform, nobody moved. I waited for her to shrug or smile, to move and leave. Then what I saw next terrified me.

A single tear rolled from the corner of Jessie's eye. She turned her head and wiped her hand across her face, staring at the ground, nodding slowly to herself. She was heartbroken. Her quest for a companion had failed her, the isolation suffocating around her. I understood, because I felt the same thing.

"Okay," she whispered.

Then her hand shot out toward Analise, tearing the gun from her hands. She cocked the weapon and raised it toward me, her eyes staring down the barrel, not with fire, but with sorrow.

Drew and I jumped, surprised by the motion.

"Hey!" Drew said. "What are you doing? We did as you asked!"

But Jessie kept her eyes on me. "You know who I am. You'll find me, and you'll slow me down."

I stared helplessly back at her, trapped in the crosshairs.

"Wait!" Drew sputtered, but it was just noise around us.

"I'm so sorry," she whispered.

I didn't move. Nothing I could do would stop her. If she wanted me dead, then there was nothing left to do but die. A strange feeling of weary acceptance came over me, welcoming the silence her bullet would bring.

And with a final spark of sadness in her eyes, she pulled her finger on the trigger.

It happened all at once. The deafening gunshot ringing out against the tiles. Drew's yell as he jumped in front of me, his arms outstretched. I expected him to fall into me, to be knocked backwards from the impact. But instead, I saw a pool of deep red erupt on Jessie's shirt, just below her collarbone. She stumbled backward, the gun slipping from her grip.

My mind clicked as time slowed. Somewhere else on the platform, someone had fired a shot. It was not Analise, who stood next to Jessie empty-handed and staring bewilderedly at the wound.

In the corner of my eye, I saw a figure at the far end of the platform, at the base of the stairs where Drew's gun had landed.

As I turned my head to face them, it took me a moment to understand what I was seeing.

I saw the man from Jessie's memories who had playfully tapped her nose at the kitchen table. His eyes weathered, his auburn beard graying, his daughter giggling as she begged him to guess what she was thinking without fail.

I saw the man standing in his long dark coat, his beard now white, his wrinkled hands shaking as the smoking gun was lowered.

I couldn't believe it.

It was Roger.

The gun clattered to the ground and the old man turned, burying his face in his hands.

In front of me, Jessie had collapsed. She was too stunned to look at who had fired the bullet, the blood gushing from the lethal wound, a red streak dripping from the corner of her mouth as she coughed. Analise, crying, knelt to hold her head, but the moment she touched Jessie, she froze, blinking as if in a daze.

Jessie looked up at me with sadness in her eyes. The light was fading quickly. I stood there, once again watching her die, once again feeling helpless. She was slipping away and there was nothing I could do, nothing she could do. Both of us, completely powerless.

And then, with a final breath, she was gone.

There was silence. Drew, Analise, and I stood numb, watching the blood trail across the platform. Drew extended his arm behind me, and I reached to his other shoulder, tears sliding silently down our cheeks, the adrenaline dissolving in our blood. On the other side of the platform, Roger sobbed forcefully, doubled over on his knees. "No, no…."

Within moments, flashes of red and blue reflected off the white tiles of the subway, the distant radio walkies of police crackling in the night air. Finally, a train rolled by, the last one of the night, headed out somewhere beyond the city.

MEMORY.

I sat next to Roger on a bench at the edge of the platform, both of us wrapped in white blankets from the paramedics. He did not move or look at me, bent forward with his elbows on his knees, staring helplessly into his hands. Tears soaked the white hairs of his grizzled cheeks. In front of us, a handful of police officers worked the scene, taking pictures, ducking in and out under the yellow police tape. Jessie's body had been taken away, but a chilling trail of red remained, soaked into the concrete.

"She was my daughter," Roger said, still staring at his hands.

"I know. I'm so sorry."

At the other end of the station, I watched as two police officers gingerly picked up Drew's gun and slid it into an evidence bag. Their voices undulated under the low wash echoing from the weathered tiles.

"How did you find us?" I asked him.

"I saw her walk by outside the pub this afternoon," Roger said. "I couldn't believe my eyes. I followed her to that big office building and waited outside."

He must have seen Jessie leaving Sentry after she pushed Drew, I thought, on her way back to Pexler.

"I didn't know what to say. If I should try to interact with her at all. Then I saw you two arrive and go into the building, too. And later you all came out running toward the subway station, and… then I saw her point that gun at you." Emotion began to overtake his thin voice. "I failed her," he said with a small shake of his head. "I left her there with her mom in that wasteland. I didn't think I could raise a child. And after that day she pushed me, I knew what she was, and I was scared." He wiped his cheek, almost whispering. "I ran away. I abandoned her. I made her who she was."

His shoulders heaved as he sobbed quietly into his hands. I slid my hand onto his back, resting lightly on the white blanket. The thought of his skin mere millimeters below and the devastation it could bring didn't matter anymore.

We sat like that for ten minutes, Roger reeling in his guilt as I absorbed it next to him, the companionship neither of us had ever had. Before us, the police were beginning to pack up their things. Somehow, this crazy night was slowing to an end.

Eventually, Roger sat back up, both of us facing forward and watching the officers jot down their final notes, leaning into their walkies to relay the final steps. Like it was all just a play, and we were simply audience members, with no stake whatsoever in the outcome.

I glanced curiously up into the beaming fluorescents above the platform.

"Do you think any of this is actually real?" I said, half smiling.

Roger gave a small chuckle next to me. "I guess we'll never know for sure."

★★★

Up at the street level, Drew was sitting at the back of an ambulance as a paramedic finished wrapping his upper arm in gauze.

"You're lucky," she said, "the bullet didn't graze too deep. Should be healed in a couple of weeks."

"Thanks, doc," Drew said. He turned to look at me as I approached from the subway exit. "Any scratches on you?"

"No," I said, taking a seat on the bumper next to him. "Thanks to you."

"Hey, promise me something."

"What's that?"

"We never do crazy shit like this again."

I held my bare hand out. "You have my word."

Drew looked down at it and smiled, clasping it back. Then, suddenly overwhelmed, we leaned in and wrapped each other in our arms. Tears slid down my cheeks as I felt my older brother's solid warmth, the physical reassurance that he was still here. When we let go, I saw his cheeks glistening as well. Trying to stabilize the rise of emotion in my chest, I looked back to the subway entrance, studying the police coming up the stairs, the eerie quietness of the city almost stifling.

"Can I ask you something?" Drew said.

"Yes?"

"What did you see?"

★★★

IT WAS JUST AFTER six AM when a car arrived to pick us up. As we snaked between the glassy black buildings in the dark, I could see the faintest hint of sunlight warming the frigid horizon. Drew and I rode in silence in the back, exhausted, and having nothing more to say. But rather than sleep, my mind continued to turn the contents of Jessie's memories over.

The little blonde girl, smiling up at her sister. The panic she felt when that little girl had vanished, leaving an empty sidewalk, and the vast possibility that she could be anywhere. The sunken, ugly eyes of the rat, snarling at her before she snuffed the light out in them.

What would I have done, had I been face to face with Lester Drake again after knowing everything he'd done? Again, I felt the mix of terror and wonder as I thought about the fact that this man no longer existed. And the wonder, the fascination, in and of itself, was horrifying. It was like a car crash I couldn't look away from, thinking of his worthless body dropping like a sack of shit off a building.

Drake was an icon of darkness, a monster, as textbook as evil could be. But what about the others? The absent father, the negligent mother, her abusive lover. Each one, chipping away at Jessie and her sister's lives, shaping her into what she would become. These dark forces were everywhere in the world, and I knew it well. I could see it in the memories of the witnesses, victims, suspects I'd pulled at the police station over a year ago. But I knew that some of them had walked free. I'd chosen to let those thoughts go. What more could I do? It was out of my hands, I'd thought at the time.

That was the difference, I thought now. The difference was that Jessie had refused to accept that as truth. But it had fused with her desire for power, and with each offender erased, it was justification for her extreme use of her ability, her questionable actions in an effort to achieve her goals under the guise of righteousness.

The thing that troubled me most of all, the conflict still clinging in my throat, was that I wasn't sure it had been completely wrong.

Looking out the window at the early morning taxis passing by, I thought again of the young brown-haired girl. Who would she have been if none of these people had hurt her? If they had been removed before they'd had their chance to make their dismal mark on her life? In a flash, I could picture Jessie and Analise in their first versions, the ones I'd met at the rooftop lounge, laughing together. Only instead of Analise, it was Mia, alive and grown, smiling as she took a selfie of the four of us at dinner. Jessie, sharing a drink with me at the bar, smiling at me on the restaurant stairs, her brown eyes shining, leaning forward to kiss my cheek.

Monsters create monsters. If I could pluck one domino to stop the others from falling, even if it meant becoming a fallen piece myself… was it actually the right thing to do?

★★★

THE CAR PULLED UP to the silver office building, and Drew and I unloaded onto the sidewalk where a few workers were just beginning the morning trickle into the lobby. Up to level forty-five we went, sore and baggy-eyed, but we had agreed there was one last thing we needed to do. We treaded quietly down the empty hall of Suite B, my eyes glancing regretfully at Melanie's darkened room. Then we stepped into my office, closing and locking the door behind us.

Drew took his usual spot before the wide window, watching the sunlight breaking the horizon and bathing the buildings of the city, bouncing off metal like silver fish scales. He looked different now, standing there with his hands clasped behind his back. Before, he had always postured himself like the ruler of the world, surveying his territory. But today there was something different. Something softer, almost grateful.

I sat at my desk, my chair feeling unfamiliar, like it had come from another era altogether. Quietly, I started the computer, the screen lighting up under the reflection of the window behind me.

I brought my hand to my pocket and pulled out the flash drive. Drew turned his head slightly, glancing down at it. I had removed it from Jessie's pocket just before the police had funneled down onto the platform. Now, I handled it reverently, like a relic, as I pressed it carefully into the USB port.

The drive was mounted. The database screen blinked back at me on the monitor, waiting for me to upload the files back safely onto our servers, where they had been purged the day before. It had been our plan to restore these profiles as soon as possible this morning. But I found myself hesitating, the mouse waiting under the palm of my hand. Then I clicked and initiated the upload process, watching the progress bar work quickly.

Sitting back in my chair, I thought I would feel relief. But my head would not settle. The palms of my hands sweat. My eyes rested on the file for Thomas Portmeau, just one name on a long ledger.

"If I don't use my ability to make the world a better place, how am I any better than the people on your lists?"

On the wall opposite the window, the clock ticked loudly as time passed by. Drew turned again to look at me, studying me as I stared at the screen.

"And you, letting these people live their lives. How are you any better?"

I felt his hand on my shoulder.

"Do what you need to do," he said.

Without speaking, we both understood what that was. I reached for the mouse again, opening a new browser tab. I felt Drew step away, returning to the window as I began an irreversible sequence.

In the new tab, I went to the web address we had been given, the upload link to Jessie's contact. I gathered the top-level files from the server, re-typing my admin password. As my fingers tapped the keys, I could feel that fierceness, that fire, burning in my blood. I selected the files and dragged them to the upload page. And in that last moment as I looked at the screen, like a man holding a match over kerosene, I could feel, more confidently than ever, that this was the right thing to do.

I clicked send. And in a matter of seconds, the transfer was complete.

I sighed, leaning back into my chair. On the screen, the confirmation message flashed.

"It's done," I said. I turned to my brother to see what look he might have upon his face. Regret. Defeat. Resolve. Pride.

Instead, I turned to find him lying on the floor on his side.

A cloth was wrapped around his head and gagged his mouth, his hands bound behind him. His blue eyes were wide with fear, as he began to murmur in panic.

And then, everything broke.

The soreness of my body was gone but replaced by an overwhelming confusion, swimming around my head like a pressurized can. I groaned as I leaned forward, cradling my head in my hands, breathing through clenched teeth.

Time had stopped, yet it was everywhere. The neatly sorted memories slipped forward, overlapping one another, both real and fake. Even as I brought my head up to survey the room, my vision was clouded with snapshots of memories. Which is why I was unsure of what I was seeing in reality, blinking rapidly to try and clear the fog.

Out the glass door and down the hall was a brown-haired woman, standing at the entrance to the hallway. Her hand held the door open as she turned to give me one last look. Those fierce brown eyes, that self-assured smile. She no longer had a bullet wound or a trail of blood leading down her shirt. The seam of my office door distorted her face, running between her eyes, giving her an almost blurred quality.

I rose from my chair to walk after her, but I could barely control my feet, could not keep myself upright. I collapsed at the base of my office door, my hand pressed against the glass as my breathing raised patches of moisture along the plane. The hallway was like a giant prism, light and darkness refracting around the woman standing at the other end.

I tried to recollect the mess of memories flowing in my head, to remember what series of events had led me to this moment. But it was like trying to lift an immense weight, an incredible effort just to move a single memory out of the way and look for the next.

And then I saw it. Her face, swimming in a memory it did not belong in. In a crowded English pub just down the street, I was sitting at the bar, stooped over my beer, spilling my heart out to the old man in the wool coat next to me. But the moment I sat up, straightening as I turned to him, I saw it was not Roger who sat next to me.

It was Jessie. Smiling as she listened, her hand resting on my wrist.

My body released a wave of cold sweat as I looked back to the hallway, but the brown-haired woman was gone. In my pocket, my phone vibrated, and I clumsily extracted it. On the screen, there was a message from Jessie's number.

The text read:

Come find me one day when you're ready.

***

OUTSIDE THE LOBBY, THE camera above the door caught a brown-haired woman stepping out into the first hour of the sun's golden light. The sidewalk was bustling with people, their heads ducked down as they headed to their next destination. For a moment, the woman stood there at the lobby door, taking in the gold-lit skyscrapers standing like giants before her. A city of millions of minds swimming up and downstream.

Then, she put on her sunglasses and tightened her scarf, and disappeared into the mass of people heading down the sidewalk, fading away with the rest of the world into the city light.

PUSH.

Acknowledgements

In writing my first book, I've learned it takes a village. My heartfelt thanks to my first beta readers: Wren, Matthew, Annie, and Kat. To my editor, Rachel Moulton, thank you for your keen eye and your intervention on my love of adverbs. Matthew, your endless support and encouragement means more than you can ever know. And to the online community of indie authors who have shared their experiences and advice in regards to the journey of self-publishing, thanks for leaving a trail of breadcrumbs so the rest of us can tag along as well.

About the author

C.J. Finch is the pen name of composer and sound designer, Kristen Hirlinger. She releases music under the pseudonym Tannins, and lives in Los Angeles with her partner and bossy tortoiseshell cat.

For updates on future releases, visit cjfinch.com and follow C.J. Finch on Instagram: @cjfinchbooks

www.ingramcontent.com/pod-product-compliance
Lightning Source LLC
Chambersburg PA
CBHW051138130726
47988CB00005B/1897